DEATH
WILL HELP
YOU LEAVE HIM

Other Books by Elizabeth Zelvin

Death Will Get You Sober

ELIZABETH ZELVIN

DEATH
WILL HELP
YOU LEAVE HIM

St. Martin's Minotaur

A Thomas Dunne Book | New York

A THOMAS DUNNE BOOK FOR MINOTAUR BOOKS.
An imprint of St. Martin's Publishing Group.

DEATH WILL HELP YOU LEAVE HIM. Copyright © 2009 by Elizabeth Zelvin. All rights reserved. Printed in the United States of America. For information, address St. Martin's Press, 175 Fifth Avenue, New York, N.Y. 10010.

www.thomasdunnebooks.com
www.minotaurbooks.com

Library of Congress Cataloging-in-Publication Data

Zelvin, Elizabeth.
    Death will help you leave him / Elizabeth Zelvin. — 1st ed.
        p. cm.
    ISBN 978-0-312-58266-1
    1. Alcoholics—Fiction.   2. New York (N.Y.)—Fiction   3. Domestic fiction.   I. Title.
    PS3576.E48D435 2009
    813'.54—dc22

                                                              2009016574

First Edition: October 2009

10 9 8 7 6 5 4 3 2 1

For Brian, always

ACKNOWLEDGMENTS

Heartfelt thanks to my blog sister Sharon Wildwind for help in honing the manuscript; to Detective Marco Conelli, NYPD, for help with the cop stuff; to the Atlantic Center for the Arts in New Smyrna Beach, Florida, for treating writers and other creative artists like royalty; to my fellow ACA residents, Ann Penn, Tom Sweeney, Paul Takeuchi, Evan Piercy, LaTisha Redding, Nathaniel Kerr, and Jayne Blankenship, and our master artist S. J. Rozan, for inspired critique; and to Susan Schulman, who makes the concept of a dream agent so much more than a dream.

Thanks, too, to the Guppies and other friends and relatives who housed, fed, and drove me around, came to my signings, and bought my books on my 2008 book tour, especially Polly Iyer and Elaine Johnson, who did all of the above for several days each.

I also want to thank all who contributed to my first book trailer video: Intimacy on Madison Avenue, for the sexy undies; Rocco's on Bleecker Street, for the delectable pastries; the Jamali Gallery in SoHo; singer/songwriter Bernice Lewis, for permission to use her wonderful song "As Soon as It Stops Raining"; Ron Miller, for the voice-over; and especially Janet Koch, for putting it all together with expertise, creativity, and professionalism.

Any writer who sets a work of fiction in New York City today takes liberties with its geography and sociology, whether deliberately or simply because the city changes faster than a book gets published. Novelists make stuff up. We call it literary license.

DEATH
WILL HELP
YOU LEAVE HIM

ONE

I scootched into the back of my best friend Jimmy's Toyota. His girlfriend Barbara's dripping umbrella almost impaled me as I fell onto the seat. I shook myself like a dog.

"Tell me again," I said. "Whose apartment is it? And who's the corpse?"

"Her pigeon's boyfriend." Jimmy swiveled to look at me. Bad idea. The car skidded on the slick, wet surface of Third Avenue.

"Watch the road, Jimmy," Barbara ordered.

The maniacs who drive New York taxis wove and dodged all around us as we headed uptown.

"Bruce, I appreciate this." Barbara twisted around to see me better over the high back of the passenger seat. "I wasn't sure you'd come out in the rain in the middle of the night."

"Hey, no problem. Pigeons have boyfriends?"

"My Al-Anon sponsee," she elaborated. "Luz. It's her apartment. She found her boyfriend dead on the floor when she came home. And don't say 'corpse.' She was hysterical when she called me, and the cops are there."

I knew that. I had a guy of my own that I called when I thought I might not make it through the night without a drink.

"So when do Al-Anons call their sponsors?" I asked. "Short of sudden death."

"When somebody else's life starts flashing before their eyes," Jimmy said.

Barbara swatted his upper arm, not hard enough to endanger us.

"Cut it out, that's not fair."

"When they can't stop saying, 'I'm sorry,'" he said. "You know it's true, petunia."

A sudden cloudburst sent runnels of water streaming down the windshield. Jimmy clicked the windshield wipers into high gear. I admired the blurry red and green glow of the traffic lights and started to wake up.

"Cops. Do they think it's murder? If so, 'I'm sorry' wouldn't be the smartest thing to say."

"That's why she needs us," Barbara said. "When Luz called me, she said, 'Frankie's dead, and they think I killed him.'"

"Uh, doesn't she have anybody closer?" I asked. "Family?"

"Aunts," Barbara said. "Dozens of them. She said some of them are there already, but I don't think their English is so hot. Anyhow, she thought they'd be intimidated by the police, and we wouldn't."

"You wouldn't," Jimmy said. "They scare the shit out of me."

He was exaggerating, but I felt the same. Barbara could get scrappy when a situation got past her very low indignation threshold. Jimmy always had to brace himself for flak. Not that she ever wanted to be rescued.

"Okay, that explains you two," I said. "And you needed me to come along because?"

"If we can't find a spot, someone's got to stay with the car. I'm not about to double-park in front of a building that's crawling with cops."

"Silly me," I said. "I should have known." Cars outnumber parking spaces by two to one anywhere in Manhattan.

"Turn here, Jimmy," Barbara said. "That's it, on the left."

We couldn't have missed it. The police cars, lights flashing, gave it away. Jimmy slowed to a snail's pace and started circling. The rain dumped another few thousand gallons of water on the car. I peered through the streams of water flowing down the side windows. Hydrant. Motorcycle. Dumpster.

"There." The space, between a rugged SUV and a flashy pimpmobile, was tight. But Jimmy wiggled the car into it. Oh, good, I get to see the murder scene. And interact with the police. And, if I knew Barbara, get much more involved than I intended.

"Hand me my umbrella," she ordered.

"Whoa, wait a minute," I said. "Before we go up there and dive in the deep end, at least tell me this woman's story. The condensed version." Barbara on a roll could show the Ancient Mariner a thing or two.

"Frankie was a major druggie. He'd just gotten out of rehab."

"Dealer?" I asked.

"Not sure. He was definitely abusive. She never had a black eye or a broken arm," Barbara said. "She wouldn't admit he ever touched her, but I bet he did. He was also jealous and possessive, snooped, bullied, played a lot of mind games."

"And you couldn't just tell her to throw the bum out."

"Are you kidding? I'm a counselor, not Dear Abby. Besides, it wouldn't have worked. She was totally hooked."

"And he wouldn't leave on his own?"

"Actually, he did," Barbara said. "Repeatedly. Always in the middle of the night, after he'd gotten her all worked up."

"That's when she'd make those sponsor calls," Jimmy said.

"Right," Barbara said. "And a few days later, he'd waltz back in, swearing he'd change, and she'd believe that this time he meant it."

Right. Pigs may fly. But first you have to go down to Kitty Hawk and build them some wings.

Jimmy locked the car doors. Hunching his shoulders against the rain, he marched up to the uniformed cop at the door to explain who we were. Barbara and I hung back, huddled under her umbrella. A persistent trickle of rain dripped down the points. Some of it landed down the back of my neck.

"You're gonna owe me for this," I said.

"Wait till you meet Luz," Barbara said. "You'll want to help her, I promise."

"Barbara! Bruce!" Jimmy beckoned from the inadequate shelter of the stubby overhang above the front door. "Come on! We can go in."

Barbara hurried toward him. I scuttled after her, trying to keep my head and shoulders under the functional part of the umbrella.

We followed the uniformed cop Jimmy had been talking to up a flight of stairs. Yellow crime scene tape barred the battered elevator door with its elderly brown paint job and graffiti scars. On the second floor, another uniformed cop stood guard beside a half-open apartment door. Our cop stuck his head in and said a few words. A minute later, Luz burst out the door. She was little, maybe five foot one or two. Cute, too, with bouncy black curls and dark brown eyes made brilliant by welling tears. The police towered over her. She flung herself on Barbara and burrowed into her embrace.

"Oh, Barbara, you came! Thank you, thank you. I'm so sorry I got you up, I wasn't sure if I should call, but I didn't know what to do. And Jimmy and your friend too, so late at night." She had a hint of a Puerto Rican accent, no more than a softening of the sibilants and lengthening of the short vowels. Wassn't. Jeemy. She flashed the bright eyes at me briefly. "You are Bruce, yes? Thank you so much for coming." To Barbara, she said, "I can't believe he's gone."

"Shh, shh, it'll be okay. Poor bunny—I'm so sorry."

She enveloped Luz like a down comforter. After a minute or two of rocking, Luz stopped heaving with sobs. She wiped mucus off her upper lip with a damp wad of crumpled tissues. She made as if to lead us into the apartment, still holding Barbara's hand. The cop at the door stopped us.

"I'm sorry, miss, you can't go back in right now. This apartment is a crime scene."

"Then where—" Barbara began, already protective and belligerent. Jimmy's reflexes were just as quick. He put a warning hand gently on her upper arm.

"It's all right, Barbara," Luz said. "We can go to the neighbor's. Mrs. Hernandez, just down the hall. See, the open door? My aunts are already there."

"That's right, miss." The cop nodded, approving. "You'll all be more comfortable there."

"But the detectives?" she asked. "They said they wanted to speak with me more."

"They'll come to you," the cop said. "Detective Garcia and Detective O'Brien will come over to your neighbor's when they're ready."

Luz led us down the hall. Mrs. Hernandez, resplendent in a quilted red satin bathrobe, flung the door wide as we approached. Her gold slippers were tipped with wads of fur, as if a couple of kittens crouched on her toes.

"Come in, come in," she urged. "*Madre de Dios*, what a terrible thing." She sounded as if she was thoroughly enjoying herself. "My *pobrecita*, come and sit with your *tias. Señora, señores,* welcome to my home. It is good this *niña* has *amigos.*"

She led Luz to the couch, where two pillowy aunts made room for her. She waved us toward an overstuffed armchair and a couple of kitchen chairs.

"I make you coffee," she announced.

From the smell of it, she had already made it, and it was Puerto Rican coffee, Bustelo or one of those brands. That was fine with me. Alcoholics Anonymous floats on a sea of coffee, most of it a lot worse than I expected Mrs. Hernandez's to be.

The aunts, buzzing like bumblebees, swarmed around Luz as soon as she sat down.

The matriarch with silver hair piled high like Madame de Pompadour was Tia Margarita, who held Luz's hand. On her other side sat Tia Wanda. The rest of them were Tia Gloria, Tia Gladys, and Tia Maria. They all wept and wailed, exclaimed, and exhorted Luz to do a number of contradictory things at once. Lie down and rest and drink strong coffee. Have a good cry and pull herself together.

Jimmy and I accepted coffee, saying *gracias, muchas gracias* like good New Yorkers who had grown up half a mile south of Spanish Harlem. Barbara refused. She appreciated so much all the trouble Mrs. Hernandez had gone to, she would love to accept the coffee, but unfortunately she had a very bad *dolor* of her *estómago*, the doctor had strictly forbidden her to drink anything with *acido* in it. Barbara was too polite, or more likely, too codependent to decline merely because it would keep her awake all night. Jimmy whispered in my ear, " 'No' is a complete sentence." An Al-Anon slogan.

"*Acides*," Luz put in.

"*Acides*."

Mrs. Hernandez's face brightened.

"I make you *café con leche*," she said. "Lots of hot milk. That way, no *acides*."

I knocked the coffee back like a shooter.

"Do you think I could go out in the hall and smoke?" I muttered to Jimmy. "It's not like we're actually doing anything."

"Hey, we're showing support," Jimmy said. "Sure, go suck up a death stick." Jimmy was the only alcoholic in the known universe who had never smoked. My sponsor had quit when he got sober. I knew my long affair with nicotine would be over sometime, maybe soon. But not tonight.

Out in the corridor, I leaned against the wall and lit up. Down the hall in Luz's apartment, people came and went. Cops, crime scene guys, whatever. A lot of equipment went in. Even the uniform on the door got drafted to fetch and carry. I wondered if I'd catch a glimpse of Luz's boyfriend. I had scored a gram or two of coke in the bad old days from a dealer named Frankie. He wasn't Puerto Rican, though. Italian, maybe. I had almost finished my cigarette when they brought lover boy out in a body bag. I didn't get to see his face.

I lit another cigarette off the butt of the first. As I coated my lungs with tar, a commotion broke out in Luz's apartment. I heard loud, angry voices. Harsh male bark, scolding female snap and yammer. Above the sharp official voices rose an argumentative rattle of syllables and a keening howl or two. Sounded like they'd rounded up a straggler. Sure enough, a woman in NYPD blue emerged, her hair wisping out of her cap and her cheeks flushed with anger. She gripped her voluble captive by the elbow. The miscreant was tiny and wrinkled, with a ramrod spine and blue-black hair too glossy not to be real. Her eyes blazed, and a flood of Spanish poured out of her. As the cop marched her toward us, Barbara's head popped out of Mrs. Hernandez's door.

"The aunts say Tia Rosa is missing. Have you seen—ah, you

have." She called back into the room, "Luz, they've got her. Maybe you'd better come and find out what happened."

Luz slipped through the door.

"*Tia Rosa, qué pasa?* Please let go of her, officer. She's upset, she didn't mean any harm."

"We found her in the kitchen," the cop said, stiff with outrage. "Cooking! We told everybody they had to leave the apartment. It's a crime scene."

"She didn't understand," Luz said. "Don't you have anybody in there who could talk to her in Spanish?"

"I thought the NYPD was supposed to be culturally diverse." Barbara's two cents.

The officer's face went an even brighter red. She muttered some disjointed words about Detective Garcia. Sounded like the one Spanish speaker had been in the can when Tia Rosa slipped into the kitchen.

Luz turned to me and Barbara.

"She was making *pasteles*. I don't know if you have tasted them." She gave me a shy smile.

"I have," Barbara said. "They're delicious. And I know they're a big deal. Like chicken soup and wedding cake rolled into one."

"They take all day to make," Luz said, managing a doleful giggle. "Usually, they are for Christmas. She says the *tias* were determined to outlast the *policias*."

"Oh, for heaven's sake," the exasperated officer said. "Go on, take her into the neighbor's. Vamoose, *no problema*," she said, shooing Tia Rosa toward Luz, who held out comforting arms.

"*Mi pasteles!*" Tia Rosa wailed. Another flood of Spanish.

"She says she left the pot boiling on the stove," Luz said. "She wants someone to bring her things so she can cook in Mrs. Hernandez's apartment."

"For God's sake, this is a murder scene!" the cop exploded.

Before she could go on, a short, muscular man in plainclothes came up behind her.

"What's going on?"

"Detective Garcia!" She started to explain, but Tia Rosa's shrill voice overrode hers.

"It's okay, Norma, I've got it." Garcia turned to Tia Rosa with a little bow and listened attentively. He probably had an aunt just like her. "She wants her big pot and her spices," he said.

"*Y la yautia para la masa,*" Tia Rosa shrilled. "*Y los plátanos, y el lechón para el relleno.*"

Another plainclothes cop appeared, a big Irish guy who could have been Jimmy's cousin.

"See to it, Officer Patton. There's no harm in being courteous."

Officer Patton looked as if she couldn't decide which she wanted to do first, bite nails or file a suit for gender discrimination. But she wheeled and marched back to Luz's apartment without another word.

"Are you okay?" I asked Luz quietly. This couldn't be easy for her.

One corner of her mouth quirked up in a little smile.

"You are very kind to ask," she said. "I think it does me good not to be sad and scared for a few minutes." The smile blossomed into a radiant grin. I caught a glimpse of what she'd be like happy. "And we will eventually get to eat *pasteles.*"

The smile faded as Detective O'Brien said, "It's time for you to talk to us, Ms. Colón. Detective Garcia and I will need somewhere to talk to you privately."

"My apartment?" Luz said. She looked scared again.

Garcia shook his head.

"Still a crime scene. It'll have to be your neighbor's. But she'd better go back to bed, and your aunts will have to stay out of the way."

"And my friends?"

"They can wait for you outside," O'Brien said. He looked vaguely familiar, apart from his likeness to Jimmy and hundreds of other Irish Americans. If I hadn't been staring, wondering where I'd seen him, I would have missed the tiny complicit look he exchanged with Jimmy. AA, then. Jimmy knew a ton of people from the million meetings he'd attended in fifteen years. In Alcoholics Anonymous, the Anonymous meant you didn't let on in front of civilians. Those guys were like the Masons. Oh, yeah. Once again I'd forgotten momentarily that now I *was* those guys.

"Do I need a lawyer?" Luz asked.

O'Brien, all cop now, grinned, the menace thinly coated in joviality.

"I don't know, ma'am. Do you?"

"You don't have to answer questions without an attorney present," Garcia said, "but we would appreciate your cooperation." His tone was soothing.

"I don't want a lawyer," she said. "I'll only get more nervous if we put it off."

Jimmy gave her a little shake of the head, meaning, Bad idea. She didn't see it. As the two detectives ushered her into the apartment, she gave a despairing backward glance, not at Barbara, but at me. I felt irrationally pleased. I wished I could do something to help her.

We retreated down a couple of landings and crept right back up again. At one point, the cop on the door snuck out, probably to smoke, and we got to put our ears against the apartment door for a minute. Luz's voice floated out to us.

"I am telling you all I know." It sounded like she was crying. "How could I have killed him? I loved him."

As Luz told us later, it went more or less the way we would have expected. The two detectives took her over her story two or three times. They made it clear they would check everything she said and regarded anything that couldn't be checked with a certain skepticism. Why didn't she and Frankie spend the evening together? He had gone to a meeting. What kind of meeting? An AA meeting. Where? She didn't know. Garcia had wanted to make something of it, but O'Brien shut him up. Where had she been? She had gone to the library, then stopped by her aunt's house on the way home. Which aunt? Tia Wanda. She had wanted them to get Tia Wanda to confirm it on the spot. The detectives had declined to brave the aunts in the kitchen, saying they'd get Tia Wanda's story in due course.

Then they turned to the crime scene. Luz had come home to find Frankie dead on the floor. The apartment's only door had a deadbolt, a keypad arrangement, and a security bar. None of them showed signs of tampering. It looked like Frankie had let the killer in. Luz had found the security bar lying on the floor when she came in. Of course, she had keys and knew the code. At least they didn't accuse her outright. For one thing, they couldn't find the weapon. He had been stabbed. They told her they would have to take all the kitchen knives for testing.

Did she know that Frankie had done time for drugs? Was he still using? Was he dealing? They pushed hard on the drug angle. She was indignant, insisting Frankie was clean. But maybe that wasn't such a bad thing. If they suspected his death was drug-related, it took the pressure off Luz. She was too cautious to spill the parts of the love story that screamed motive. Like how he threatened and maybe even hit her. Like how he kept leaving.

We were on the landing with our noses to a crack in the stairwell door when the apartment door opened. We heard Garcia say, "Okay, let's wrap it up here for tonight. You can let the ladies out of the kitchen and tell them to go home."

The three of us retreated down the stairs. Halfway to the next landing, Barbara stopped short.

"This is silly. We wait for Luz, to make sure she's all right. No discussion."

Mrs. Hernandez's door swung open just as we reached it. A fleet of aunts sailed out like fishing boats at high tide. Sidling past them, we could see Luz on the sofa. Tia Margarita held her hand. O'Brien stood over them.

"We're not finished with you," he said. "If you want to leave the city for any reason, you'd better ask first."

Barbara bounced right up to him.

"Look, she's exhausted and overwrought. Can't you let her just go home with her aunt? Or me, if you want," she added to Luz. Luz shook her head, then bent it briefly toward her aunt.

"Yes! Let her go!" Tia Margarita said. She sat bolt upright as if to shame the sagging couch for its posture. "My *paloma* needs sleep. She is sick with sorrow over this worthless man. She had nothing to do with his *drogas terreras*. Leave her alone! You are wasting your time here. She was not his enemy. Why don't you go and bother his wife?"

His wife? Frankie had a wife? My mouth dropped open. So did Barbara's. The detectives froze like bird dogs, and their noses quivered. No wonder, Barbara said later, that Luz had never seemed to worry about where Frankie went when he stormed out, only whether he would come back.

"He wanted to get the marriage annulled," Luz said in a weary voice. Her head bent, she stared down at her lap. "She wouldn't let him." She raised her eyes, her chin lifted. "He only went to her because he felt sorry for her. He never loved her. It wasn't a true marriage. He slept on the couch."

Yeah, right. And I've got a bridge for you, sister. I held my breath. Any moment now, the detectives would realize they'd resumed the interview with all of us right there listening.

"You knew about the wife," O'Brien said. If she hadn't, suddenly finding out would be a terrific motive for murder. If she hadn't known all along, how would Tia Margarita have known?

"It was old news." Luz sounded defiant. "She meant nothing—not to him, not to me."

"Children?" O'Brien persisted stolidly.

"No! He wouldn't have them—not with her. I tell you they had nothing."

"You knew her?" I didn't trust Garcia's polite tone for a second. "You had visited her home?"

"No, of course not. But I knew Frankie. He told me ev—" She stopped abruptly. She'd spotted the catch, as we all had. If he had told her everything, she would have known about the drugs. "He told me what I needed to know, and I needed to know he loved me. The wife—old news. Maybe she hated him, maybe she didn't care. Go and ask her."

It was after three in the morning when we finally emerged. The rain was still coming down in sheets. Luz kept going over her interview, arguing the points she was afraid had failed to convince the detectives.

"Frankie never told me where his meetings were," she said. "I told them his home group was in Brooklyn."

Jimmy shook his head.

"Maybe better not to have volunteered any information."

"I didn't know what to do," Luz said. "I thought to show them I am willing to cooperate."

"What's done is done," Barbara said. "You did the best you could."

Tia Margarita tugged at Luz's elbow, saying something about *la mañana*. Save it for the morning.

"*Si, tia, pronto!* They upset me very much."

"We can't do anything about it tonight," Jimmy said very gently. "Time to get your Aunt Margarita home to bed. Can we drive you home?"

But Tia Margarita refused Jimmy's offer to drive her and Luz to her home in the Bronx. It was too far, she protested, and too late at night. We must go home and get some sleep. A few taxis zoomed past, all occupied and headed for nicer neighborhoods. East Harlem was not an easy place to hail a cab at the best of times. Finally, he called them a car service on his cell phone. When it arrived, he more or less forced a twenty-dollar bill into Tia Margarita's hand. He pried her fingers open and wrapped them around it, then took her off guard by planting a kiss on her gnarled knuckles.

"You're a good boy," she said, patting his cheek.

In the meantime, Barbara gave Luz a prolonged hug. "It'll be all right. Anyhow, there's nothing you can do about any of it tonight except be good to yourself."

"And pray." Luz wasn't quite crying, but she gave a watery sniff.

Barbara being Barbara, a couple of questions popped out.

"You really didn't know about the drugs?"

"Not until he went to rehab—like I told you. Just, you know, in the past—bad company, he said."

"And you knew about the wife? It didn't bother you?"

Luz sniffed again and made a brave attempt at a grin. "Oh, I felt horribly guilty."

"But you were sure she was no threat to you," Barbara persisted.

"Absolutely sure."

Once we were on our own in the car, Barbara said, "And you don't know all the things she didn't tell the cops. He was jealous. He used to snoop in her e-mail. He wanted to make sure she didn't have any secret lovers. Completely paranoid. She tried to make a joke out of it, poor thing."

"And that thing about his going to church with her?" Jimmy prompted.

"Right." She swiveled in her seat. "She called me in floods of tears about that. He said it was bad enough he had to listen to that God stuff in AA, and she had to be an idiot to think just because he was clean he'd sit around with a bunch of old ladies with droopy boobs and silly hats." She added sharply, "It's not funny."

I hastily rearranged my face.

"I know it's not." I did, really, but the habit of irreverence was hard to break.

"And another time? He said he'd sweated blood in rehab so he could start a new life, and he was damned if he was going to do it with a stupid bitch like her clinging to his ankles and dragging him down."

Not exactly the spirit of recovery.

"A guy like that gives sobriety a bad name," Jimmy said. "I could have killed the asshole myself."

"Now, there's a motive," I said. "Suspects, two million sober alcoholics."

"Don't even joke about it," Barbara said. "To tell the truth, I used to worry that he would kill her. He had a terrible temper. No impulse control." Barbara can never resist the clinical term. "I didn't even like it that he knew I was her sponsor. I was afraid he'd decide it was my fault she wasn't submissive enough and come after me."

"What did Luz have to say about that?" I asked.

"Oh, she kept assuring me he was harmless. It gave me chills every time she said it. Talk about denial."

"And what about the wife?" Jimmy asked. "Was Luz lying? Deluded? Or what?"

"Good question," Barbara said. "I haven't the slightest idea."

TWO

I woke up early, too wired to go back to sleep. My body was zonked, but my brain was wide awake. Sleeping in got harder when I gave up passing out. I thought a little about Luz and her problem and a lot about what I was going to do for the rest of my life. I did office temp work to pay the rent, but that was a recovery job, not a career. In AA, they suggested no relationships the first year. So I was single. I wasn't lonely. How could I be? I had Jimmy and Barbara, my AA sponsor, and two million sober alcoholics breathing down my neck.

When the phone rang at nine, I was cleaning my apartment. Sobriety, housework, up at the crack of dawn. I hardly recognized myself. I had made a few improvements to the place since I got out of detox. I had exchanged the mattress on the floor for a futon on a pale wood platform. The boxes of neglected possessions that had stuck to me like moss the last few years of my drinking were gone. Some stuff had ended up in the worthy-cause thrift shop on the corner, the rest in the nearest Dumpster. I didn't miss any of it. I'm not a moose. I don't need moss.

The phone kept ringing. Probably Barbara, to tell me the game was afoot. She had a theory that playing detective would keep me from getting so bored with sobriety that I relapsed. Now I just had to locate the phone. Barbara, in a fit of helping, had organized the crap out of the whole apartment. I couldn't find anything. I was baffled until I had the bright idea of following the cord away from the phone jack. I finally unearthed the phone in a tangled pile of clothes destined for the Laundromat. I didn't have to pick them up to smell them.

"Yeah."

"Bruce! Are you really up at this hour or is that a clone with a different childhood?"

"Yeah, it's me. Hi, Laura." I hadn't seen my ex-wife or heard from her since I got out of detox. I'd left a message on her machine, telling her I'd stayed sober. Her deep, throaty voice still turned me on. "What are you doing up yourself?" Laura and I had spent much of our marriage in bed. I'd say the percentages of time spent making love, getting high, and in a stupor ran about even.

"I haven't been to bed."

"Did you take your lithium?"

"I'm much more fun without it."

She had a point. The beginning of Laura's manic swings felt like carnival in Rio. On the other hand, the later stages could get scary.

"Besides, the lithium was making me depressed." It had a certain logic. The suicidal end of her depressions had scared me more than the psychotic mania.

"It might not do that if you took it in the dose the doctor ordered."

"Oh, Bruce, you're no fun since you stopped drinking." She had always delighted in jerking my chain. "Why don't you come over?"

"If you promise not to try to get me high. And I'm serious." That had been our catchphrase in the bad old days. "I'm serious" meant time to stop being playful. Put down the kitchen knife. Unlock the handcuffs. Give me back my underpants. Get away from the ledge.

"Okay, okay. I'm allowed to seduce you, I hope. You haven't gone and joined one of those sexaholic programs while you're at it?"

"Not even on my list," I assured her. It was about the only one that wasn't.

"Come out and play, Bruce." The deep voice managed to sound like a wistful little girl's. "I want to see if those reformed drunks have ruined you."

"Recovering," I corrected automatically. "All right, I'll be there in a couple of hours. I have to finish vacuuming."

"Vacuuming?" When she squealed, her voice went up an octave. Peals of laughter followed. "Oh, Bruce, my sides ache, I don't know when I last laughed so hard."

"Thank you for sharing." That's right, call me a clown and laugh at me. "Don't bust a gut. I'll see you later."

I took the subway down to lower Manhattan. Didn't jump the turnstile. I had an awful feeling that when I got to Step Nine, the amends step, my sponsor would tell me I had to make restitution to the MTA for all the times I had.

Laura had a loft in SoHo. One of those New York institutions, like my rent-controlled apartment. The glass-half-empty kind of guy that I used to be might say a loft was just a big open space the size of a warehouse with all the pipes showing on the ceiling and no privacy except in the bathroom. From a glass-half-full perspective, the place was vast and airy and flooded with light from the high windows on all four sides. Laura had the whole fourth floor and the luck to be surrounded by lower buildings.

Nobody else I knew could still afford SoHo. The starving artists had all moved on. But Laura was a trust-fund baby. She made arty jewelry, using feathers and crystals and copper wire and industrial detritus. But she didn't have to work. Just as well. She was usually either shuttling through bipolar swings or high as a kite. She could afford Chivas Regal. And she got all the pills she wanted from a tame doctor known throughout the tristate area as Dr. Feelgood.

The entrance to Laura's building was a scarred narrow door squeezed in between a chi-chi gallery and the kind of clothing store that displays no more than three garments, all black, and never has any customers. Above the lintel someone had painted THE GATES OF HEAVEN. It used to say ENJOY THE DOPE, ALL YE WHO ENTER HERE. But the tenants were aging, and they'd developed a little discretion. The buzzer hadn't worked at any time since the day I met her. I backed into the street and squinted up at her windows. Saturday was tourist day in SoHo, and traffic was moving slowly.

I put two fingers in my mouth and gave a piercing whistle.

"Laura!" I bellowed.

One pane in the wall of windows swung open. The rusty handle she used to crank it open fell off and plummeted to the street. It narrowly missed the heads of a passing family from Wichita. I knew they were from Wichita because their T-shirts said so. The handle hit the ground at some velocity and bounced into the gutter, where I intercepted it. When I looked back up, Laura's head was sticking out the window. She shook the fluffy mane of hair that had ended up in my mouth many times in our snuggling days. Oh Lord, had she dyed it magenta again? Laura on a manic swing took looking like a SoHo artist to an extreme. The Wichita family had stopped dead in their tracks, blocking foot traffic. They craned their necks upward. One of the kids, an acned preteen, snapped off a shot on his digital camera. We had made their day.

"Sorry!" Laura shouted. "It always falls off. Here, catch!"

She tossed a clanking bunch of keys my way. The gawking tourists took a hasty step backward. They needn't have worried. I had had plenty of practice. I had never had my own key. Even when we were married, Laura had insisted on what she called her freedom. One man's cheatin' woman is another's free spirit. I had gone along with it without much thought.

Laura's building had an elevator, grit encrusted and sour smelling. The battered old cage creaked and whined as it took me up to the loft. When Jimmy used to visit me here, he would ride up and down, pretending he was a Welsh miner. Down into the pit, he would intone. And now back up into the light again. Laura bought him a canary one Christmas.

The elevator door opened directly into the loft. As always, I blinked coming into the light. It was kind of like coming out of a mine. I hadn't been here for a while. I looked around. Nothing had changed. The king-size water bed still stood in the middle of the room. Laura might be the last person in New York who still had one. The time it sprang a leak was a night to remember.

Laura met me at the elevator door. I stumbled over a familiar gap in the oversized shaft right into her arms.

"Let me look at you." Laura's idea of looking involved hands, teeth, and tongue.

"Hey, hold it. You're not reading Braille." Her bare feet, decorated with magenta nail polish and coin-silver Indian rings she might have bought on the street, balanced on mine like a life-size dancing doll's. I kind of shook her off me. I circled her upper arms with my fingers and held her at arm's length.

"You've lost weight." Her arms felt like matchsticks. "Have you been doing H?"

"No!" She looked at me with wounded outrage. An alibi face. I knew it well. I'd worn it many times myself. I grabbed her left wrist and turned the arm smooth side out. I knew exactly where to find her veins. No fresh track marks. Good.

Instead of pulling away, she reeled herself in, bringing us chest to chest. She ground her pelvis against me.

"That's not the most alert part of me anymore," I remarked.

"Wanna bet?"

She bent her head forward and shook the flyaway magenta mane so it just brushed my face and neck. My skin sprang to attention. To be honest, so did that other part. She had always had that effect on me.

I drew back to the boundary of my personal space and made eye contact.

"Admit I look good," I said.

"Let's go to bed." No more foreplay. To be fair, she had refrained from offering me a joint.

"A little conversation first?" I pleaded. "A cup of tea?"

"Bed," she insisted.

That extra octave down lent her the authority to get what she wanted. I'd have needed a special Twelve Step program to resist. Laura Anonymous. Step One: I'm powerless over Laura, and my life has become unmanageable. Her voice, her hair, that breakable quality. Her wild manic energy. Nothing about Laura felt wholesome. I think we got legally married to spice things up with the biggest contrast we could find.

I surrendered.

Twenty minutes later, I floated on my back, sated and drowsy. The water bed rocked me with a barely detectable sloshing motion. I managed to find my lips with the cigarette without opening my eyes. Laura's bed would never be a no-smoking zone, thank God. The phone rang. Let it. It wasn't for me. The body of water beneath me sloshed left, then right as Laura heaved herself out of bed. Her toe rings jingled as she ran across the polished floor. Imagine a New York apartment you could run in.

In the old days, Laura had kept the phone right by the bed. She didn't like to stop what she was doing. Like almost everybody else, she'd switched to cell. It played the first line of "Yellow Submarine." I began to get tired of it as the clatter and clang of flying aluminum told me she'd mislaid it last while cooking.

Stubbing out the cigarette, I rolled over on my stomach and pulled a pillow over my head. One of the few things Laura was careful about was keeping ashtrays by the bed. You really don't want to burn a hole in a water bed. The clattering and the Beatlesque electronics stopped, but I couldn't hear her voice. I decided I wanted to. I raised a lethargic hand and knocked the pillow off the back of my head. I could still barely hear Laura's voice. She was whispering. Something else I'd forgotten: Laura whispering meant Laura cheating.

I didn't know how I felt about that. Marriage gives you a license to have sex with that person that never expires. Divorce didn't seem to change that. But the vows we'd made were void. Besides, Laura and I had never been monogamous. Both of us had times when we weren't interested at all. Hers came during her depressive swings, mine at moments when Jack Daniel's and King Chivas took all of my attention. Each of us assumed the other found comfort elsewhere. Still, I didn't much like the idea of Laura talking to a boyfriend with my body fluids still slick on her thighs.

"Laura!" I called, deliberately loud. "Come back to bed." She didn't answer. I propped myself up on one elbow. She still stood naked in the kitchen, clutching the cell phone to one ear and making shushing motions toward me with her free hand.

"Get off the phone." I took a perverse pleasure in insisting. "Come on back to bed."

She stamped her foot and flapped an emphatic hand. I could read the signals: Leave me alone. Pipe down. I would have kept

prodding, but she pointed to her lips. Without sound, she enunciated, "I'm serious." I collapsed back onto the bed and waited for
her to come back.

I had almost dozed off when she slid under the covers. She snuggled in next to me. Her skin had cooled in the wide open spaces
of the loft. I could feel her sharp little bones. She tugged at the
antique Amish quilt that had cost as much as I made in a month of
temping. Only a husband—in this case, an ex—would have tugged
back, grumbling wordlessly about having to share. She wouldn't
give up. I rolled over to face her. Locked in each other's arms, we
had plenty of room. The magenta hair tickled my nose. I didn't
mind. She smelled of patchouli. The faint breath of the Sixties reminded me how much I'd liked hallucinogens before things started
going irrevocably bad.

"So who was it?"

"Do you really need to know?" She sounded defensive.

"Just making conversation."

A silence fell. I could hear the faint hum of the refrigerator.
Somebody flushing. What sounded like a herd of buffalo thunder-
ing across the ceiling. That would be the upstairs neighbor's Great
Dane, who got to play whenever he wanted to.

"I've been seeing someone."

"Uh, do we talk about these things now?"

Her arm tightened around me. She walked her fingers up my
spine.

"I don't know. Do we?"

I thought about it as she blew a few warm breaths on my neck
and twiddled my left ear.

"I don't mind if you don't." I had no intention of telling her
anything. Not that I had anything to tell. I did, however, want to
hear about this guy. What had once been jealousy seemed to have
evaporated. "So tell me. What's his name?"

"Mac." She pushed the short syllable out grudgingly, like a little girl caught lying. It made me feel tender. I pushed the flyaway cloud of hair back from her face and put my lips against her forehead.

"How long have you been seeing him?"

"About a year."

"You're so tense." I began to lick along her hairline, working my way from left to right. I could always do anything with Laura. Sex didn't embarrass her one bit. And if you've met anyone more uninhibited than a bipolar on an upswing and off her meds, you're even farther from Kansas than I am.

"So what's he like?" I murmured, spitting out a curly strand. She twitched her head away, though her hips against my groin sent me a different message.

"Oh, you know."

"No, I don't," I said.

"You didn't used to talk this much," she said peevishly. "What is this, the Inquisition?"

"Hardly." I burrowed down toward the foot of the bed, keeping my hands on her and stroking as I went. "Would the Inquisition do this? Or this? Or this? Jeez, Laura, you went magenta all the way."

"Ow!" She jerked away.

"What did I do?" I had only pressed the palms of my hands against her thighs. They'd always been soft and satiny in spite of her thinness, and I knew them well. "Did I hurt you? Let me look." I flipped the quilt back.

"No!" She tried to pull it back over her, but I was stronger. In the dusty afternoon light, I could see her creamy thighs were marred by some nasty-looking bruises. A couple were the blue-black of recent marks, but the rest, in various stages of discoloration, swirled green and yellow and lavender against the pale surrounding skin. I might have imagined it, but I thought I saw finger marks.

"But is it art?" Okay, I get flippant when I'm stuck.

She blew a little air out through her nostrils and made a soft sound in her throat. For a second, I thought I'd succeeded in amusing her. But she pulled her legs away and sat up. Arms around her knees, she drew herself up into a little defensive ball. Even depressed, the Laura I knew did not go small. With horror, I saw a tear roll down her right cheek. But Laura never cried. Well, yeah, during a major depressive episode. This was not that. This was not good at all.

"Dammit, Laura," I sputtered, thinking of half a dozen things to say and rejecting them all.

She gave me a little lopsided grin with absolutely no attitude in it. This was pathetic. I felt like crying myself.

"It's okay," she said.

"No, it's not!" I shot back. "Does he hurt you?" I might have been jumping to conclusions. I'd had some strenuous and even kinky sex with Laura myself. But this looked like abuse. It made me very angry.

Her beautiful voice got wispy without going up the scale at all.

"I can't help it, Bruce. I'm in love with him. I know he's not good for me, but I can't leave."

THREE

"I can't believe you talked me into this," I bellowed over the clamor of the train.

Jimmy and I swayed as we hovered over Barbara in classic New York subway straphanger position.

"Who, me?" Jimmy knew damn well I didn't mean him. "I'm a stranger in a strange land myself."

"No way would I venture into the wilds of Brooklyn without you guys," Barbara screamed. "I need Jimmy to cover my back when I brave Catholic rituals. And Jimmy needs you for moral support. Anyhow, we're doing it for Luz."

Luz sat across the aisle of the subway car, wedged up against a guy in floppy gangsta pants. His body language suggested he had his Walkman ratcheted all the way up on a heavy megabass beat. She saw us conferring and raised her eyebrows in inquiry. Barbara shook her head and patted the air with her hand: nothing, never mind, don't worry.

We were on our way to Frankie's wake.

Barbara beckoned me to bend over so she could get her lips close to my ear. It didn't stop her from yelling, the way people do on their cell phones.

"Bruce, have you ever been to a wake?"

"Not a wake," Jimmy corrected, "it's a viewing."

"Same thing nowadays," I said. "They don't make funerals like they used to." Except in the movies, I'd never been to the kind of wake the word evoked. This one would be held in a nice, sanitized funeral home, not the front parlor. The deceased wouldn't come back to life in the middle of the night. And no booze. Just as well.

"I'm a nice Jewish girl," Barbara said. "I like it better when the corpse is stowed away before the party starts, and they give you plenty of bagels and chopped liver to take the edge off your grief. It creeps me out to have to look at the departed all decked out in his best suit and looking almost but not quite like himself."

"You guys hustle them underground in twenty-four hours," Jimmy said. "That seems strange to me."

"We lived in a hot climate until the Diaspora," Barbara said. "I hope this expedition isn't a big mistake."

So did I. Luz would be braving Frankie's family. And we'd be crashing the party. But she had been determined to come, and Barbara equally determined to support her.

"I have to say good-bye to him," Luz had insisted.

Jimmy and Barbara had tried to persuade her to make her farewells at the funeral instead. The funeral mass would provide no opportunity for a scene. Jimmy especially hoped fervently that Luz didn't want a scene. "I don't want any trouble" is his personal motto. I'd gone headfirst into plenty of trouble in my time. In this case, I felt what Barbara would call detached. I'd never known Frankie, to my knowledge, and I'd only met Luz the other night. Jimmy was right, though. We'd all feel safer in a church, with

— 28 —

everybody facing front, their eyes on the priest and their minds on Jesus and or at least their own mortality.

Luz remained stubborn.

"I have to see him up close one last time. If I don't, I'll always remember him on the floor in his blood."

She had said the same thing again this morning, in tears, over a fortifying greasy-spoon breakfast on the Upper West Side before the four of us boarded the train. Barbara had handed her a pack of tissues. Jimmy had made one more attempt to talk her out of going.

"What about his wife? It will be so uncomfortable for you."

That was putting it nicely. She must know on some level that she was setting up a potential social catastrophe.

"She's never seen me. You know how it is. The widow is overwhelmed, so many people come up to her, they take her hand, they say how sorry they are. She says thank you, thank you. She doesn't ask who they are—if she doesn't know, she pretends she does."

"She's got a point, Jimmy," Barbara said. "They won't give us name tags."

"You're willing to go up and take her hand?" Jimmy asked. Good question.

"If I have to." Luz's shoulders hunched. I thought of a mule pulling a plow through a rocky field.

"What about his friends, Luz?" Barbara asked. "It won't be just her family, you know. The place will be crawling with people who do know you."

"The ones on my side won't betray me. The ones on her side don't know me." She made it sound simple.

Jimmy and I both let out what Barbara calls our ACOA sighs. Jimmy's would have blown a strike on a bowling alley. She, being an adult child of Eastern European Jewish parents rather than of alcoholics, said, "Oy *vey iz mir.*" We all accepted the inevitable.

"What if the two detectives we met are there?" I had kept my mouth shut up to this point, but it wouldn't hurt to consider strategy.

"Oh, I am so tired of them," Luz said. "They keep coming back and asking the same questions."

"It's an opportunity," Barbara pointed out. "Not just for them, but for us. If Luz didn't kill Frankie, this viewing is our best chance to meet a whole flock of people who could have."

"If?"

"Cops' 'if,' our 'since we know,'" Barbara said.

"Oh, Barbara," Luz said, looking at her sponsor with touching faith, "it will be wonderful if you can find out who did it. Then the police will have to leave me alone."

Jimmy kicked me under the coffee shop table.

Still, it might be kind of interesting. In spite of the ominous presence of the corpse, the viewing would play out as a social event. We'd have a chance to talk to people who'd been close to Frankie and might have had their own reasons to kill him.

Jimmy had already told me privately that he doubted the stabbing was purely "business" from higher up the drug-dealing chain.

"Dealers have guns," he'd said, looking grim. He didn't have to say that investigating would be a helluva lot less of a lark if professionals were involved. Or that this wouldn't deter Barbara.

We couldn't completely rule it out. Frankie might have tied off loose ends before he went away to rehab for twenty-eight days. Or he might have left his affairs in a mess to cause trouble the moment he came out. He could even have gone to rehab to avoid preexisting trouble. It wasn't unheard of. What if he'd cheated someone he owed drug money to? What if he'd sold bad drugs to users, either adulterated with some inactive ingredient or cut with something toxic? Luz had believed that Frankie meant to get and stay clean.

She was new to the program. She was still on that pink cloud they talked about, dazzled by the bright and shiny miracle of recovery. The rest of us knew too many addicts whose bullshit had never diminished, no matter how long they didn't use.

Frankie was more than just a drug addict. He was also a guy who hit women. He'd been violent with Luz even after he got clean. How many other women had he hurt? How many women had it in for him as a result? Or the women's friends and family? And what about the wife? I hoped Luz was right that the wife had never heard her name or seen her picture. If she had, I hated to think what might happen when we walked into the funeral parlor. He must have cheated before. And maybe he'd battered his wife as well as his girlfriends. Her family, whom we were about to meet, would have plenty of reason to hate Frankie. In spite of myself, I felt detective fever taking hold. It didn't have the kick of getting high, but it had its own fascination. Part of me could hardly wait to meet all these people.

The funeral home was so far into Brooklyn that the train emerged from its tunnel to run along an elevated track. We rattled along above dingy rows of storefronts and rubbish-strewn empty lots. Cramped backyards flashed by, stuffed with a tangle of last summer's flowers, persistent weeds, beat-up lawn furniture, and decrepit children's toys. After making about a hundred local stops, the train decanted us onto a deserted platform high above the street. A rickety set of iron stairs led downward. Ahead of me, Barbara slipped her hand into Jimmy's. That would have been fine if the stairway had been wider. She tripped on his heels and nearly knocked him over.

"Sorry!" Barbara said.

Jimmy wrenched his hand away to grab the railing, remarking mildly that if he intended to die in Brooklyn, he'd pick a more interesting way to go. Luz giggled nervously. I thought better of offering her my arm. But I waved her ahead of me. I figured if she lost her footing, I could catch her before she plunged forward. And if she tripped and fell backward, she'd hit my chest rather than the sharp edge of one of the metal steps.

Jimmy winked at Luz.

"Codependency is always having to say you're sorry, even when you didn't do anything."

Luz laughed a bit more naturally, and a couple of little wrinkles between her eyebrows smoothed out. It occurred to me that she must be wary of both of us, no matter how much Barbara sang our praises. With her history, Luz might expect any man, even us, to switch without warning from charm and affection to rage and using his fists.

The funeral home stood on a king-size corner lot in a residential area a few blocks off the shopping street that ran below the elevated tracks. The neighborhood looked prosperous. Detached brick houses squatted amid manicured patches of lawn and bunchy foundation plantings of rhododendron and azalea that were probably spectacular in the spring. The funeral home must get plenty of business. The place had more square footage, more abundant plantings, and more expensive paving, trim, and roofing than anything else on the block. The front door, of polished oak, sported a brass lion's head knocker and a doorbell that played the first couple of bars of Bach's "Jesu, Joy of Man's Desiring." It wasn't locked, anyhow. Jimmy pushed it open as the music ended. We walked into a sumptuous entrance hall that fulfilled the promise of the exterior. The decorators had pulled out all the stops: crystal chandeliers, etched-glass wall sconces, and mahogany furniture with dark red and gold velvet upholstery. If we'd taken off our shoes, our toes would have sunk right into the lush Persian rugs.

A gentleman with a bald head so shiny it looked polished greeted us with an inaudible generic murmur and an outstretched hand. He wore a dark suit with the faintest whisper of a pinstripe, matching silk tie and breast pocket handkerchief in a subdued burgundy, and a professionally mournful face. We all shook. His hand felt warm, fat, and solid, like a bunch of tightly packed sausages. We glanced around at the three or four doors that led to different reception rooms.

"Like gladiators wondering which one leads to the tiger," Jimmy whispered in my ear.

Luz muttered Frankie's family name, Iacone. I hadn't heard it before. So he was Italian. And Luz was Puerto Rican. That alone meant trouble. Diversity is a fact of life in New York. So is ethnic clannishness, whether or not it's considered "correct" to say so. At any rate, this Frankie might be the Italian guy I'd done business with. I would know for sure as soon as I checked out the casket.

The undertaker beckoned us to the nearest door on the right. Sorry, funeral director. It swung open with a discreet swish. The room, thank God, was crowded. By the modulated exhalation of Jimmy's breath, he was equally relieved. We couldn't see the coffin, no less the widow. When Luz stopped short, the rest of us had to brake suddenly in order not to crash into her. We had agreed we wouldn't call attention to ourselves if we could help it. Knocking her over would not have made a good beginning.

"I can't!" Luz flung a look, wild with panic, at us over her shoulder.

Jimmy put a hand on her other shoulder in wordless reassurance.

"I'm afraid it's too late to change our minds, baby," Barbara said. "We're right behind you."

Jimmy started to whistle through his teeth, unconsciously as usual. I recognized the off-key Civil War military march, one of his favorites. Barbara dug an elbow into his ribs, and he shut up. Luz lifted her chin, straightened her spine, and must have told herself some variant of "Forward, march!" But before she could take more than a step or two into the tightly packed mass of people filling most of the room, a dark, solid figure pushed its way out of the crowd to loom over us.

"Luz. You shouldn'a come. You shouldn' be here."

She had told us that those who knew her wouldn't betray her. She hadn't said they wouldn't be hostile.

"Vinnie." She waved a hand feebly toward us. "This is Frankie's cousin Vinnie. My friends. Barbara and Jimmy. And this is Bruce. Please!" Her voice pleaded. Don't make trouble. Don't give me away. "I just want to say good-bye."

Vinnie frowned. His bushy black eyebrows almost met above a massive beak of a nose. I doubted even a broad smile would make more than a centimeter of breathing room in the middle. He dwarfed Jimmy, who is burly and far from short. In fact, he looked like a real bruiser who probably worked out every day and bench-pressed three hundred pounds. His black hair sprayed out around his head in curly tufts. Tightly knit fuzz sprouted above his collar and knotted tie and popped out below impeccable French cuffs. His heavy gold cuff links and navy blue suit looked expensive. Drug money? The suit might have been tailored for him. Like Jimmy, he'd be hard to fit. But he still looked like a thug who had robbed a banker for his clothes.

"You shouldn'a come," he repeated.

Luz started to cry. The tears welled up on the lower rim of her eyes and spilled over to roll one at a time down her cheeks, like raindrops on a windowpane. Vinnie changed his tack.

"Okay, okay, f'Godsake don't cry," he said gruffly. "Ya here, ya here, but you gotta pull it together." His eyes, under the heavy lintel of his brows, slunk left and right around the corners of his face like spies in an old noir movie. Like us, he didn't want Luz to make herself conspicuous.

Luz did her best to comply. She squared her shoulders, shook away the drops on her cheeks with a quick toss of her head, and somehow sucked the remaining tears back up into her body. All without making a sound. She still looked miserable.

"Can I see him?" she mewed.

Vinnie clucked his tongue in an exasperated kind of way.

"I better take you." He swiveled to scout over the heads of the crowd. "Sooner the better, none a the family's over there right now." He shot a baleful glare at Jimmy, Barbara, and me under the brows. "You come too," he ordered. "Stay close."

Luz fell in behind him like a duckling following its mother as he bulled his way through the clusters of mourners. We flanked them, slightly to the rear. I did not want to trip on this guy's heels. Vinnie provided a muttered commentary over his shoulder as we passed each knot.

"Fellas from the neighborhood." I guess that meant childhood friends. The fellas, four or five of them, glowered silently at each other. Adjacent to them, a separate knot of women, dressed and made up to the nines, chattered away like starlings. They must be the wives, presumably invisible to Vinnie. I strained to hear them as we brushed past, so close I could smell powder and perfume.

"Netta's holding up pretty well."

"It hasn't hit her yet."

"She's gotta put up a good front for Massimo and Silvia. They're shattered."

"Not that Frankie ever gave them a day's peace of mind, or Netta either."

"Stella!" The other four reproached her in unison. Evidently plain speaking was not welcome.

"That one I could talk to," Barbara breathed as we brushed past. She twisted her head as far around as it would go, trying to fix Stella in her memory. I stared too. Round face, high domed forehead like a Renaissance madonna under light brown hair pulled back tight. Petite and nicely rounded, with a lively expression and intelligent eyes.

Vinnie jerked his chin at a couple of men, maybe in their midthirties. They had on expensive-looking dark suits, morose expressions, and identical ears that flared out memorably from their heads.

"Netta's brothers. Them you wanna stay away from."

No argument from me on that one.

The next bunch showed the first hint of ethnic diversity in the room. Their skin tones ranged from fishbelly white through café au lait to French roast. A variety of face and body types to match.

Vinnie growled deep in his throat, like a suspicious dog preparing to defend his territory.

"Them even I wanna stay away from."

At the same time, one of them, an African American with a gleaming shaved head and skin the color of golden oak, looked up. I heard Barbara mutter something about cheekbones to die for. Women. The man caught Luz's eye. She stopped short.

"Ishmael. I—I didn't know you'd be here." She sounded frightened.

"Shee-it, Luz, same to you, girl. Looks like Frankie getting himself reformed didn't work out so good." Ishmael grinned without humor. I told myself that his teeth couldn't possibly be filed to a point. The hard eyes and the way he seemed to enjoy his own meanness just made it look like they were.

Luz drooped where she stood. It was probably the best possible way to deal with him. This guy had alpha male written all over him. Either you assumed the position or you got your throat torn out.

"No," she said, nothing but sadness in her voice, as if she had taken his taunt literally.

Vinnie had already taken himself at his word and moved on.

Luz stood bowed in front of Ishmael as if rooted. By tacit consent, Jimmy and I flowed up behind her to put a bulwark at her back. We crowded Barbara to the rear. Not that she'd thank us. Barbara can get kind of sassy in her cool counselor persona. Claims she's met plenty of drug dealers as well as addicts and held her own with them. She thinks she's tough as nails. The truth is, she meets only the safe ones with the clipped wings. At least she had the sense to zip the lip for once.

"We'll get together soon, have a little talk about old times," Ishmael said. I don't know which was more menacing, the mock-jovial voice or the eyes like stones. "I know where you live."

Jimmy shook himself loose first. He nodded curtly to Ishmael as he turned away, sweeping Luz up with a solid arm around her shoulders. I put my hand under Barbara's elbow. To my relief, she let me steer her away from trouble.

"Come on. Vinnie's waiting for us," Jimmy said. "Looks like he's cleared a path to the casket."

I peered at Frankie on his bier. He had worn that determined jaw and grim mouth long before the undertaker had wired it shut. His slicked-back dark brown hair revealed the arrowhead of a widow's peak. His eyebrows had a distinctive half-moon arch. They made a statement. Yep, I had definitely copped rock from this guy a time or two. It didn't make me mourn his passing. Even though he was in the program. Did anonymity run out with death, like an expired credit card? Or did it sit there accumulating mojo, like an unpaid traffic ticket?

Barbara peeped at him from behind Jimmy's reassuring bulk. As she'd said, she wasn't at her best with the embalmed. With a little gasp and moan, Luz fell to her knees on the padded rail. Jimmy stepped forward and knelt unselfconsciously beside her. Barbara hooked her arm through mine. I'm too compact to hide behind, but I didn't mind if she snuggled up. Vinnie made a little bob and crossed himself but then backed off. He would have communed with his dead cousin earlier. He probably wanted to get away from the Other Woman and her friends too. Us.

"I can't help it," Barbara whispered, "'casket' makes me think of Snow White."

I turned my head to grin at her.

"Feeling Jewish?"

"Shhh. Dissociated. Like I'm at the movies. There really is no way not to look, is there?"

Frankie's family had spared no expense. The glossy hardwood coffin with its burnished brass handles reflected track lighting and the flames of tall white candles set in massive candelabra, also brass. The effect was theatrical. The coffin was lined in puffy pale blue satin, like a baby boy's cradle. Its cover curved over the lower half of the body, with a glimpse of blue satin just visible, folded back at the waist. At least two dozen elaborate floral arrangements had been placed around the bier. A couple of wreaths were draped over the closed part of the coffin. Two giant urns, elevated on stilt-like tripods, stood sentry at the head and foot. Lilies predominated. Their heavy, languorous scent filled the air. In the close air of this pompous and depressing room, I understood why they call that smell funereal.

Frankie lay with his hands folded across his chest. The waxy fingers curved around a silver crucifix on a chain.

"Do you think his parents knew about the dealing?" Barbara murmured. "I bet they were enablers."

Protecting him from the consequences. Keeping the addiction going. What had Frankie's parents thought of his going into rehab? Had they denied he needed it? Had they thought he would live happily ever after? Would they have resented the cheerfully intrusive tone that rehabs take with families?

Frankie's face had that look of a good fake of a human expression that the embalmer's art can bestow. It was not reposeful. You could see why they call the dead stiffs. I eased myself around toward the head of the coffin, pretending to examine the flowers more closely. I figured I should take the chance to read the cards. If this murder had been personal, the killer might have sent flowers. Barbara had the same idea, except she really did want a better look at the flowers too. She stuck her nose right into the lilies. Then she had to wipe a dab of pollen off her nose and pinch her nostrils to avoid sneezing her head off.

From where I stood, I could see Luz's face. The dramatic lighting cast its beam on her. She looked literally transfigured by grief. The tears fell unchecked. I glanced around to make sure nobody who looked like family was nearby to wonder who this unknown Niobe might be. While I watched, she put a hand out to caress his cheek and then snatched it back as if she'd burned it.

Barbara caught my eye and mouthed, "Enough." Jimmy still knelt next to Luz. I started to turn away, momentarily off balance as I swiveled. Something cannoned into me at thigh level. I clutched at plump, soft flesh encased in dark maroon satin and organza: a little girl, formally dressed.

"Oops, sorry!" As I relaxed my hold, a little boy crashed into her. He was equally formal in a pint-size dark blue suit. First communion garb. This time, I cracked my calves against the edge of the kneeler and almost did a backflip onto the open coffin. Jimmy, getting up all in one solid piece, blocked my fall. Barbara reached out to steady me. Luz, still crying and praying, ignored the commotion.

The two children regarded us with unwinking stares. If they'd been cartoons, their captions would have read, "Who the hell are you?" and "You don't belong here." The little girl had liquid dark eyes, rounded, chubby cheeks and a thick, bow-shaped upper lip like a cartoon goldfish. Her brown hair fell in fat ringlets below a matching satin scrunchie. The boy had a grim mouth for such a young face. His ears flared like those of the guys Vinnie had identified as the wife's brothers.

"Is that your uncle Frankie?" Barbara asked.

"It's my papa," the boy said.

"He's not really here," the little girl added. "He's in heaven." She put a chubby thumb in her mouth and started to suck.

The boy tugged at her arm until the thumb came out, glistening with saliva. She started to wipe it on her satin dress. He clutched at her wrist to stop her. Whisking a starched handkerchief from his breast pocket, he dried her hand. She used her free hand to poke him in the stomach, giggling when he said, "Ow!"

She darted away. He ran after her. We all looked at each other. Jimmy shrugged. I hoisted one eyebrow. Barbara turned to Luz as she got to her feet, moving like an old lady with a bad back.

"Children?" Barbara said. "He had children? Luz, did you know?"

Luz turned toward us a face that looked deader than Frankie's.

"They were the only reason he stayed so long. But he was working it out. He was beginning to understand that maybe a loveless marriage wasn't so good for them either."

"But you said—you lied to us. Much worse, you lied to the police. Luz, that is really, really bad."

"I'm sorry, Barbara. I would have told you, honestly, only—I lied to the aunts. I couldn't tell them I was sleeping with a man who had a real Catholic marriage. I just couldn't. And then, Tia Margarita was there when those detectives asked me. I'd have told them when they came back, but they didn't ask me again."

By now the police would know. The detectives would have interviewed the family. They didn't have to go back and ask her again. The fact that she'd lied about it simply became a part of their investigation.

"I don't mean to guilt-trip you," Barbara said. She reached out to rub Luz's back a little, as if to erase the disappointment and reproach she couldn't hide. "I know how bad you feel already. But— the couch?"

"He swore to me, and I believed—believe—him," Luz said defiantly. "It was an empty marriage. Emotionally, it was over."

We all stood there in embarrassed silence for a minute or two. I felt relieved when Frankie's cousin pushed his way out of the crowd again. Other mourners were beginning to drift toward the coffin, too.

"Come pay your respects to Massimo and Silvia now," Vinnie said. "And then you should leave."

Obediently, we followed him.

Frankie's parents sat on a dark red velvet couch. A glass-topped side table held a box of tissues and an ornate brass lamp whose dark red shade cast a morose ruddy light on them. The father's hands were tightly clasped, as if a moment's relaxation would make him disintegrate. The mother's lap held a heap of crumpled tissues. As we approached, she twisted a strip of tissue in her fingers, over and over. Both wore unrelieved black and had silver hair, lackluster as if sorrow had dulled it. They looked shriveled and old. I had a hunch that Frankie's death had withered them. The cluster of sympathizers around them parted to let us in. I hoped the parents wouldn't recognize Luz as Frankie's unwelcome girlfriend on the side. When I glanced at Barbara, I saw her lips move as if she was praying the same thing. If they'd seen a picture of Luz or heard her name, nobody's Higher Power could avert a scene. No, I take that back. In the program, they said, "Be careful what you pray for." God could probably provide a fire or a heart attack to take the focus off this unfortunate meeting.

It looked like no *deus ex machina* would be needed. Jimmy, taking the lead, held out his hand first to Massimo, then to Silvia, and shook.

"I'm sorry for your loss." His voice held a tactful blend of sympathy and respect.

I followed suit. Then came Barbara, who impulsively laid her other hand over Silvia's as she held it.

"I am so sorry about your son," she said. "Losing a child—terrible for you." Even when the child was a scumbag like Frankie.

Luz came last, her voice hoarse and practically inaudible as she muttered her condolences.

"You were friends of my son?" Massimo asked. "Thank you for coming."

"Thank you for coming," Silvia echoed. "Have you spoken to Netta yet? She is so sad."

We nodded and murmured as we backed away. I didn't have to feel ashamed, but I did. One more unwelcome but authentic feeling from the folks who brought you sobriety.

Luz gulped, maybe with relief. Jimmy heaved one of his ACOA sighs. Barbara had tears in her eyes. I hoped she wouldn't break down. Barbara didn't cry prettily like Luz. Puffy eyes, a red nose, and a lot of mucus would not improve the present situation. I hoped we could avoid the wife. But the crowd fell away around us, leaving a straight path to where she sat. Enthroned on a gold velvet wing chair, she was surrounded by women of all ages. Two leaned over the back of the chair. Two more crouched at her feet. One had pulled a folding chair close and held her hand. On the other side, a woman enough like her to be her sister rubbed her back. She looked up as we approached, dull misery in her eyes. Better that than recognition or hostility. With automatic politeness, she pushed up against the chair arms to rise in greeting. The women pushed and pulled her down again, conveying with little pats that she had the right to remain comfortable. But we had seen enough.

Frankie's wife was pregnant.

FOUR

Frankie had lied about sleeping on the couch. Luz almost fainted. She hadn't known.

"I want to go home," she moaned as we propped her up.

"Let's get her out of here," Barbara said through gritted teeth. "Now!"

We forged through the crowd. Barbara kept the wilting Luz on her feet and moving. Jimmy's bulk provided a privacy screen. I scurried around the edges like a pilot fish escorting a shark. Vinnie had disappeared. The rat.

Barbara kept murmuring without conviction that it was all right, it was going to be all right. Somewhere in there she had crossed the line. She'd taken on Luz's catastrophic life and dragged us with her. When I got sober and she and Jimmy let me back into their lives, I had no idea I would do as much leaping before I looked just following Barbara around as I'd ever done getting wasted.

We reached the foyer. The front door looked like the gates of paradise to me by this time. But Luz started tugging Barbara toward a discreet RESTROOMS sign.

"I can't go outside like this," she said. "I look like sheet." Agitation increased her accent.

"Can't we just go?" I whined.

I hoped Jimmy would talk them out of this detour. But he was whistling through his teeth and looking at his guardian angel, who had hovered above his left shoulder since we were kids. He didn't always believe in it, but in moments of stress, he checked in.

"You'll feel better when you've washed your face," Barbara told Luz. To us, she said, "I'm going to pee, and you should too. It's a long ride back to Manhattan."

"Yes, dear," Jimmy said. "She doesn't have to face that grueling subway ride, though. I'll call a car service." He got his cell phone out of his pocket as Barbara drew Luz toward the Ladies'.

"You should go too," she told Luz, pushing open the textured glass door.

"Thank you for sharing," I said as the door swung closed behind them. "Come on, Jim, let's get some air."

We emerged into the afternoon sunshine. A lot of people had fled the funereal atmosphere inside. Small groups loitered on the flagstone walk.

"Praise the Lord! Smokers!" I nodded toward a tight circle with heads together and the smoke from their cigarettes rising from the center. Collectively, they looked like a wigwam in winter. "Look like a bunch of oddballs, too."

"Program people," Jimmy said. "Let's join the party. Ask them for a light."

Sure enough, the password was, "Hi, I'm Jimmy. I'm a friend of Bill." Code. Bill W. was the founder of AA. They eased back and made room for us in the circle.

"Friends of Frankie, too, I guess."

"Yeah, we were all in rehab with him." The speaker was a wiry little guy, maybe part Asian and part African-American, with a shaved skull that made him look like a very scary baby and tattoos up and down his muscular arms.

"We liked him," a woman said. "This is such a bummer. I can't believe he's dead." She shook back blond hair showing dark at the roots. "Hi, I'm Marla."

We all chorused, "Hi, Marla."

I understood why Marla was rattled by Frankie's death. You expect addicts to die. Hell, I had expected to die myself at any moment. But when somebody dies clean and sober, it's a shock.

"I think I know you," Jimmy told the wiry guy. "Marshall, right?"

"It's Mars now, I call myself Mars—the god of war."

"Mars knew me when I first got sober," Jimmy told us.

"Before that, man. The TC?"

Therapeutic community. One of those places they locked you in and turned you into a straight arrow who would make a Mormon missionary look radical.

"Oh, right," Jimmy said. "Of course. That was a hundred years ago."

"We escaped together." Mars grinned. "Remember?"

"Hey, wait a minute," I said. "I was there. I did that too."

Mars and I gave each other a closer look.

"That was you, man? Shit, I guess it is. You was one sarcastic dude, I remember that better than your face."

"That was you?" I said. "I can kinda see the resemblance. You had hair back then. And skin."

Mars raised his arms and contemplated his tattoos with pride.

"Now I gots Art, man. That be Art. So you stayed the course, Jimmy my man? From that time in AA, what, ten years ago?" He shook his head in admiration.

"Fifteen," Jimmy said.

"Not me," I admitted. "Waited to see how the big guy liked it first."

They all laughed.

"Woke up last Christmas Day in detox on the Bowery," I added. That got a bigger laugh. It always did. "Day at a time ever since."

"Way to go, man," Mars said.

The others muttered the stuff that sounds so asinine from the outside, like "Keep coming back" and "Easy does it." Sometimes even I got the warm fuzzies when I heard it. Oh, well, everything's a trade-off. My liver for my sense of irony.

"And here I am just gettin' outa rehab one more time," Mars marveled. "Seems like I purely like the shit too much."

"Jimmy! Bruce!"

Barbara and Luz stood framed in the dark doorway, blinking in the light.

Barbara beckoned to us.

"'Scuse us a second." I ground out my cigarette with my shoe.

"You go, Bruce," Jimmy said. "Bring them over. Tell Barbara I want her to meet an old friend."

Delegated. Why not? Jimmy had them eating out of his hand. He loved program people. I guess that over the years, AA friends made up for the friend he'd lost. That would be me. Failed best friend and perennial fuckup Bruce Kohler. Not a cheery thought. The black cloud that still followed me around sometimes made its presence felt.

"Ladies. What's happenin'?"

Luz gave me a wan smile.

"You should have seen this ladies' room," Barbara said. "I've seen some fancy bathrooms, but this one took the cake. Gold swans on everything—well, brass, I guess—swan faucets, swan soap dish, a swan boat tissue dispenser. But wait till you hear what happened.

Poor Luz—it was awful, wasn't it, Luz? I made her splash cold water on her face, then we went into the stalls."

"I appreciate the blow-by-blow description," I said. "I know you wouldn't want us to miss anything."

"Give me a chance," she said. "It's important what we did, because we were both still in there when the door banged open and we heard the clatter of stiletto heels."

"I couldn't stop crying," Luz admitted. "I didn't want to come out."

"And I was too emotionally exhausted to pull my undies up," Barbara declared. "So I sat there sort of spaced out, but I snapped out of it when I heard the Brooklyn voices. 'Poor Netta, I feel sorry for huh,' the first one said. 'She was supposed to stop throwing up by the second trimester, but no such luck.' Then the other one said, 'Didja see how she was crying? All of a sudden, Frankie is a saint. Dja think it's true about him having a girlfriend?' And the first one said, 'Well, duh. They found him in somebody's apartment, and I don't think it was the cleaning lady.'"

"I was so embarrassed," Luz said. "I thought I would die if they knew I heard them."

"They were horrible," Barbara said. "You could tell they enjoyed dishing the dirt, even though Netta must be their friend. And in between, they're going, like, 'Wanna Tic Tac?' 'Nah, I've got gum,' and chewing through all of it."

"They thought I'd killed him," Luz said. "One of them said, 'She must have done it, don't you think?'"

"'Must of done. Doncha,'" Barbara corrected. "They were awful women with awful voices. One had a giggle and the other had a snicker, and I don't know which was worse. The one said, 'Netta tole me Frankie swore there wasn't anybody. All those times, he just went uptown to get those drugs.' And the second one goes,

'Oh, that's a great excuse. Don't worry, honeybunch, I was at the crack house so it proves I love you.' Listen to me—'she goes'—that's how they talked."

"Go on," I urged her. "So she goes, like—?"

Barbara grinned.

"The snickery one says, 'Men! When the cat's pregnant and big as a balloon, the mouse goes and finds somebody else's mouse hole.'"

"She didn't."

"I swear she did. And the giggler says, 'Puh-lease! I almost swallowed my gum.' I thought, I hope you choke on it. I suppose there is a silver lining—they obviously didn't suspect that Luz had come to the viewing."

"Hardly enough silver to line a toilet seat," I commented, "but I guess it's better than nothing. What happened next?"

Barbara hesitated and looked at Luz.

"It's okay, Barbara," she said. "I know you think the same. The woman said, 'She's better off without him.'"

"There wasn't much more after that," Barbara said. "They must have been cousins, because one said, 'Don't tell that to Uncle Massimo and Aunt Silvia' and what a shame when they thought he'd finally gone straight, and the other one said Aunt Silvia might think so but Uncle Massimo was smarter than that and he knew Frankie."

"They said no more," Luz added, "but I thought they would never leave."

"I could hear them messing with the little cut-glass bottles of lotion and spraying their hair," Barbara said. "Finally, I realized they must both be waiting for their turn to go. There were only two stalls. So I came out. If I hadn't, they'd probably still be in there yakking and squirting themselves with free products. They were such slobs. They dropped their hand towels on the floor, and they didn't put the tops back on the lotion bottles either."

"Then at last we leave," Luz said. At least she had recovered enough to talk normally. Back inside there, she could barely drag the air up from her lungs. I guess she was in her own kind of withdrawal. She'd been as hooked on Frankie as a junkie is on smack.

"Barbara, c'mere," Jimmy called out. "I want you to meet somebody."

"We can leave now, if you want, Luz," I said. She had had enough for one day. "Jimmy called a car—it should be here soon."

"Luz?"

"It's okay, Barbara, I'm fine. I'll wait for you right there." She flicked her chin toward the street.

"Leave her alone," I said. "It's all right, Luz. If you need us, we're here."

Barbara and I went over to the recovery crowd. Jimmy made the introductions.

"My partner, Barbara." Partner, not girlfriend. Nice. Correct. And he omitted the fact that she wasn't an alcoholic, so they wouldn't all freeze up.

"You were all in rehab with Frankie?" Barbara nodded toward the building where the body lay. "Poor guy. What could have happened? How did he do in rehab? Do you think he meant to stay clean? Or am I breaking anonymity?"

"No anonymity no more," Mars said solemnly. "He dead." The others nodded.

"Not at the beginning," said a chunky, short Hispanic guy with slicked-back hair. "I roomed with him. He'd been dealing, right?"

The others nodded.

"He played it close to the chest, but I thought maybe he was hiding out."

"Wouldn't be the first time," Mars commented, and they all nodded again, the way people do in a meeting when they identify with someone's story.

"I can't get over it. I just saw him," Marla said. "We held hands during the Serenity Prayer. I'm a chronic relapser, can't seem to get beyond five months."

"Yeah, yeah," Mars said. "We heard it before."

"Fuck you, ballhead," Marla said without heat. "Ya mother."

She and Mars grinned at each other.

"We were all in group with him," Marla said. "He was pretty mokus at the beginning. Like he didn't know where the hell he was or how the hell he got there."

"He was angry," the Hispanic guy said.

"Yeah, but after a while, he started listening," Marla said. "It was like he wasn't sure whether or not recovery was bullshit, and he couldn't decide which scared him more."

"Frankie was scared?" Barbara asked. It didn't jibe with what we'd heard about Frankie.

"Not to hear him talk," Mars assured her. "Big Frankie wasn't scared a nothin'."

"Right," said Marla. "Not dealers, not the drugs, not the counselors. Just maybe everything, underneath, like the rest of us. And now—poof! I still can't get over it."

"Scared of himself," a tall black woman put in. If heroin chic turned you on, she was stunning. She pushed up the sleeves of her heavy sweater, uncovering stick-thin arms striped with track marks.

"How about women?" Barbara asked.

"He talked in group about his wife and girlfriend," she said. "That's her, right?" She nodded toward Luz, eyeing her with tolerant contempt. "And the other one in there knocked up." She was sharp. A survivor, like any addict who's not dead.

"Did he say anything about hitting?" Barbara asked.

"Not to me!" The black woman bared her teeth. "I tole him I'd cut him if I caught him being mean to women."

Bluffing. A knife sharp enough to cut into human flesh would have been confiscated when she got to rehab. And however street-wise, she'd been knocked around. Like most addicted women, she'd lost some teeth.

"Yeah, he did," chipped in a runty little guy, almost stunted, with a pale, pinched Irish face and flaky, faded ginger hair. "Some things you only tell the guys."

"The girlfriend. He beat on her?" Marla said. They all looked at Luz, who gazed out into the street, watching an SUV try to paral-lel park in a space big enough for a Volkswagen. "I guess I'm glad I didn't know. I kinda liked Frankie. Some things he said, I could identify with. And then he croaks and doesn't get a chance to make amends."

"Did anybody particularly not like Frankie?" Barbara asked. "I mean, so it was noticeable."

They all looked at each other before anybody answered, but I couldn't read the looks.

"Oh, no," the Irish guy said. "We've all done bad stuff when we were wasted. Everybody thought he was okay."

"Yeah, Frankie was cool," the Hispanic guy said.

"We were, like, all in it together," Marla said.

"Like Kevin said." The Hispanic guy nodded at the Irish guy. "Frankie wasn't the only one there who beat up his wife."

"His wife? He beat her too?" Barbara asked.

"Yeah, he spit it out one day in men's group."

"Nobody's perfect," Mars said.

FIVE

When the phone rang, I was having a drunk dream. Jimmy and I were at the beach. We lay on chaise longues in the sun. We were drinking Chivas Regal straight from the bottle. It felt so real. My unconscious had perfect recall. The first shock on the tongue. The slow burn down the esophagus. The warm glow in the belly. The elbow going on automatic. Then pleasurable stupor gave way to dismayed realization that now I'd have to start sobriety all over. I came abruptly awake. I lay flat against the mattress, feeling like the dead man with sixteen men on my chest.

"Oh, shit," I said aloud, both glad and sorry I hadn't picked up after all. The phone was ringing. I groped. Dropped it. Scrabbled for the receiver. Managed to hoist it in the general direction of my ear.

"Yeah," I barked. I squinted at the red glow of my digital clock on the dresser. Half past two in the morning.

"I've got a bucket of water and a razor." The deep voice dragged.

"Oh, God, Laura." Suicidal. I bit back, Do you know what time it is? "What happened?" Silence. "Talk to me."

"Sometimes words aren't worth the trouble."

"You're depressed." No shit, Sherlock. I hated when this happened. But I couldn't blow her off. She had never done it. But each time, she might. "Is anyone with you?"

Besides the procession of men in her bed, Laura often had a dysfunctional friend or two crashing in the loft. Mental patients she knew from various treatment programs. Drinking and drugging buddies. Artsy farts she'd met at craft fairs: jewelers and potters who lived in Vermont or Maine and needed a place to stay. They didn't know talking Laura down in the middle of the night came with the package.

"Mac was here, but he left."

The unsatisfactory boyfriend. I managed not to say, Did he leave before or after you got out the razor?

"Come on, Laura, you know you want to live." I wasn't so sure it was true, but it couldn't hurt to say it. "You have talent, you're beautiful, you have friends who love you."

"I don't care. It's all bullshit." Every word thumped me in the gut. Reason said I wasn't responsible. Reason didn't help. If Laura killed herself, it would be my fault. I sat up in the bed. I wished I had a cup of coffee. It would be a long night.

"Laura, put away the razor."

"Or I could cut myself."

"Please don't do that, Laura." I heard my pleading tone, which never helped, and steadied my voice. "Cutting doesn't help."

Laura had done this bizarre thing since her early teens. She'd score her arms with a razor, hatching the skin with dozens of little slashes. Borderline personality, Barbara said when I asked her once. It's what they do.

"It does too. When I cut, at least I know I'm alive." Laura said what Barbara said they say.

"So you do want to stay alive." I grasped at the offered straw.

"Not necessarily." Arguing with a depressed person was frustrating. "I want to feel something, anything. But then I can't stand the feelings. They hurt me, Bruce. You can't make them go away, can you? There's nothing but the razor and the bucket."

"What about your medication?" By this time, I felt hopeless myself. Depression is infectious. I don't know how shrinks stand it.

"It doesn't work, not really."

"That's not true," I argued. "I've seen it work for you." But only when she took it as prescribed. And didn't mix it with Ecstasy or crystal meth.

"The doctors play with my head. I'm tired of being a statistic."

True and not true. Barbara always said one should validate the feeling and correct the cognitive distortion. Now if I could just remember what the hell that meant, maybe I could say the right thing.

"You feel out of control when they're figuring out the medication. I understand. I know it feels scary. But they are trying to help you."

"Then you take the medication!" she shot back. "Maybe it'll help you."

God grant me the serenity, I said in my head, to accept the things I cannot change. The Serenity Prayer is so deep you can't deny it's true. Courage to change the things I can.

"Laura, listen to me." What to say next? It came to me, one clear thought. "If you don't put away the razor and the bucket, I'm going to call 911."

Oh, shit, I was having a spiritual experience. If you pray, the answer will come. I had always assumed folks who said "God talked to me today" were wackos. Maybe this was what they meant. "Call 911" wasn't a burning bush, but it was something.

"No, no, Bruce, don't do that, please don't. I don't want them to take me away."

I could tell she was crying. Now I really felt swell. And the wisdom to know the difference.

"Then put away the razor," I said. "Wrap it in a paper towel or something and throw it in the garbage. I'll stay on the line while you do it. I'm right here."

In the past, I'd always grabbed a cab and rushed down there. Or before that, when we actually had a relationship, I'd have been there already. If I gave in now, it would be tears and threats till morning.

"I don't have a paper towel."

"Then use a napkin. Go on, do it."

Of course she had more razor blades. I had checked her medicine chest on general principles when I'd been down there. If nothing else, she used them to chop up cocaine. But throwing it out had symbolic value. This whole thing was a ritual. I'd never varied my role before.

"I'm looking for a napkin. Is it okay if I put down the phone?"

"Sure. Whatever."

Amazing. I actually had the upper hand. I could hear her rattling around her kitchen.

"Okay, I did it. I even threw coffee grounds and part of an onion on top so I wouldn't fish around for it. Now what should I do?"

My God, now she was seeking my approval. If I didn't watch my step, I'd find myself back together with her. I had regained enough sanity since I stopped drinking to know I didn't want that. No way.

"Take the bucket and dump the water down the sink."

"There are dishes in the sink."

I sighed. A childlike, compliant Laura was no less difficult to deal with than the manic sex goddess or the depressed voice of doom.

"So they'll get wet. Or go into the bathroom. Dump it down the bathtub. Or the toilet. Your choice." She put the phone down without comment. Laura was oblivious to irony at the best of times. Sometimes it amazed me that we'd ever gotten together. While I waited, I put the phone back down on the dresser. I lay down head to foot on my bed so the cord would reach and tucked the receiver against my neck so I didn't need my hands to hold it. I yawned so wide my jaws ached. I might even get back to sleep if Laura let me go.

"Bruce, will you come down?" It would have been a childish whine if she'd had an upper register. No matter what she said, it sounded sexy. God grant me the serenity, because some things never change.

"No."

Wow. I couldn't believe it. No was a complete sentence I'd never used before. I still felt addicted to Laura. But maybe there was hope for me.

The next evening, I met Jimmy for dinner and a meeting. I was reluctant to tell him about the midnight phone call. I still felt protective of Laura. I didn't want Jimmy judging her. He's not a judgmental kind of guy. But he will tell you what to do to stay sober. I didn't want to hear, "Give her up, or you'll drink again." So we talked about alcoholism, as usual.

Her name came up anyway.

"Did you drink when you were happy, or did you drink when you were sad?" Jimmy asked. Rhetorical question. The answer is always, "Both."

"Speaking of sometimes happy and sometimes sad," he said, "what's with Laura?"

"Is that the clinical definition of bipolar? Sounds a little under-stated to me," I said. "Honestly, I don't know."

"Are you seeing her?"

"You don't 'see' Laura. You close your eyes and surrender."

Jimmy closed his own eyes and muttered, "I will not get preachy. I will not get preachy."

"You better not, big guy." I gave him an amiable punch in the gut. "Anyhow, anything you could say, I've told myself already."

"Can I say just one program slogan?"

"You already have." I tapped the side of my head. "I channel you these days. 'People, places, and things,' right?"

"Glad to hear you've been listening," Jimmy said. "She still stocks the pharmaceuticals, then."

"I don't want any," I protested.

"Yet."

"I know, I know, I think I'll never have another craving I can't overcome, but that's just the disease talking dirty to me. Can we talk about something else?"

"Okay, forget program, but Laura is still Laura. She could always suck you in."

"I'm setting boundaries," I protested. "And don't grin at my vocabulary, dammit. Anyhow, she's got a boyfriend."

"Oh, man, you've got it bad."

"I do not."

"You do so."

"Do not."

"Do so."

When we were kids, the next step would have been a tussle. The two of us rolling around on the ground. Or the floor, depending where we were. We were getting old.

"It's not like you think," I said. "I'll never end up back with Laura. But you've never had an ex. You don't know what a habit it is. I worry about her. I don't think this new guy treats her right."

Jimmy raised a skeptical eyebrow. "Not candy and flowers, you chump. She's got bruises."

"You can't save her, bro," Jimmy said. "That's what 'powerless' means. Do you know how many times that little Luz called Barbara in the middle of the night? First time she said he'd left, we thought, okay, he left. She's in shock, it's a big deal. We wanted to do whatever we could to help. Talk her down, invite her over, tea and sympathy and take her to a meeting. By the fourth or fifth time, we realized it was a dance they did. He was never gonna leave, not for real."

"But he did leave," I pointed out.

"Yeah, being dead will do it."

"Barbara doesn't think she did it. How about you?"

"Man," Jimmy said, "I have no idea. She's so little, and she swears she loved him, whatever that means when the guy knocks you around."

"Plus the mindfuck. Leaving but not leaving, jerking her chain for the fun of it. I think this Mac guy of Laura's does the same thing. I can't stand to think of her putting up with that."

"You married Laura," Jimmy said. "You know her a lot better than any of us, including Barbara, knows Luz. Could you see her murdering Mac if it got bad enough?"

"That's not it." I swallowed hard, a lump in my throat and a little flutter in the pit of my stomach. This getting-in-touch-with-your-feelings shit sucked. "I'm afraid she'll kill herself."

"Like I said, you've got it bad. If you don't watch out, you'll find yourself in Al-Anon talking about your 'qualifier' and how to detach with love."

He'd given me the answer: Al-Anon. So I didn't ask the question. But how the hell could you detach when you saw someone you cared about doing ninety downhill on a dead-end street?

— 61 —

SIX

I lay on Jimmy and Barbara's living room sofa, envying Frankie. Dead or alive, he didn't have to sleep on the couch. Home meant drunk dreams and midnight calls from Laura. So I'd stayed over. It had seemed like a good idea at the time. The couch looked great on the outside, six feet of butter-soft leather in a color decorators called merlot. As close as I got to a bottle of wine these days. But down under the skimpy thin-enough-to-fold mattress, like any other foldout couch my spine had ever met, it resembled a medieval torture device. When I called it the rack, Jimmy pointed out that it didn't stretch my body out in opposite directions.

"Okay, what did they call the one that stuck metal bars and bumps up into your back?"

Being Jimmy, he went straight to Google. And as usual, he fell right in.

"Hey, listen to this. 'We custom-build a range of torture and medieval restraining devices including thumb and toe screws, cages, belts, and shackles.' And it gets a lot of hits."

"Thank you for sharing. Next you'll tell me 'there but for the grace of God' and I should put your damn sofa on my gratitude list."

"Very good, son." Jimmy chuckled. "You're beginning to get it."

I was, but it made me grumpy.

"Coffee," I said.

"Coming right up," Barbara said, appearing from the kitchen like the Good Witch of the North. She had intelligently brought the whole pot. "If you'd gone home last night, you would be stumbling around making your own right now. Or wondering if you had the strength to make it to the nearest Starbucks."

Much too grumpy to admit she was right.

"I miss passing out and waking up at noon," I complained. I grabbed the three mugs dangling from her fingers and held them in a cluster between both hands while she filled them.

"No, you don't," Jimmy said.

At the same time, Barbara said, "God, I get tired of the ambivalence stage of the change process."

I had to laugh. "I hope you don't tell your clients that."

"Hell, no, I save it for you."

"Thanks a bunch," I said.

"Speaking of clients," she said, "unlike you guys, I have to go to work this morning. We need to talk about what to do next to help poor Luz. We could track down some of those people we met at the funeral, get them to speak some ill of the dead so we can figure out who the suspects are."

"Hey, I work," Jimmy said. "Reminds me, I have to catch a client before Hong Kong goes to bed."

"Well, before you do," she said, "why don't you look up Frankie's family? Iacone is an unusual name, isn't it?"

"Yep," said Jimmy, his fingers already flying. "Less than a hundred listings in the online white pages, and that's without specifying a state."

"What kind of Italian do you think they are?" I asked. "Sopranos Italian?"

"You watch too much TV." Jimmy grinned.

"The whole country watches too much TV," I retorted. "Is that a yes or a no?"

"Not sure."

"The wife's brothers looked pretty scary," Barbara said. "The ones Vinnie warned us to steer clear of. But we shouldn't stereotype."

"I know, I know," I said, "not every Italian is connected." We knew plenty of guys in AA who got pissed off when people kidded them about the Mafia. On the other hand, Jimmy had once heard a recovering hit man qualify. "But Frankie's dead, so somebody's got to be a bad guy."

"I understand it would be truly stupid to march up to Frankie's scary relatives and start asking questions," Barbara admitted. "At least until we know for sure they're *not* that kind of family. That's why I thought maybe I could approach the women. Inquiring minds want to know, but they also want to stay alive. Even if they really are Sopranoish, the women live in a different world where they can pretend to believe the ugly stuff doesn't happen. At least, that's how it is on TV."

"Don't forget the guy dealt drugs," Jimmy said. "We all saw that other set of guys at the funeral. The ones even Vinnie wouldn't go near. You don't want to mess with them, and 'you' means all of us. They've never heard of Miss Marple, Barbara, and they won't think you're cute."

"So how do we find out if it *was* drug related?"

"Leave it to the police," Jimmy said.

"Listen to him, Barbara," I said. "No fooling." Back when I used to score from Frankie and his pals, the only reason I wasn't scared shitless is that I went in high and came out higher. In our fucked-up minds, a "good" dealer was one who'd let you sample product.

"So what *can* we do?" she said. "We can't let Luz end up convicted of murder. It's so unfair. She said to me, 'It hurts so much that Frankie's gone, and on top of that I have to worry about getting arrested for killing him.' She's terrified of going to prison, and I don't blame her."

Neither did I.

"What did you tell her?" I asked.

"I told her she didn't kill him, so they can't prove she did."

"You watch too much *Law & Order*," I said. "Innocent people get convicted all the time."

"They *show* too much *Law & Order*. And that's what Luz said."

"So go back to whodunit," Jimmy said. "Who apart from drug dealers had a motive?"

"Even Luz couldn't claim that everybody loved Frankie," Barbara said, "so no one would have hurt him."

"Shouldn't Luz be in on this conversation?" I asked.

"Some things I'd rather not say in front of her," Barbara said. "Like I was thinking—what about the aunts?"

"The matriarchal aunts? Now there's a creative thought."

"Why not? They've got the backbone for it. They love Luz, and they must have hated it that she was going with a druggie."

"Too smart not to suspect the hitting, either," Jimmy added. "Not that Luz would thank you for fingering her aunts."

"So we'll rule them out. How about the wife? Netta."

"A pregnant woman dragged herself all the way from Brooklyn to East Harlem," I said, "to stick a knife in the father of her children?"

"When you put it like that," Barbara said, "it sounds unlikely. But it wouldn't be the first time. Or maybe someone did it for her."

"Okay, then. Who's on your list?"

"I meant to look at the guest book at the funeral," Barbara said. "Then Luz fell apart and we had to get her out of there. All those names and addresses wasted!"

"Now here is where you're going to fall at my feet and adore me." Jimmy rocked back in his chair and beamed at her. "They put up a Web site."

"What?"

"A Web site," Jimmy repeated. "According to Dictionary.com, 'a set of interconnected Web pages, generally located on the same server, and prepared and maintained as a collection of information—"

"Clown," she said.

"A funeral Web site?" I said. "That's creepy."

"Why? People do wedding and bar mitzvah Web sites. Everybody likes to see their name in print, everybody wants to know who came. People who didn't make it get to see the pictures. They can post messages and send the family their condolences."

Come to think of it, it wasn't half as creepy as the medieval tortures Web site.

"They have pictures?" Barbara said. "Let me see." She squeezed herself around behind Jimmy's chair and clung to his back so she could look.

Jimmy removed her arms from around his neck without comment. He was used to being draped in nice Jewish girl.

"Yeah, there's an online album. Plenty of snaps of Frankie with the family."

I followed lazily. Jimmy zipped the mouse around and brought Iaconefuneral.com up on his nineteen-inch screen. He scrolled down the menu on the home page. Slideshow. Guest book. Prayers.

"Wow, this is a lot better than a real guest book. You can actually read all these names and addresses. It's too many to take in."

"I'll print it out," Jimmy said. "I think if we cross-check pictures and people's posts and the address list, we can sort a lot of these people out."

It was weird to see Frankie looking jovial, with his arms around a slimmer Netta and the little girl and boy we'd met.

— 67 —

"This does not look like a guy who ever slept on the couch," I said.

"Hey, what if one of those women was in love with Frankie?" Barbara said.

"Then wouldn't she have been more likely to kill Luz? Or Netta?"

"Not necessarily. These things can go all different directions. We have got to get to know these people better," Barbara said, "or we'll never figure it out."

"Maybe she was in love with Netta," I said.

Jimmy and Barbara looked at me, then at each other.

"Naaah," they said simultaneously.

"Okay, I was being flippant," I said. "Not in Brooklyn."

"Or how about this—could another man have been in love with Luz? She would have told me," Barbara said, "but what if it was somebody she hardly noticed? Guys you're not attracted to don't count."

I winced.

"Barbara, I love you, but some thoughts are better saved for your women's group."

"What, you don't want to know the secrets that lie in the heart of a woman?"

"When I do, I'll let you know."

"I really have to get to work," Barbara said. She unglued herself from Jimmy and started back through the living room. "I'm going to be late as it is."

She gathered up the empty coffee pot and mugs, a couple of books, a sheaf of papers, and her handbag.

"Oh!" She stopped dead in the center of the room, her arms full of stuff. "I just remembered. Luz knew one of the dealers. Isaac? Ezekiel? Ishmael!"

"Barbara," Jimmy said, "these are dangerous people."

"But if we're careful—I mean *really* careful, Jimmy—it's just talking."

He shook his head and spoke to me.

"She doesn't get it."

"She could talk to Luz about it," I said. "If Luz wants to contact him—her life, her risk."

"If you're going to start calling me 'she,'" Barbara said, "I'm outta here."

"Give me a kiss first, pumpkin," Jimmy said. "I'm sorry, I didn't mean to 'she' on you. I get scared when you don't realize what chances you're taking."

She dumped the armful of stuff—not on the good carpet, and the mugs and pot rolled, but didn't break—and ran back to give him a quick but fervent smooch.

"Now I really have to run." She was almost at the door when Jimmy's exclamation stopped her.

"Ha!"

"Something on the funeral site?"

"No," he said. "Look at this. Iacone's Bakery. Making Brooklyn lick its lips since 1946. Nice Web site."

"That doesn't sound much like organized crime, does it?" Barbara said.

"Not connected, just cannoli," I said.

"It doesn't prove anything," Jimmy said. "Crime families nowadays go in for legitimate businesses. They could be laundering money as they make the biscotti. Hey, these look good. *Il pasticciotto, il bocconotto, la sfogliatella.*" He rolled the words out sonorously. "Nice pictures."

"Show me," Barbara said.

"What about work?"

"It's okay if I'm late. I'll stay late if I have to. Hey, these look good," she said. "That settles it, this is my assignment. I'm going out to Brooklyn to that bakery. I'll take a day off next week. I'll schmooze with whoever works there, dig up whatever I can about the family, bring you back some pastries—everybody's happy."

"Our old friend Mars mentioned a couple of meetings he hits regularly," Jimmy said. "And I got the numbers of the other rehab folks."

"Fast worker, aren't you?" I said.

"The two who had never gotten clean and sober before both asked me to sponsor them," he admitted sheepishly. "I told the woman she should find a woman sponsor, but it was fine to call me if she was afraid she'd pick up. The guy I said I'd be glad to do it on an interim basis, and let's see how we get on on the phone."

Barbara kissed him on the top of his head. Cute.

"They could see right away how good you are. You have what they want."

"Thanks, poppet, but I don't think I'm all that special. They hear fifteen years and they think I've got the magic bullet, that's all."

Little do they know. Fifteen years one day at a time of undiluted reality is a long, hard haul. But I didn't say it. I didn't want to sound like I was putting Jimmy down. In the small corner of my heart that's honest and maybe even a little humble, he's my hero.

"So you'll cover them," I said instead. "What about me?"

"Oh, you're going to the meetings." Jimmy chuckled. "It won't hurt you to get around, see some different faces, hear new stories."

I'd latched onto Jimmy's home group and found a few meetings near my apartment. I'd gotten into a groove.

"Besides," he added, "I have to put the program first. If I'm sponsoring somebody, it doesn't feel right to milk him for information."

Barbara drooped.

"I'm Luz's sponsor," she said. "I'm only trying to help her. Do you think I shouldn't be doing this at all?"

"No, pet, I'm not taking your inventory," he said. He grabbed her hand and smacked a couple of kisses into her palm. "You do what feels right to you. I'm only talking about myself. I'm me and you're you, okay?"

"Ohhh," said Barbara, bouncing back. "Is that what they've been trying to teach me in Al-Anon all these years?"

"I don't have a problem finding out what meetings they all go to when I talk to them on the phone. They might be anywhere in the city. Some of the numbers had the 718 area code." That could be Brooklyn or the Bronx or Queens. "I'll do the groundwork. Then Bruce can bump into them at a meeting and make friends."

I noticed he had no doubt I'd be willing to pump a program person for information. I didn't really mind. Sobriety was hard enough without getting too deep. Working the steps. Actually becoming the kind of person who had nothing to be ashamed of.

"Or I could always relapse," I offered, "then I could play detective in the rehab."

"No!" they said in unison.

I didn't really mean it.

SEVEN

In AA, everything's an anniversary. In a couple of weeks, I'd be ten months sober. I still hadn't told my mother. I kind of hoped she'd figure out for herself that I'd stopped drinking. But the few times I'd seen her, she hadn't said a word. Since my dad died, she didn't keep so much as a beer in the house. I used to carry at least a six-pack in with me. You'd think she'd notice. But growing up with a drunk for a dad and marrying another, Ma had become adept at not seeing what she didn't want to know.

The Long Island Rail Road chugged through the little towns of Nassau and Suffolk counties, bearing me inexorably toward East Islip and revelation. I couldn't deny my mother was on my Eighth Step "list of all persons we had harmed." In Step Nine, you make amends. My mother would have a heart attack if I handed her a check for all the cash I'd filched from her handbag from the age of eight on. And I knew the money was the least of it.

I had grown up in ethnic Yorkville. My father, like many of the neighborhood's alcoholic dads, worked at the Ruppert Brewery. It's long gone now. It didn't survive the morphing of the neighborhood into the Upper East Side, though the rent-controlled apartment where I still lived did. Dad died of what his death certificate politely called liver failure when I was in my twenties. He'd left Ma pretty well provided for, between a union-negotiated pension and a surprising amount of life insurance that he'd bought while tanked and never bothered to cancel. But apart from rent, she couldn't afford Manhattan.

Dad was mostly German American, but Ma was Irish, like Jimmy's folks. She'd picked East Islip because they had a chapter of the Ancient Order of Hibernians. The Our Lady of Knock division. I am not making this up. Not that she went to any meetings or events. Ma had a low tolerance for intimacy. No friends, no risks, no feelings. She complained if the cat snuggled up against her on the sofa. So maybe it wasn't all my fault that I hadn't found a way to tell her my big news before now.

I took a cab from the Islip station. There's a bus, but no way was I getting into this without cigarettes. Four or five taxis waited along the curb as I emerged from the train. I picked the one whose driver I could see ignoring his own NO SMOKING sign. I'd phoned to tell Ma I was coming. She hadn't bothered to dress. Ma hardly ever appeared in anything but a Fifties ensemble of flower-print housecoat over fraying white slip, shambling felt slippers, and old-fashioned hair rollers. She couldn't have crossed the street to mail a letter in that outfit. The rollers suggested that she had somewhere better to go later on. But she never did. If I wanted to remind myself she ever wore anything else, I had to visualize Dad's funeral. To which I'd gone drunk.

"You want a cup of tea?" she greeted me. She turned away from the open door and shuffled toward the kitchen.

"It's great to see you too, Ma." I closed the door, clicked the lock, and caught up with her. "Hold up a minute."

I leaned over and kissed her cheek. She looked surprised. Then, plodding along like Slow and Steady the tortoise, intent on winning the race, she resumed her course to the stove, where the teakettle shrieked and rattled.

"I got cookies." Oreos, my childhood favorite. A flash of memory startled me: my mother and I sitting at our kitchen table in the city, both of us scraping the cream off the inside of our Oreos with our front teeth and laughing. She looked big, so I must have been little. It occurred to me that my mother had probably been depressed for the past twenty-five or thirty years.

I dunked the supermarket-brand tea bag she supplied a few dozen times, going for maximum caffeine. Ma was too Irish not to boil the water all the way, but too cheap to buy better tea. I fished out the string with the little tag, which had fallen into the cup the way it always did. I plunked the sodden tea bag into a spoon and wrapped the string around it to squeeze out the last few drops of infused liquid. All part of the ritual. I sipped my tea.

I didn't know where to start. Ma wouldn't help me out, either. She never asked questions, not "What did you do in school today?" or "Doctor, am I going to live?" If the silence went on too long, she might start telling me something she'd heard on the news. I'd better just spit it out.

"Ma, I've got something to tell you. I've stopped drinking."

She sipped her tea. What did I expect? Earth to Ma.

"Ma? Say something."

"Yeah, yeah. Your father went on the wagon a few times."

I told myself to stop grinding my teeth.

"No, Ma, I mean I'm really sober." Clean and sober, but she'd never had a clue about the drugs. No point in enlightening her now. "I'm going to Alcoholics Anonymous." She wouldn't ask me how long. "It's almost ten months."

She actually put her teacup down.

"I went to that Al-Anon once." Now she'd surprised me.

"Really? I didn't know that. How did you like it?"

"It was okay, but the women were all talking about how their husbands drank. I had enough of that at home, so I didn't go back."

I thought of telling her it wasn't supposed to be that way. She'd heard only what she could hear.

"How long did you go?"

"Just the once." It figured.

That covered the topic of recovery. A wave of despair washed over me. Given my family, how could I ever become a normal human being?

The gray silence stretched out. At this point, I always used to go in the fridge and pop a beer. I took another Oreo and racked my brains for something to say.

"I saw Laura the other day." Laura was the only one of my girlfriends my mother knew, because she was the only one I'd married.

"That tramp."

"What's that supposed to mean?" I had said the same words in the same tone countless times. All my life.

"She wasn't the kind you marry." She's said that a few thousand times too. It was one of the few subjects she had a strong opinion on. Not counting stuff like whether Leno was better than Letterman. I remembered belatedly how profoundly my mother irritated me. No wonder I'd considered the six-pack a necessity. Two, if I stayed more than an hour. The fact that she was right about Laura didn't help.

"Well, I did marry her." I sounded sulky even to myself. "So if you can't say anything nice—" How dumb could I get? Telling Ma "don't say anything" was like telling George Bush to be stupid. She had it covered.

I pushed my chair back with a scraping of wooden legs on the squeaky linoleum.

"I gotta go. I just stopped by to tell you about the drinking." I felt too embarrassed to use the word *sobriety*. Odd, considering how long Ma had known me. She'd wiped my baby butt like any other mother. I don't know what I expected. That she'd cry and fall on my neck? That she'd tell me I'd made her proud? That she'd ask a question?

I snatched up my jacket, which I'd thrown on a chair when I came in, and left. It took all my self-control not to slam the door. So much for good intentions. No amends today. But I was mad at myself, not her, all the way back to Penn Station. As they say, the program works.

EIGHT

"Let's go out," said Laura.

Another Saturday afternoon at her place. I lay stretched out on her water bed. I was full of black truffle frittata, emptied of desire, and perfectly content to spend the next two hours in a state of suspended animation.

She stopped pacing up and down and peered out the window.

"You expecting someone?" I asked.

"No, of course not." She paused to light a cigarette, then forgot to put it to her lips. I had seen her take her medication, so it wasn't that. She had what Barbara's Yiddish-speaking grandmother called *shpilkes*. Ants in the pants. "I just need to get out of here for a while."

"Am I allowed to come?" I inquired.

"Of course, dummy."

"Any particular destination?"

She shook her head, then stalked over to the heap of clothes we'd discarded in the dash for the Pole. She scooped them up in clumps, shook them briskly, and disentangled hers from mine. She tossed mine in my general direction.

"Hey!" The belt buckle almost took out my eye. "Not the head, not the head." A direct hit could do damage.

"Then get up." She hopped on one foot, pulling on a pair of panties that were little more than a thong. Overdressed for her. "Come on, Bruce, don't make me wait."

She'd said the same thing a lot more sweetly half an hour before. With a resigned sigh, I reached for my pants.

On the street, Laura sniffed the air like a dog scenting game and set off at a brisk pace, heading south. I trotted after her, threading my way around the knots of tourists and gallery-goers. What was she up to?

"Yo! Laura! Wait up!"

She stopped, tapping her foot in a show of impatience. The tourists rightly considered her one of the sights. More than one raised a digital camera, then hastily lowered it when she glared. In full manic regalia, she qualified as a work of art. Blue hair this week. Eyeliner, lipstick, finger- and toenails to match. Decked like postmodern halls with a parure of her own design. The necklace covered most of her chest like King Tut's pectoral. The matching earrings hung almost to her shoulders. The tiara perched impossibly on the top of her fluffy mane. The elements included exotic feathers and the wings of butterflies that had died naturally. *No animals were harmed in the making of this jewelry.* She didn't mind killing a flock of spring-loaded ballpoint pens and a clock or two, though. She'd electroplated the innards of both and soldered them on for a sculptural effect.

"Come on!" She jerked her head toward Canal Street. The earrings swayed like chandeliers in an earthquake.

"What's the hurry?" I complained. "You said we're not going anywhere special."

"We're not," she snapped. She set off again before I managed to catch up.

"So why does it matter when we get there?" I asked her receding back.

At Canal Street, we turned west. I was surprised. Chinatown, which on a Saturday afternoon is alive with vendors selling fresh fish and produce and always fun if you like silk brocade and lacquered ducks, lay to the east. In spite of her disclaimers, I suspected we had a goal.

We ended up on a narrow, undistinguished street in TriBeCa, not far from West Street and the river. She had stayed ahead of me all the way. Some stroll. She halted in front of an old-law tenement, six stories with grimy windows and a fire escape obscuring the brick façade, squeezed between two warehouse buildings that might or might not have been converted to residential lofts. TriBeCa—Triangle Below Canal—hadn't even been named when prices started going through the roof in SoHo. For the first time, she looked hesitant.

I squinted up at the building. Nothing to explain her interest jumped out at me.

She nuzzled up to me and took my arm. Suddenly we were a couple again.

"Could you get up on that?" She nodded toward the fire escape. It started on the second floor. The bottom ladder hung down just far enough from the ground so you had to drop. Unless you were a cat, you could break an ankle.

I looked at her.

"Oh, Brucie, don't be slow. I know, I'll go first. I'll climb on your shoulders, and you'll give me a boost."

First? Thank you for sharing.

"And we'd do this because—?"

She pouted and started biting her nails. I put my hand on her wrist. It was still so thin my thumb and fingers met. I drew her arm gently down. Who knew what they put in that gunk she painted her nails with? Blue shit. Ground lapis lazuli, maybe. It was that bright a blue. I wondered if lapis was poisonous.

Laura stuck her bottom lip out farther. She said nothing. The lip was also blue. I'd nibbled on those lips, sans makeup, less than two hours ago. I didn't feel much like it now. To tell the truth, I wanted to shake her. But I'm not that kind of guy.

"Talk to me, Laura. Tell me why we're here, or I'm leaving." Set limits. Don't enable. How did this crazy woman manage to turn me into such a wimp? "Who lives here?"

I thought she wouldn't answer. But after a long moment, she pushed it out in a sulky baby voice.

"Mac."

"Oh, Laura, f'Godsake! What do you think you're doing?"

The lip twitched.

"That's it. I'm going." I wheeled and took the first step. It could have led to a journey of a thousand miles. But she grabbed the back of my shirt, none too gently, and pulled me back. She was that kind of girl. Woman.

"He's not there," she protested. As if that made a difference.

"Oh, yeah? How do you know?" Now we were two big babies.

Her eyes shifted. A dusting of glitter overlaid the blue on her eyelids. I resisted being distracted.

"How do you know?" I repeated.

"I called before we left," she muttered.

"Ha! So we were coming here all along. You just didn't bother to tell me." After you're sober ninety days, you get to be self-righteous about lying. No, the program doesn't say that. "That's it, I'm leaving."

Five minutes later she teetered on my shoulders, straining to reach the bottom rung of the dangling ladder. At least she had on blue ballet slippers. She could have worn Doc Martens. Or hiking boots with spikes. I kept looking up and down the street. Not a soul appeared. I could have used a good excuse to cut this crazy expedition short. Laura didn't care. Once she'd scrambled onto the first platform, she pulled me up after her, as nonchalant as a catcher in a trapeze act. If you can call about six feet square of rusty iron bars with lots of space between them a platform. We barely fit, and I almost dropped my cigarettes. Yes, I needed a smoke. A guy's gotta do something with the anxiety. Prayers to my Higher Power for guidance in breaking and entering didn't seem quite appropriate.

"He never locks it," Laura said. She whipped out a small screwdriver I didn't know she had. She had stuck it in a garter I didn't know she was wearing. Our wedding garter, as it happens. Blue. She pried up the window expertly. Clearly, she'd done this before. I hoped to hell this guy Mac really had gone out. I didn't think I'd have much to say to him if we met this way.

"Come on!" Laura said. She had pushed the sash window up. Her fingers, grimy with New York City soot, grabbed at my shirt again. The front this time. She swung first one leg, then the other, over the sill and pulled me into the room.

I don't recommend breaking and entering sober. Every time a floorboard creaked, the hairs on the back of my neck stood up. I had to pee. While I slunk from point to point, Laura acted as if she had every right to be there. She opened drawers, slammed doors, and strode from room to room. The apartment wasn't that big. We'd landed in the bedroom: big messy unmade bed, guy laundry on the floor. Mac must have money. His furniture hadn't come from Dumpsters or even thrift shops. More than one hardwood tree, probably endangered, had died for the sleigh bed and matching dressers and night tables. A closet that would have been walk-in if it weren't so crammed with stuff held jackets, suits, and shirts with designer labels, enough L.L.Bean–type outdoor things for a polar expedition, and so much sports equipment that I had to dodge back to avoid a leather bag of golf clubs that wanted to crush my toes. As I righted it and pushed it back in, a tennis racket in a heavy wooden press made a pass at my head. I shoved that back onto the shelf it came from. That dislodged a bag of neon chartreuse tennis balls. As I grabbed at the bag, it fell open. The balls went bounding around the room.

"Bruce! What the hell are you doing?" Laura spoke at normal volume, albeit in pissed-off tones.

"Collecting dust bunnies," I said. I lay prone and at full stretch with my right arm under the bed. My fingers scrabbled at a couple of runaway balls. Lint clung to my sleeve.

I retrieved the balls at some cost to my rotator cuff, wiped them on my shirt, and popped them back in the bag.

"Get up!" Laura said. "Don't be an idiot."

I would have been glad to comply, but it was too late. If I could reverse time, I'd go back to before we broke in. Preferably before we climbed the fire escape. Hmm, how could I see the glass half full in this situation? Oh, yeah. Mac wasn't home.

"Look at this." Her voice held only pleased surprise. "This must be new."

I shoved the bag of balls back into the closet and put my shoulder to the door until I got it closed. I shook off a staticky athletic sock that clung to my pants leg like a scared kitten in a tree and picked my way over to where she stared at a drawing on the wall. It seemed to be a signed Picasso.

"Original?"

"Of course."

I already didn't like Mac. Now I hated him.

Laura turned away and started rummaging among the tangled covers on the bed.

"What are you doing?"

"I just want to see—oh!" Her face tightened into a grim frown. "Damn!"

"What's the matter?"

She ignored me. She yanked back the covers. The incriminating evidence lay on the sheet: an extremely wispy pair of feminine bikini panties and a barely-over-the-nipples lace bra. Laura ground her teeth.

"Not yours?" I asked. Considering how blithely she'd jumped into bed with me, I didn't quite see the problem.

"Idiot!" That must be me. "Bastard!" That must be him.

"I'm going to pee," I said.

The bathroom hadn't been cleaned in a while. An open bottle of aftershave, a brush clogged with tufts of graying hair, and a box of condoms sat on the edge of the sink. The toilet seat was up. I unzipped with one hand and swung open the medicine cabinet door with the other. I'm always interested in pharmaceuticals, even now when I can't perform any hands-on research. The guy had a lot of unlabeled pills. He probably bought them off the Internet. I would take a closer look in a minute. I was about to flush when I heard an elevator ping beyond the wall. Then a heavy door slammed. Uh-oh. We were busted.

I lowered the toilet seat and lid in soft slow motion. Hastily zipped up, nearly pinching off a capillary in my finger. Tiptoed to the door. I eased it open just a crack. No point in calling attention to myself.

Mac's angry voice carried fine. I needed to take my eye from the crack and put my ear to it to make out everything Laura said. The cringing, little-girl tone shocked me.

"Mac, please don't be mad at me. I need you—I needed to know."

"I've warned you before, Laura. What I do is not your business."

"I can't not care. Please! I love you so much. Don't you love me just a little? Don't you like it when I do this? Or this?"

Now I cringed. She was coming on to him.

He didn't buy it.

"Ow! You hurt me!"

"I'll hurt you a lot more if you come snooping again. I said stop it! Stop it!"

Laura's anguished wail tore me up. What was he doing to her?

"You will listen to what I say!" *Slap.* "You will not stick your nose in my business!" *Slap.*

Oh, shit. I couldn't cower in the bathroom and listen to this. I had to do something. I pushed open the door and marched out, hoping I looked tougher than I felt. From the hall, I could see both the entrance door Mac had come in by and the open bedroom window. I wanted to make a run for it. But I couldn't leave Laura there getting beaten up. As kids, Jimmy and I had fought like puppies. We'd tumbled and snapped but never really hurt each other. In my teens, I'd been in plenty of fights. I had a scar or two and memories of a few close calls when I'd been lucky not to get killed. But all my berserker recklessness had come straight from Jack Daniel's. In sobriety, I'd discovered my inner wuss. Too bad. I squared my shoulders, visualized John Wayne, and swaggered into the living room.

Mac was big. Not square and solid like Jimmy, but tall and broad and thick like the Hulk. He loomed over Laura, arm raised to begin a backhand swing he had probably perfected on the tennis court. She cowered before him, face averted to avoid the blow. My stomach clenched. One of the knuckles poised to swipe wore a big, ugly ring with corners on it.

"Hey! Now wait a minute!"

Both of them froze. Then Mac swung around without lowering his arm.

"Who the hell are you?"

I stood my ground.

"You leave my wife alone."

Mac laughed, a bark with a growl in it like the Hound of the Baskervilles.

"The drunk? Hey, bud, you're trespassing in my apartment. Or does it bother you if I say *Bud*?" His mock-solicitous tone oozed contempt. "And I do believe you mean your *ex*."

I ground my teeth. I felt my jaw joint slip a notch with a little click.

"Leave her alone."

"Why?" Mac laughed again. "I'll do anything I damn please with *my* girlfriend in *my* apartment." He reached out and drew her to him, flinging a heavy arm around her shoulders. You could have sawed enough planks for a picnic table out of it. "Wanna watch me fuck her?"

Rage propelled me forward. I sprang toward him with both fists clenched. A deep growl rumbled in my chest. I felt like a bantam in the ring with an ostrich, but I couldn't help that. I didn't even bother to curse. He could have the F word. I'd have his heart and liver out. I'd kill him.

"Laura!" It came out like a battle cry. Like Lancelot yelling, "Guinevere!" Like Tristan screaming, "Isolde!" Even though I didn't love her anymore.

I hope for Lancelot's and Tristan's sake that those ladies didn't do what Laura did. When Mac put his arm around her, she'd plastered herself to his side as if she'd been glued there. Now she broke free and leaped in front of him. She crouched in a defensive stance, hissing like a pissed-off cat. At me.

I skidded to a stop.

"Laura?" It came out in an incredulous screech.

"Go away, Bruce! You'll ruin everything." She stamped one blue ballet slipper.

Me? Ruin what? A perfect *pas de deux*? An expert beating?

"But . . . but . . . but . . . ," I sputtered like a Harley with a bad load of gas.

"Don't be an idiot," she said.

Mac said nothing. He folded his arms like Mr. Clean and looked sardonic. He did it even better than I did.

I reached out across what felt like the Grand Canyon and tried to take her hand.

"You're getting hurt," I said. "You deserve better than this. Come on, let's get out of here."

She swatted my hand away and stepped back. Mac moved in to meet her, a solid wall at her back. Her flyaway blue curls only came up to his chin. He put both arms around her waist from behind. His thumbs just brushed her nipples. With a malicious grin, he locked his gaze on mine and gave each of them a tweak between thumb and forefinger. She let him.

"Let's get out of here," I repeated, because I had to try.

She wiggled her butt against what I bet was a Hulk-size hard-on. I thought her eyes were sorry.

"Just go. Please."

I looked from the bedroom with its open window to the door Mac had come in by. I weighed the loss in dignity climbing back out onto the fire escape against having to march past them to exit by the door. Steps up to the gallows or dead man walking down death row? At least the door wouldn't break my ankle. They watched in silence as I left.

NINE

"She let me walk away!" I banged my fist on the nearest hard surface. A big glass vase rattled on the coffee table. Barbara removed it.

"Hey, that's Lalique," she said. "My father bought it for my mother in Paris on their honeymoon."

I had dropped by to pick up Jimmy's printouts from the funeral Web site and let off steam. Impotent rage still roiled my gut.

"I know it hurt, baby," Barbara said, "but you and Laura aren't married anymore. She doesn't owe you anything, and she's not your burden."

"She was scared of him!" I pounded the table again. This time a glazed ceramic pot bounced. "Sorry. Take the pot away too. I'm so mad."

"That's okay," Barbara said. "My sister made that one in arts and crafts when she was thirteen. You can break it if you like."

"Thanks." My sense of humor will always trump my inner drama queen, and Barbara knew it. She'd always thought Laura's craziness had doomed our marriage as much as my drinking. I folded my arms, tucking my fists into my armpits where they couldn't do any more damage. "The guy's an eight-hundred-pound gorilla, and she snuggled up to him like what's-her-name and King Kong."

"What do you expect in an addictive relationship?" she said. "He's like her drink."

"She wasn't like that with me," I objected.

"So she wasn't addicted to you the way you were to her," Barbara said.

"She always pretty much led you around by the dick," Jimmy added.

They both looked sorry for me. I couldn't have that.

"Thanks a heap." I cocked a finger and shot at Jimmy. He fired back. The imaginary recoil nearly knocked him off his computer chair. I clutched my chest and staggered. Ham on wry, that's me. "Can we please change the subject?"

"Murder," Barbara said. "Luz and Frankie were a lot like Laura and Mac."

Hell, I was just starting to feel better.

"Don't say Laura and Mac, like they're a couple. Let's go to dinner at Laura and Mac's. Let's watch Mac slap Laura around. Though slap is a euphemism. The guy has hands like nine-pound hammers. He doesn't have to make a fist to have a fist."

"You can't save her, Bruce. But Luz has got a chance, now Frankie's dead—if she doesn't end up convicted of his murder."

"Okay, okay, I said I'd help."

Half an hour later, I took the Christopher Street subway stairs two at a time and plunged into the maze of Greenwich Village. The Village had been a kind of Mecca for Jimmy and me when we were spaced-out adolescents trying to transcend the neighborhood. Before we got old enough for bars, we'd hung out in pizza places and hamburger joints where they'd sell us a pitcher of beer. The toughs we usually hung out with in Carl Schurz Park wouldn't be caught dead downtown among what they called fags and weirdos. To feel sophisticated, we only had to take the subway. In fact, we used to get girls by inviting them downtown on dates. It didn't take much to thrill a Catholic girl who thought patent leather shoes were sinful.

The Village had changed a lot since we were kids. The starving-artist scene had moved to cheaper neighborhoods. Many of the kinky little shops had gone, though tattoo places and cheap jewelry stores where they'd pierce any body part you wanted were enjoying a renaissance. Shoe stores and three-dollar cups of coffee had crept in. But I enjoyed feeling nostalgic about those early walks on the wild side.

As he'd promised, Jimmy had done some homework on the program guys we'd met at Frankie's funeral. Kevin, the runty Irish guy, was gay. He'd said so up front when he asked Jimmy to sponsor him. Kevin had mentioned that our old friend Mars swung both ways and sometimes went to gay meetings with him. I didn't remember Mars being bi back in our TC days. Traditional therapeutic communities are heavy on testosterone. Barbara says their idea of sensitivity to sexual orientation nowadays is to put all the gay guys in a gay men's group so everybody knows who they are. If Mars was already into boys, he probably kept it to himself.

So here I was, walking in the door of a gay AA meeting. I felt a tad self-conscious. But I didn't think some guy in eye shadow would put his hand on my crotch.

The meeting was big even by New York standards, where fifty passes for a medium-size group. It was held in a big chapel on the ground floor of the church, rather than in the basement. Hanging scrolls of the Twelve Steps and the Twelve Traditions blocked most of the stained-glass windows and the giant cross in the front of the room. Tactful.

The qualification had just started when I walked in. The pews all faced front, so my chance to see if I could spot Frankie's rehab buddies wouldn't come till the break. I sat down near the back. I felt uncomfortable, but no more than at my usual meetings. My eye fell on Tradition Three on the right-hand scroll: "The only requirement for membership is a desire to stop drinking." Gay meeting or not, I had a right to be here.

The speaker didn't look or sound particularly gay, if you think all gay guys flop their wrists and call each other Mary. His heavy drinking started when he came out to his family and they threw him out. He had a partner named Herb. Otherwise, it was the same old story. Partied hard, fucked things up, hit bottom, came to AA kicking and screaming, gradually began to like it, slowly got his act together. Wouldn't trade a single day. Grateful. It all came down to that. Grateful and humble. Those words still made me squirm. But in some corner of my cynical heart I aspired to them myself.

As the speaker wound up and they started passing the basket, I craned my neck, trying to spot the rehab guys. That bald head, shiny as honey and about the same color, might be Mars. When he stood up, I saw the tattoos. And when the fellow next to Mars turned his head to talk to him, I saw it was Kevin. They squeezed out of their pew and joined the flow toward the coffee, cookies, and doughnuts in the back. I didn't want to be too obvious. So I got my caffeine fix before I positioned myself so our hands would meet over the Krispy Kremes. Mars and I both went for the last one in the box. Perfect timing. We checked, fingertips hovering above the box, and made eye contact.

"Go ahead," I said.

At the same time, he said, "No problem."

Our hands dodged a bit, like two people trying to pass each other on a narrow street. I let him get the doughnut.

"They didn't tell me sobriety would turn me into Miss Manners," I remarked.

"Sure do need that sugar we used to drink without even noticin'," Mars said. "Just got outta rehab, and seems like I can't get enough a that sweet stuff. Bruce, right? Saw you out in Brooklyn the other day."

Out of the corner of my eye, I had been watching Kevin pile cookies on a napkin. At Mars's words, he looked around.

"Jimmy's friend," he said.

"And you're poor Frankie's friends from rehab," I said, as if I hadn't been stalking them. "Sad thing, huh? If he felt half as bad as I did coming off the booze, it is a shame. He bought it after all the trouble and before he got to enjoy any of the benefits."

"How long are you clean again?" Kevin spoke thickly around a mouthful of doughnut.

"Almost ten months."

"That's fantastic," Kevin said with evident sincerity. "I've never gone that long. What's it like?" I didn't want to talk about me. But the admiration felt good. I hadn't had anything you could possibly call an achievement in a long time.

"Some days aren't bad. But I'm still dealing with the wreckage of my past," I admitted. An AA phrase. "I guess Frankie never had a chance to put things right."

Kevin nodded.

"Yeah, that's the part that's always sent me back out. I can't deal with it—too messy. So first it's a six-pack, then a few shots in the bar—well, more than a few—and before I know it I'm on a dark street corner again looking to score."

"Gotta do something different this time, man," Mars advised.

"I know." Kevin shook his head. "It doesn't help that half the fellows in the bar *are* the wreckage of my past."

"People, places, and things." I tried not to sound pompous. "I wonder what Frankie would have done if he had lived. They say no relationships the first year. But he already had the girlfriend uptown and the wife in Brooklyn. That situation alone probably made him drink and drug. And the dealing—sometimes they won't let you get away from the places and things. They've got some ugly ways of getting the message across, too."

"Too true," Mars said. "Frankie kind of boasted once or twice that he'd always been able to handle the Mr. Bigs. But before, he'd always done what they wanted. Cut the stuff, get it on the street, get the money back to Mr. Big, make sure you can account for every nickel. And keep your mouth shut."

"Amen to that," I said.

"Frankie did keep his mouth shut pretty good," Mars said.

"Yeah," Kevin agreed, "no names, no hints. You know how some people hint around when they know they should shut up but they can't stand to keep a secret? Frankie didn't do that."

"No trail of bread crumbs," I said.

"Exactly."

The trouble was, to find out who killed Frankie, we needed bread crumbs.

"He said he always paid his debts," Mars said.

"What did he mean?" I asked. "He didn't owe any money to the suppliers further up the line? Kept out of trouble? Or he didn't let anyone get over on him? He could have meant he always got even. Say, if someone cheated him."

Or cheated on him, I thought. Frankie had been jealous, even paranoid. Snooped in Luz's e-mail. Made wild accusations, then walked out. The asshole. Luz, poor fool, was devoted to Frankie. She couldn't have faked how devastated she was by his death. If she'd stabbed Frankie in her own apartment, she would have confessed. She had apologized for calling Barbara in the middle of the night and asking her to come. That was a pretty small misdemeanor compared to murder. Then again, the police might not see it the way Jimmy and Barbara and I did.

"How is that little girl?" Kevin asked. Great. Now a runty Irish gay guy was going telepathic on me. "I felt sorry for her."

"Yeah, so did we," I said. "That's how come we went to the funeral with her." Don't overexplain, I told myself. Stay cool. "She'll be okay."

She'll be better off without him, I thought. Should I tell them how he hurt her? No. Either Frankie had copped to his ugly side in group, or they didn't need to know. Maybe he'd admitted in the men's group that he'd hit her once in a while. But to a guy like Frankie, what I'd call emotional and verbal abuse would be no more than making sure a woman knew the score. I could imagine him tallying up imaginary slights and errors. Would he call knocking her around or stripping the varnish off her verbally a way of paying his debts? I wouldn't put it past him.

"She'll be better off without him," Kevin said. Telepathic.

TEN

Barbara and I took the Toyota to Bensonhurst.

"I'm glad we didn't take the subway," she said as we sped across the Brooklyn Bridge. The East River sparkled below us, and we could see the bright colors of fall foliage on the Brooklyn side. "You know what my maternal introject always says."

"It's a gorgeous day, you should be outside," I recited. I knew all about Barbara's mother in her head.

The scenic route to the neighborhood where Frankie's father had his bakery swung around the tip of Manhattan. We could see the Staten Island and Statue of Liberty ferries plowing a creamy wake through New York Harbor. And the bridge was always worth a visit. Jimmy and I had walked across it once after dropping acid. But that's another story.

Once we found the neighborhood, locating the bakery wasn't hard. The sign said IACONE & SONS, SINCE 1922. Massimo's father or maybe even his grandfather must have been the original baker.

"I guess Frankie was the only son," I said as we hesitated on the sidewalk. "No wonder Massimo was shattered."

"This sign is old," Barbara said. "On the Web site, it was Iacone's Bakery. No sons to carry on. Frankie must have broken his father's heart a long time ago. If Massimo wanted him to go into the family business, oy, had he got the wrong number." She did the punch line in a Yiddish accent. When Barbara likes a joke, you get to hear it a lot. "Do you think he'll be here?"

"Massimo? One way to find out." I started toward the door.

"Wait a minute." Barbara pulled at my hand. "We need a strategy. What are we going to say?"

"I don't know," I said. "A dozen cannoli, please?"

"Stop it!" Barbara wrenched my arm enough to make me glad I wasn't prone to dislocated shoulder. "Though we will buy something. Look at those little puffy things in the window, don't they look good? What do you think they are, almond? And, ooh, look at the display case in there. I see at least three different kinds of darling miniature cannoli—chocolate, the regular kind, and some with rainbow sprinkles on them."

I had to laugh.

"You're like a puppy that smells bacon. What happened to needing a strategy?"

"We can say again how sorry we are about Frankie. He'll remember us from the funeral as friends. And then we'll order the cannoli."

"And where in this agenda do we ask the questions, Sherlock?"

"I plan to order a *lot* of pastries," she said. "In between picking three of this and three of that, we can ask all the questions we want. Come on, we're wasting time. Let's go in."

I followed her into the store.

It was set up like a café, with lighted display cases running down one side and white wrought-iron chairs and small tiled tables on the other. The smells of sugar and yeast socked me in the nostrils the moment I stepped through the door.

Barbara stopped short. I bumped into her and had to grab her shoulders to keep my balance.

"Mmm, heavenly!" she said, inhaling from the diaphragm up.

The store was empty of customers. Behind the counter, a small woman was placing lemon tarts one by one on a tray. Her head was bent, her face hidden. A red and white bandanna covered her hair, presumably to keep it out of the merchandise. At the sound of Barbara's voice, she looked up. I recognized the round face and high Renaissance forehead. It was Stella from the funeral. The one who'd known Frankie well enough, and cared about Netta enough, to speak ill of the dead.

"Can I help you?" she asked with a friendly smile. "Oh. I know you, don't I? Not from here. I know all our customers. Oh! Frankie's funeral." Her expression grew guarded. "Friends of Frankie's?" Declaring herself as someone on Netta's team.

"Not *close* friends." Barbara went smoothly into action. She bustled toward the counter, exuding warmth and charm. "It was a sad thing. We felt it was important to show up. Mostly, we felt so sorry for Netta."

"You know Netta?" Stella was still suspicious.

"No, but we heard enough to know she must have had a pretty hard time," Barbara said. "She must have had so many different feelings when—when it happened. Those tarts look delectable, are they lemon? I want a few of everything. They all look so good!"

Stella smiled and seemed to relax. Evidently the way to her heart was through her *sfogliatella*. She must bake as well as work behind the counter.

"I made these myself," she confirmed. "I love it when people like my pastry. Do you want to taste it? This one came out a little lopsided. I'm kind of apprenticing with Massimo."

"And how does he feel about that?" Barbara asked with a fine air of insouciance. It's a standard therapy question, but most shrinks don't spew crumbs as they speak. Barbara licked a droplet of lemon filling off her upper lip. "Training a woman, I mean. I thought he might be a little old-fashioned."

"Oh, it took him a while to get used to me. I've known him since I was a toddler—I call him Uncle Massimo—so I wouldn't let him intimidate me. And when I finally made a perfect Italian wedding cake for a big customer when Massimo had the flu, he threw up his hands and decided I was here to stay."

"Decided to relax and enjoy it, huh?" Barbara grinned and licked her fingers. "This tart is delectable. We're definitely going to want some of those. Frankie never worked in the bakery? Netta didn't want him to?"

"When Netta married him," Stella said, "she thought he *was* going to work in the bakery. Personally, I think he never had any intention of going into the business. Oh, he had to work here summers when he was a kid, Massimo wouldn't have let him get out of that. Believe it or not, he wasn't a bad baker. But the moment he was old enough to stay out late and get away with not telling his parents where he'd been—well, Massimo and Silvia couldn't see it coming because they didn't want to see it. But all us kids could."

"You all grew up together?" Barbara asked. "Oh, those baby cannoli look great, let me have half a dozen each of those. Netta too?"

"We're really only a few families that lived within a couple of blocks of each other. My husband too. He's a lawyer, works in the city, not like most of them. We knew we were it for each other the day he punched a boy who'd pulled my braids and made his nose bleed. We were seven. Frankie was the one who pulled my hair. He was bigger than the rest of us, and he always had a mean streak. Hot temper, too."

"Were Netta and Frankie childhood sweethearts too?"

"Not like me and Gil. His name is Guillermo, and everybody used to call him Billy, but when he went to law school he decided Gil sounded more dignified. I don't care. Netta was the queen of the neighborhood. All the boys were crazy about her, the cousins, everybody. Frankie got her attention the most because—well, he was kind of compelling, you know? Like a snake charmer. Bigger than life."

"Charismatic," Barbara said.

"Yeah, if that means what I think it does," Stella said. "Netta kept all the boys dancing around her, thinking they might get to first base. Everybody except my Gil."

"What base did Frankie get to?" Barbara asked.

"Ah, that's a very good question!" Stella said. "Home run. They didn't announce their engagement till she was already—well, you get the picture."

"She wouldn't have—"

"Are you kidding? Her brothers would have killed her. The whole neighborhood would have made her life a misery. And believe me, they would have known. In a place like this, everybody always knows everything, even when you can't imagine how."

Now they were communicating without even finishing their sentences. Barbara was on a roll with the girl talk. I didn't want to get in the way. I retreated steadily backward. When the backs of my knees hit one of the wrought-iron chairs, I eased myself down, trying not to creak or scrape in any way as I sat.

"And once the kids came," Barbara went on, "I suppose—"

"No way. Not in this neighborhood. The older generation still thinks the Pope knows best. You make your bed, you lie on it. Even if Netta had wanted to, and I'm not so sure she did. She was still kind of hooked on him, you know?"

"Oh, yes," Barbara said. "Addicted to the relationship. But she still must have had a hard time. Did he—did he ever—?"

This time, it seemed to me she might have to finish the sentence. We had two questions: did Frankie cheat on Netta, and did he hit her? Yes to both, but did Stella know? According to her, the whole neighborhood knew anything she knew. So if she knew, anyone who loved Netta had a motive.

As they talked, Barbara pointed to one treat after another. Stella lifted them out of the case with tongs and packed them up with as much care and fancy paper as if they were Christmas presents.

"She always forgave him," Stella said. "She always stood up for him. Even when she spent nights alone—when the kids were sick, when her parents died. He didn't want this last baby. You could read the signs, you know?"

Barbara nodded. That extra X chromosome must carry the gene for second sight. They could read the signs.

Stella lowered her voice and leaned across the counter.

"I think there was somebody else. You know, not just anybody, but somebody special. Where would it have ended? You want a shopping bag for these, or should I just tie them all together with string? I can put a wooden handle on it if you want."

As Barbara handed over her credit card, the door opened and a couple of customers finally came in. I got up and ambled over to the counter.

"Massimo," I said in Barbara's ear.

"Massimo isn't working today?" she asked Stella. "We would like to pay our respects."

Stella shook her head, her face solemn.

"Massimo and Silvia are having a hard time."

"I understand. I'm so sorry," Barbara said.

"Sorry," I mumbled along.

Stella sighed.

"They look ten years older," she said. "They won't get over this for a long time. Ever."

Barbara took the pile of fragile boxes, tied together in tiers like a wedding cake. She handed them to me. Now I knew why I'd come along. We strive to serve and never to yield, or whatever the Marines say. Jimmy would know. Barbara took her receipt and then Stella's hand, which she patted and held for a second.

Where would it have ended? That was the only thing we already knew.

ELEVEN

Barbara and Luz walked along the south edge of the Central Park Reservoir. Barbara set the pace with a brisk gait she insisted was a very slow run, and Luz trotted in her wake, trying to keep up. It had not rained since the night of Frankie's death. The changing leaves glowed topaz and cherry amber. A concrete causeway bisected the shimmering water. On it, gregarious seagulls perched, taking a break from the sea, and cormorants stretched their glossy necks and spread their wings to dry. The track crossed a paved plaza, a stone Parks Department building squatting to the left and a rustic bridge arching to the right. Barbara called a greeting to a white-haired man who maintained a precarious balance as he stood on his head on a slatted park bench.

"That's the Mayor of Central Park," Barbara said. "He started running around the track in 1935. What a great old guy."

"Frankie will never get old," Luz said. Her eyes and mouth drooped, forming a mask of tragedy.

"Did you ever think about the future?" Barbara asked.

"Barbara, you taught me yourself to take everything one day at a time," Luz said. "Whenever Frankie said he loved me, I took it as a sign from God that what we were doing was okay. I guess I was wrong."

"It's not about right or wrong," Barbara said. "You did what you did. You feel what you feel."

"I feel sad," Luz said. "And angry—angry at Frankie for lying to me and then for dying. Angry at the police, and scared, too."

"What happened when you saw them again?"

"They took my fingerprints," she said. "They said they were all over the security bar. Of course they were—I always set it when I'm home alone."

"Did Frankie set the bar?"

"Sometimes yes, sometimes no. He would never admit he was scared of anything. They found it lying on the floor."

"Maybe they found signs that someone else handled it after you and Frankie. Not fingerprints, necessarily. Maybe someone with gloves."

Luz laughed briefly, a sad little sound without humor.

"Nobody wears gloves in East Harlem—not in October when the weather is still beautiful like this."

"Yeah, he would have looked kind of peculiar," Barbara said. "And if he had an iron bar in his hand, why did he need a knife? Also, he'd have had to have planned in advance, and—well, if he had to use one of your kitchen knives, it sounds like a spur-of-the-moment thing, but if he brought his own—I'm sorry, Luz. I'll shut up if it upsets you."

"No, it's okay," Luz said. "This must sound crazy, but I like it. I like that you and Jimmy and Bruce keep trying to figure it out. You're all so sure that you can find the solution." A smile, tentative but genuine, illuminated her face. "And none of you think that I am guilty."

"Of course not!" Barbara exclaimed. "If anyone knows how much you adored Frankie, it's me. Is it okay to tell you now how many times I zipped the lip? I nearly burst not giving you advice, not telling you to leave him."

"I know," Luz said. "You made your feelings clear."

"Oh, hell!" Barbara said. "Sorry, I didn't mean to."

"No, no, you did exactly right—you're a good sponsor, and you didn't try to tell me what to do," Luz assured her. "I knew in my heart that I should leave."

"No shoulds!" Barbara said. "*Should* is a toxic word. It only makes you feel unnecessary guilt." She grinned. "But yeah, you should have."

"Oh, Barbara!" Luz grabbed Barbara's hand and gave it an impulsive kiss. "You are more than a sponsor, you are a fantastic friend."

"I'm glad you think so," Barbara said. "You don't know how much it means to me. I worry all the time about whether I'm saying the right thing."

"Everything you say is perfect," Luz declared.

Barbara gave a shout of laughter.

"I wish you'd tell Jimmy and Bruce that. They love me, but they both know all my defects of character. Anyhow, the past is gone, we can't fix it. The important thing now is to figure out who did this, so the cops can't possibly think it might be you."

"What can we do?" Luz asked. "I mean you and me. You and the boys already do so much. I want to help. It is silly not to, especially as it is all to save me."

Barbara glanced sideways at her as they jogged past the Guggenheim.

"Well, I did think of something. Will it bother you if I talk about Frankie's dealing?"

"No, no, Barbara, you have the right. I am so ashamed I lied to you. I didn't know much. He would get angry—okay, I tell the truth now, he'd get ugly, start criticizing me and yell or even shake and pinch me—if I asked a question. He took me with him a few times to see Ishmael, but he swore it was simply to buy a little marijuana for himself. Ishmael was the big bad wolf, Frankie was only—is it Little Red Hood?"

"Little Red Riding Hood," Barbara supplied.

"In my heart, I knew," Luz said. "But I didn't know, because I didn't want to know."

"I understand. Denial is a defense mechanism. You can't control your unconscious. It was the same for me with Jimmy's drinking. I didn't know because knowing would have been unbearable."

"Right, that is it exactly," Luz said. "But all the signs were there. They would go in another room, and Frankie always wore this big jacket with lots of pockets on the inside when we went up there."

"Up there, you mean Ishmael's apartment?" Barbara asked.

"Yes. He had a nice apartment—leather furniture, pictures on the wall that looked expensive. Velvet drapes."

"I bet those came in handy."

"Yes, it was never daylight in Ishmael's apartment, always night."

"Do you remember where he lives? How often did you drop in?"

"Oh, you don't drop in on Ishmael. That would be a very, very bad idea. You have to call."

"Do you still have the number?"

"Oh, yes. Frankie had a lot of numbers on his PalmPilot, and the police took that away, but before that we had a Rolodex. I kept using it when he stopped, and it was in with my things, so the police must have thought it was mine. They didn't take it. Why, Barbara? Do you think of copping some drugs? Ishmael has them all—heroin, crack, cocaine, crystal meth, hashish, whatever you want. I am joking," she added.

"God, I hope so!" Barbara said. "I'm not an addict, but I'm a counselor. I'm not supposed to use illegal substances. I was always scared of the heavy drugs, anyhow. I don't like going out of control—big surprise, huh? Though I admit getting stoned was a lot of fun."

"Yes, the Al-Anons want to know what happens next. We want to be safe." Luz shivered as if the day had suddenly turned cold. "That is not always possible."

"You're right there. We can't stay safe—stuff we can't control happens all the time—and we never know what happens next. No, I'll tell you why I asked. I was thinking—I know this is a lot to ask of you, but we need to know whether Frankie was in trouble with the dealers. The police know or can find out. But they won't tell us."

They rounded the northwest corner of the track and started on the last leg. Squirrels scurried about their business in the grasses and wildflowers beside the track. A few golden leaves drifted down. Before them, the shadows of the cherry trees striped the path with shade and sunlight.

"If his death was drug related," Barbara said, "they'd have to admit it had nothing to do with you. Were you surprised when Frankie decided to go to rehab? And right before, did he seem different than usual? Nervous, watching his back more?"

"The police asked me that," Luz said. "Not more than usual. Frankie was always—what is that ACOA word?"

"Hypervigilant."

"Yes, that's it. Frankie always acted as if trouble might come out of nowhere at any time. When we ate in a restaurant, he always had to sit with his back against the wall."

"For a drug dealer," Barbara said, "I can see how hypervigilance would be a survival skill."

"And about the rehab—yes, I was surprised. One day, all of a sudden, he wants to go to this place for twenty-eight days and re-cover. Before, he would never consider it. What are you thinking, Barbara? Do you have some plan?"

"I do," Barbara admitted. "You can say no if you're not comfort-able—I really mean that, because maybe it's a crazy idea. But— the police won't tell us if anyone from the drug world had it in for Frankie, but I bet Ishmael knows. And you know Ishmael. How would you feel about calling him—didn't he say something at the funeral about getting together?—and asking if you could see him and talk about Frankie?"

"Barbara, I don't know about this. I don't think he meant that pleasantly, about seeing me soon. When he said, 'I know where you live,' my stomach did like this." She held her hand out and made a fist.

"I'd go with you, of course," Barbara said. "If there are two of us, he wouldn't do anything, would he?"

"Probably not," Luz said. "And the neighborhood is okay, es-pecially if we go in the daytime. It's uptown, on the West Side, between Harlem and what they call Inwood. Do you really think we'd learn anything?"

"Ishmael struck me as the kind of guy you don't hint around with. We'd ask. The worst he can do is not tell us."

"Or lie to us," Luz said.

"Good point."

"If you think it is important, I will do it," Luz said. "We will protect each other."

"I can bring my can of pepper spray," Barbara offered.

Luz giggled.

"Maybe not, Barbara. That would make him angry."

"Yeah, I guess we really don't want to make Ishmael angry. Even the little I saw of him, he is one scary dude. But we don't want to leave a single stone unturned. And we're the only ones who can turn this one, so let's do it. Let's give ourselves points for bravery—courage is a character asset, anyhow."

"You'll be with me when I make the call?"

"Holding your hand if you want," Barbara assured her.

"Oh! I just thought of something else," Luz said. "He won't talk to us unless we smoke with him."

"Pot, you mean?"

"Oh, yes, he always has marijuana. That is the ritual, first you have the joint, only then you can talk business. If we refuse, he might get angry, but he will certainly tell us to go away."

"I don't mind. In fact," Barbara confessed, "I'll look forward to it. I told you getting stoned was fun for me. Of course I stopped when Jimmy got clean and sober. And then I became a counselor, and who are you going to do dope with? I wouldn't get high with an addict—that really would be wrong."

"Oh, yes, you said, your counselor ethics. This whole thing would not be breaking them?"

"We-e-ell," Barbara said. "I think in this case, clearing you of murder trumps a bunch of rules. It's for a good cause, and it's only just this once. You have to swear you'll never, never, never tell anyone I did it."

"Not even Jimmy and Bruce?"

"Especially not Jimmy or Bruce," said Barbara. "They would kill me."

TWELVE

Barbara took a deep breath and let it out slowly as the door closed on her cheerful, lying good-bye to Jimmy and Bruce. They planned to dine on leftover Chinese food heated in the microwave and attend an AA anniversary meeting. She had allowed them to believe that she and Luz would spend the evening at Al-Anon. Lying to Jimmy made her feel miserable. He was so sunny-tempered and goofy, and he trusted her so much. As the elevator made its creaky ascent to pick her up, the apartment door opened again. Her heart thumped as Jimmy's head appeared in the doorway.

"Did you know," he asked, "that Frederick the Great called Empress Maria Theresa the only *mensch* in Austria?"

"No, Jimmy," she said, "but thanks for letting me know." How could you lie to a guy like that? "Here's my elevator. Have fun at the meeting!"

At the Starbucks on the corner, she found Luz sipping espresso. Barbara slid into a chair and leaned her elbows on the small, round table.

"Did you call him? What did you tell him? Did he say we could come?"

"I told him I'd hardly slept since Frankie died—that part is true—and that I needed something to help me relax. And I said my friend's boyfriend is in recovery so she can't let him know she still likes to get high."

"Oh, God, Luz," Barbara said, "what are we doing? You set us up so well that he'll expect us to buy. *Oy vey iz mir.* The part about not being able to take anything home is totally true."

"I can't take it home, either," Luz said. "Thank heaven Frankie tried so hard to hide the drugging from me that he didn't leave a stash in my apartment. The police went over every inch of it. They were worse than Tia Wanda on a cleaning mission. They took down the crime scene tape, but how do I know they won't ask to take another look?"

"Only they won't ask," Barbara said, "they'll come with a search warrant. I agree, you don't want them to find a Baggie full of marijuana."

"Besides, then we'd have to smoke it. That does not seem like such a good idea to me."

"You're right," Barbara said. "I know it's tempting to bypass the feelings, but in counseling we say the only way out is through. You need to mourn."

"Believe me, Barbara, I am mourning." Luz's eyes filled with tears.

"I know, baby, I know." Barbara reached out a soothing hand and started rubbing circles between her shoulder blades. "This is very hard for you. This too shall pass, but in the meantime, it sucks."

Luz smiled through a watery sniffle.

"I bet they don't teach you to say that in counselor school. But it is a true word."

"So what do we do, buy half an ounce and throw it away on the way home? I brought cash just in case we couldn't get out of it."

"Oh, no," Luz exclaimed. "We can't throw away money like that."

"It does go against the grain," Barbara said. "Maybe we'd better find a way to tell him what we really want. Say we'll pay him to answer a few questions about Frankie, whatever he would have charged us for the dope. An ounce, maybe. We can't be stingy—he'll know how much we need the information, and it's not as if we're going to smoke it."

"But when we first go in," Luz said, "that is different. He offers it, it's free, but it's—what would you call it?"

"A ritual," Barbara said.

"Yes, to be courteous. He would be offended if we said no."

"Like a peace pipe," Barbara said. "I just hope I can keep my mind on what we came for once I get stoned. It never took much in the old days. Jimmy used to laugh at me. Two or three hits, and I'd be on the floor clinging to his ankles and saying, 'Save me, save me!'"

"I don't think you'd better do that with Ishmael," Luz said.

"I'll try not to," Barbara said. "So I guess we both get to take a time-out—me from my counselor ethics, and you from your sorrow."

"You know what, Barbara?"

"What?"

"We will probably enjoy this." She caught Barbara's eye, and they both giggled.

Barbara looked curiously around Ishmael's apartment, trying to decide whether it was what she had expected. The heavy velvet drapes that must make it seem like night even on the brightest day, yes. The thick Persian or Turkish carpet, maybe. The art on the walls—including a De Kooning, a Botero, and what couldn't possibly be a Cézanne as well as two extremely well-done Haitian scenes and several magnificent West African masks—only because Luz had told her beforehand. The collection of teddy bears, definitely not.

"The teddy bears are new," Luz whispered.

She and Barbara stood as close together as possible, drawing courage from each other's body heat. Ishmael, wearing a rich blue caftan heavily embroidered in gold and a cap of kente cloth, gave them time to look around. The teddy bears, of every style and size, perched on the leather sofa and matching chairs, sprawled back-to-back as bookends, and flopped out of every drawer and cubbyhole. A massive teak wall unit held a sound system that Barbara thought must have cost thousands.

Ishmael flashed them a genial smile, his shark's teeth gleaming.

The better to eat you with, my dear, Barbara thought.

His cheekbones were as gorgeous, his eyes as hard, as she remembered.

Ishmael laid his palms together and bowed.

"Namaste. Ladies, come and sit. How may I serve you?"

Namaste, my right foot, Barbara thought. More like, "Welcome to my castle. I am Count Dracula."

He ushered them to the deepest couch. Its golden oak leather, a perfect match for Ishmael's skin tone, was buttery and supple. When Barbara sat, she sank into the cushions beneath as well as behind her. Not a sofa bed, Barbara thought. I bet he never has his friends for a sleepover.

Ishmael chose a roomy armchair of the same leather and sat. His long legs were crossed under the caftan, his back as straight as a Zulu warrior's.

Washing the spears, Barbara thought, riffling through her memories of one of Jimmy's favorite military periods. Didn't that mean dipping them in the enemy's blood? And here we are, planning *not* to keep our wits about us.

Ishmael took off the kente cloth cap and laid it carefully on the arm of his chair. He whipped an oversized silk bandanna out of his sleeve with the air of a prestidigitator and rubbed it across his already burnished skull.

"You will smoke with me."

It seemed to Barbara as if the paraphernalia appeared by magic.

"Sinsemilla. You won't have had any this good. Or would you prefer hash? I have a Turkish water pipe that is to a bong what the Kentucky Derby winner is to a Mexican donkey. Or—this?"

It was a crack vial. Barbara shook her head.

"No way! I mean, no, thanks. Marijuana is fine."

Without comment, Ishmael whisked out a packet of rolling papers—still using Bambú after all these years, Barbara observed—and began rolling joints, his slim, elegant fingers dexterous. When he licked the papers, his tongue caressed them like a lover's. He's doing that on purpose, Barbara thought. He's trying to see how uncomfortable he can make us, because he knows damn well we wouldn't be here if we didn't want something from him.

Ishmael snicked a roach clip onto the end of one joint and laid the rest aside. Flame spurted from his fingertips. Don't be an idiot, Barbara admonished herself, at least not till you're stoned. He had the lighter in his sleeve—he could palm it because his hands were big but not bulky. The roach clip looked like sterling silver. It had diamond chips set into it. He offered it to Luz. She cast an apprehensive glance at Barbara, who nodded. Luz set the joint to her lips and drew in a long, deep breath. Her eyes closed as she held the smoke in, then expelled it in a slow stream.

Dammit, I don't care, Barbara thought. I'm glad Luz can get

away from reality for a couple of hours. She's in so much pain. So what's my excuse? Oh, the hell with it.

Luz handed her the joint. No turning back now. She inhaled.

In a couple of minutes, she and Luz were giggling helplessly. Ishmael, who had taken only one hit to their two or three, showed no alteration in mood or self-control.

"Probably habish—habitch—" Barbara said aloud, then, "Oops!" She pressed her fingers to her mouth like a child who has said a forbidden word. Ishmael was probably habituated to the drug. Addicts and alcoholics always thought a hard head meant they were in control. On the contrary, increased tolerance was a hallmark symptom of addictions. Now she had lost her train of thought. She felt a gentle movement of the leather cushion beneath her, like a boat rocking on a calm sea. Was Jimmy in the boat with her? No, she was here with Luz. She turned her head to the side to look for Luz. The movement seemed to take forever, as if her neck had become the axle on which her head revolved like one of those slow-spinning restaurants in the sky.

Luz cradled one of the teddy bears, rocking as she sang to it in Spanish. It was the cuddly kind, with pale cream fur and golden eyes that seemed to regard Luz with compassion. Some of the bears were dressed, in outfits ranging from a sailor suit to a tuxedo, but this one wore only a blue satin bow.

"All right." Ishmael's voice came as from the other end of a wind tunnel.

Barbara had forgotten Ishmael. She turned her head toward him, again rotating it with infinite slowness on her neck, which felt as long as Alice in Wonderland's. Luz raised her head, nursing the teddy bear against her breast.

"Now," Ishmael said. "What you bitches really here for?"

Isn't it amazing, Barbara thought, how relaxed I feel around

Ishmael. I don't even mind the B word. When he says it, it's just vocabulary.

"I'm not afraid of you," she said.

Ishmael grinned like a wolf.

"Girl, that be chemical courage. Why, if somebody smart enough, he just roll it up and smoke it and be brave whenever he wants."

Luz held her teddy bear up like a shield and waggled its paw toward Ishmael.

"Tell us about Frankie," she said in a growly bear voice.

Ishmael uttered a hoot of laughter.

"I told you that be good shit. What you wanna know, little girl?"

Luz hugged the teddy bear against her chest.

"Was he in trouble?" she demanded.

A long silence fell. Barbara dreamily examined the pattern on the Persian rug. As she followed the mazelike twists and turns, she thought, this must be how obsessive compulsives feel. If I lose the thread, I have to start over.

Ishmael took a long drag on the water pipe. Barbara hadn't even noticed him setting it up. It gurgled pleasantly, and he blew out a stream of smoke. Ishmael's hash is better than my mother's corned beef hash, Barbara thought. Ooh, am I in trouble. Not like Frankie, though.

"What precisely do you mean by trouble?" Ishmael asked.

He can turn that Ebonic talk on and off, Barbara thought.

"You mean *was* he trouble," Ishmael asked, "or was he *in* trouble? Why you be botherin' yo head about that, anyway? Ohhhh, I get it. You playin' no shit Sherlock. Only right now you playin' *good* shit Sherlock."

Ha! Barbara thought. He is stoned. He just knows better how not to show it.

Luz's arms tightened around the bear.

"I need to know how he died," she said fiercely. "If you know, you must tell us."

"Or you'll what?" Ishmael jeered. He sprawled in his chair, long legs stretched out so far that his feet almost touched the women's toes. "Oooh, I'm so scared."

Get a grip, Barbara told herself. You came along to help Luz. She forced herself to speak, her voice sounding remote and unfamiliar in her ears.

"We know he was dealing," she said. "Did he cheat anybody? Sell bad drugs? Steal from—from someone up the line?"

Better not ask if he'd stolen from Ishmael. She wasn't foolhardy enough, even stoned out of her gourd, to ask Ishmael outright if he had a motive. But he might have. Maybe they hadn't thought this through enough. She had assumed that "drug traffickers," if they had murdered Frankie, were shadowy figures from the underworld, Colombians maybe, executioners for omnipotent "lords"—not a guy who lived a few subway stops from her, a guy she'd met at a funeral in Brooklyn.

"Maybe I know, and maybe I don't," Ishmael said. "What you gonna give me if I tell?"

Luz and Barbara looked at each other. Was he asking them for sex?

Ishmael intercepted the look and read it with scorn.

"I don't do no white pussy," he said.

Just vocabulary, just vocabulary, Barbara told herself.

He stood, rising up so tall and close that Barbara had to restrain herself from shrinking back. Dealing with Ishmael was like meeting a grizzly bear or mountain lion in the wild. You might end up dead, but you couldn't show fear. And if you ran, he'd run you down.

"Come on," he said. "We goin' for a ride."

At least, Barbara thought as they followed him out onto the dark street like the children of Hamelin, he hadn't made them buy the marijuana. She had failed to think of a safe way to dispose of it.

On the street, Ishmael triggered a remote, and down the block a car beeped and flashed its lights. Barbara expected something expensive but flashy, maybe a Fifties Cadillac with enormous tail fins and an airbrushed custom paint job. But the car, when they reached it, was a black Mercedes. With an ironic bow, he ushered them into the backseat, which was as soft as the couch in his apartment and smelled of new leather. Ishmael walked around to the driver's side. Settled behind the wheel, he picked up a peaked cap from the empty seat next to him and covered his shiny dome.

"How do you like that, ladies?" he said. "Now you got your very own show-fur." He reached a long arm over the backrest and patted the teddy bear, still clasped in Luz's arms. "Hang onto that. We gonna need him."

The windows of the Mercedes were tinted. It was hard to see out, although red and green traffic lights and the orange of the sodium streetlights cast a dim glow through the glass. Barbara could sense when the marijuana started to wear off, because the light show began to lose its fascination.

"I wonder where we're going," she murmured.

"Me too," Luz said. "I tell myself we must be safe as long as we are together."

"And we've each got our own Higher Power," Barbara said. "I wonder why they say there are no atheists in foxholes. I should think that would be the perfect time to have doubts."

"Barbara, you're still high," Luz said.

"I hope I don't end up with a migraine," Barbara said. "How about you?"

"Mine is wearing off," Luz said.

"I feel like a chiffon scarf blowing in the wind," Barbara said.

"If he's taking us into danger, I hope it's a long ride. I need to get a few more of my bones and muscles back."

"I don't know about that," Luz said. "Where could a long ride from upper Manhattan end?"

"Hmm. A lot of places, none of them appealing. Staten Island, New Jersey, Canarsie."

"Don't you worry 'bout them outer boroughs," Ishmael remarked. His eyes locked with Barbara's in the rearview mirror. "Don't you worry 'bout nothin'."

Barbara and Luz fell silent, and the car rolled on. Ishmael drove with precision, timing progressive traffic lights so that he never had to stop for a red. He never exceeded the speed limit or cut in blind ahead of a van or truck. Even Ishmael, Barbara thought, if he wasn't careful, could get stopped by the wrong cop for DWB—Driving While Black.

Ishmael took the curve through the bottom of Riverside Park onto the West Side Highway. Barbara turned her head to look at the motorboats, yachts, and houseboats bobbing in the Hudson at the Seventy-ninth Street Boat Basin. The motion didn't take forever this time. Maybe the high was wearing off.

"I'm starving," she said.

"I am hungry," Luz said at the same moment.

They both giggled.

Ishmael tossed a couple of Snickers bars over his shoulder in their general direction. Evidently, munchies were part of the service. Barbara tore the wrapper off hers and crammed it in her mouth.

They reached Chelsea Piers and the parklike stretch below it, where the whole waterfront had been developed and landscaped in the past few years. It was too late for joggers, but a few dog walkers panted along, their dogs straining at their leashes, eager for the next fascinating sniff. Barbara wondered if, after all, they would leave Manhattan. The lights on the Jersey side of the river twinkled. Ahead lay the Battery Tunnel, beyond that, the swing around the tip of Manhattan to the Brooklyn Bridge. To the east lay Queens, the airports, and all of Long Island. Would they turn east to the maze of streets in the Village? What was open at night in lower Manhattan?

As they approached the covered walkway that arched over Chambers Street, Ishmael turned on his left blinker. Although the intersection was deserted, he waited for the light. The car wove its way without hesitation through the skyscraper canyons, so crowded with life and color during the day. Not the Stock Exchange, not the Fed, not the courts. They passed 26 Federal Plaza and the police headquarters on Centre Street. Barbara wondered what would happen if she yelled, "Help! Help!" But they had not been taken for a ride in the abduction sense. They had come of their own free will, tit for tat.

"How do we know you'll tell us the truth?" she demanded, raising her voice for Ishmael.

"You just gonna have to trust me." His voice carried a teasing lilt, but the eyes in the rearview mirror remained hard as stones.

Ishmael pulled up in front of an Art Deco tower on Broadway, a few doors above the monumental bronze bull that declared the extended Wall Street area a temple to economic expansion. Why don't they replace it with a giant bear when the market is down? Barbara wondered. Silly, she answered herself, in a bear market they can't afford it.

"Come on," Ishmael said. He clicked their right hand door un locked from the driver's controls with one hand as he pushed his own door open with the other.

Barbara realized only then that they had been locked in the backseat with no controls of their own. In that respect, the Mercedes resembled a police car. She stepped out onto a yellow line. Ishmael had parked perfectly, twelve inches from the curb, but illegally. She wondered if he had a license. It was hard to imagine Ishmael taking his driving test and flunking the first time, like everybody else. He walked around the hood and reached in on the passenger side. In one flowing motion, he tossed the chauffeur's cap on the seat, threw a laminated card on the dashboard, and scooped up a high-end Eagle Creek backpack that must already have been stowed under the seat. She squinted to read the card. She doubted Ishmael was a member of the Police Benevolent Association, but it was a great way not to get a ticket.

Luz climbed out of the car, still clutching her teddy bear. As she stood upright on the sidewalk, she tilted, wobbled, and clutched at the open door for support. Barbara slithered out past her. She too grabbed the door, but only to give herself a boost.

"Are you okay?" she asked. "Dizzy? Hey, I don't think you need the teddy bear."

"Keep it," Ishmael ordered. "Here. One for you." He pulled a bear with a red bow from the backpack and pitched it underhand to Barbara, who caught it purely by reflex. "Follow me. And keep your mouths shut."

They marched after him like a short string of boot camp recruits with a martinet of a sergeant—except for the teddy bears. A chain barred the revolving door of polished brass and glass. USE DOOR ON LEFT AFTER BUSINESS HOURS, a sign advised. Ishmael pushed open the left-hand door. Reaching over Luz's shoulder, Barbara caught it on her extended palm before it swung back. He never was a Girl Scout, she thought. If you have to move the branch, you hold it for the next person so it won't spring back in their face. The image of Ishmael in a uniform of Girl Scout green made her smile, but not excessively. The marijuana really was wearing off now. Where are we going, she wondered, and why on earth are we carrying bears?

The vast lobby was dimly lit. Slick marble walls rose to a distant ceiling with gilded plaster moldings. A uniformed guard was seated at a massive reception desk that looked like rosewood, topped with a marble counter big enough to skate on. As they reached the first of several elevator banks, he got up and came toward them.

"Paton, Schein, and Arrowhead," Ishmael said as the guard's lips parted. "Mr. Arrowhead is expecting us." It sounded like a law firm and probably was. Barbara had a program friend who worked the night shift in a big corporate firm as a paralegal. As Ishmael spoke, she noticed that he had shed his caftan along the way. He must have bundled it under the car seat when he picked up the backpack. He was now dressed in a crisp white shirt, blue blazer, and chinos. The Mercedes was roomy enough to store an endless assortment of props, like a car for circus clowns. Ishmael, it occurred to her, was primarily a showman. His theatricality kept him prosperous and out of jail. Nor did it hurt the success of his special effects that his usual audience was high.

The guard, though not in an altered state, seemed to take them at face value.

"Please step over to the desk first," he said.

In a movie, this was where Ishmael would have reached for a gun. Instead, he raised his arms obligingly as the guard wanded him.

"And your backpack?"

"Empty," Ishmael said, opening it so the guard could see. The man was thorough, unzipping each of the many pockets and running his fingers inside.

"Now stand on that spot for ten seconds, please. State your name and who you got the apperntment with for the camera."

Ishmael faced the small red eye, squared his shoulders, and enunciated clearly, "James Washington. To see Ronald Arrowhead."

"Ladies?" the guard said.

Were they supposed to recite their real names? Barbara looked at Ishmael for guidance. He winked at her.

"Nancy Drew," she said. "Mr. Arrowhead."

Luz suppressed a giggle.

"Lola Montez," she said.

"Fourteenth floor," the guard said. "Second elevator bank. I'll ring Mr. Arrowhead and tell him you're coming."

They were in. Barbara experienced a thrill of irrational satisfaction, as if she understood their agenda here and cared about furthering it. They rode the elevator in silence, the surface of its polished brass door reflecting their wavering images as if in a pool of water. When they reached the fourteenth floor, Ishmael said, "You stay right here. You don't move. You don't snoop." As Barbara opened her mouth, he added, "You don't ask no questions. And gimme those bears."

The law firm, if that's what it was, had the whole floor. Ishmael pressed the buzzer next to glass double doors behind the vast desk in the dimmed and deserted reception area. A long buzz responded. A lock snicked open. Ishmael disappeared into the corporate corridors, the teddy bears under his arm. Their flopping heads and the red and blue bows peeked out from the crook of his elbow.

"I don't think I'm high anymore," Luz said.

"Me neither," Barbara said. "I wish I hadn't eaten that Snickers bar."

"And that was it," she told Bruce and Jimmy later. Conscience, her chronic difficulty with discretion, and love of a good story had combined to render her unable to resist confessing their adventure. "We never got to see Ronald Arrowhead or find out who he was."

Jimmy's dancing fingers on the keyboard were already far ahead of her.

"Major philanthropist," he said. "Patron of two orchestras and three museums. And here's the firm. Just what it looked like, corporate law. Fortune 500 clients only."

"I'm surprised it was deserted," Bruce said out of a vast experience of temping. "New associates in those firms bring their sleeping bags. And the paralegals and support staff work shifts. You must have gotten out at the executive floor."

"So Mr. Arrowhead could get his drugs delivered," Jimmy said. "It makes sense."

"He must be a good customer," Bruce said.

"I think the painting behind the reception desk was a real Chagall," Barbara said. "At least Ishmael kept his word. Before he let us out of the car on Eighty-sixth Street, he told us he hadn't heard a single whisper on the street about Frankie being in trouble over drugs or any rumors about his death. As far as he knows, it wasn't a drug hit, and he told us he would know. So all's well that ends well."

"You're damn lucky it did, Ms. Nancy Drew," Jimmy grumbled. "If you ever do it again, I swear I won't bail you out when you get caught carrying drugs inside of teddy bears or anything else. That would really put the kibosh on your counseling career. And no more dope. Promise."

"I promise," Barbara said. "Honestly, Jimmy, I do. But I must admit it was fun."

THIRTEEN

I lived in two worlds these days. Three, if the brokerage houses and law firms where I temped counted. I spent a lot of time at Jimmy and Barbara's, lolling on their couch and trying to figure out who stabbed Frankie to death. Not for justice. I could have stuck a knife in him myself, if I was that kind of guy, for what he'd done to Luz. She was so little and cute. On her lips, even a word like *fingerprints* made music. Feengerpreenss. If she'd only let herself go. Frankie had turned her into a hermit crab. She'd peep out and then scuttle back inside her shell. She even missed the brute. I wished I'd been there when she and Barbara got stoned. Maybe not, if I couldn't have some too. But still.

Whatever Barbara thought, it wasn't fear I'd die of sober boredom that drove me either. Sleuthing was addictive. Once you asked the question, not knowing the answer felt like a chronic itch between the shoulder blades. You just had to twist and stretch and try to scratch it.

So Frankie hadn't been on the run from his suppliers. His

customers might be another story. It was easy to cheat a druggie. Add oregano to the dope. Baking soda to the coke. Those were benign compared to what some dealers cut the shit with. You could get killed buying doctored product on the street. On the other hand, if you wanted to stay in business, it didn't help your reputation if your customers started dying.

The police already knew about Frankie's dealing. That meant at least one prior conviction. The Rockefeller laws meant mandatory sentencing. Even if the judge was your mother's boyfriend— or your mother—you got no leniency. If Frankie had to choose between being a three-time loser and getting clean, he might have turned crab himself. Pulled a nice safe rehab over his head. Was the law closing in on him? The homicide cops must know, even though like any TV watcher I knew narcotics was another branch. It was all on the computer nowadays. But Frankie had come out of rehab. Gone to his AA and NA meetings. Knocked Luz around, the bastard. Had he gone on dealing? If so, the law hadn't caught him at it. Some dealers prided themselves on not doing drugs. Most thought alcohol didn't count. It counted. So did pot and your Aunt Violet's Valium.

Frankie might have meant it when he checked into rehab. We all meant it for about fifteen seconds. But good intentions could slide away fast. He had managed to make Luz believe he went straight for love of her. I didn't buy Frankie as a screwed-up nice guy. Maybe he thought he did love Luz. It didn't stop the violence or keep him from blaming her. She said the wrong thing. She didn't jump high or fast enough. It made me sick.

So what about the wife? Stuck in Brooklyn, spewing up in the morning and making the kids do their homework, she'd have been pissed off if she found out that Frankie played away from home. The guy Vinnie, the cousin, had warned us off her brothers. Was this a Godfather-type family? We knew nothing about those guys.

I tried to imagine what I'd do if I was the vengeful kind of brother. Say, if someone treated Barbara the way Frankie treated Luz. Not stabbing. I'd have wanted the guy to hurt, not die. I'd have beaten the shit out of him and thrown his goddamn cell phone out the window so he couldn't call for help. I'd have stomped on his fingers and taken that iron security bar to his ribs. And laughed all the way back to my apartment.

When I went downtown to Laura's, I entered a different world. When Laura and I were married, we lived in a warm bath of sex, drugs, and rock and roll. And you could hold the rock and roll. Her mood swings were my roller coaster, and I lay back and enjoyed the ride. Sure I screamed, but with pleasure, like a kid at Great Adventure. I don't know why we got divorced. Well, I do. One day Laura said, "I'm bored. Let's get a divorce." And I went along with it just like I did everything else she proposed. Drinking and drugging every day didn't leave me much energy to buck the tide.

So what the hell was I doing, clean and sober but still getting out of the train at Spring Street and walking over to West Broadway on a Saturday afternoon? She called. I came running. Not as fast as in the old days, especially when she cried suicidal wolf. I couldn't pack up the whole tent and stay away. But I tried to set some limits. I could call Jimmy or my sponsor or go to a meeting if the Laura song rang too loud in my ears. In high school we'd had to read the one about the poor schmuck who made them tie him to the mast with cotton in his ears so he wouldn't go overboard when he heard the original Sirens. Those were the gals who got you dashed on the rocks. Or were they the ones who turned you into pigs? I had no intention of turning into a pig. Been there. Done that.

It wasn't like the old days. I didn't want to get inside her skin anymore. I wouldn't have cared about her sleeping with Mac if the guy had been good to her. Maybe. And when I caught her keys and took the elevator up to the loft, I knew it wasn't my real life. Just a short vacation.

"What have you been doing with yourself all week?" she asked. We lay in the water bed, spent and lazy. She ran a finger down the left side of my chest. Right where an Aztec priest would make the incision to cut out my heart.

Thinking about murder. Eating too many miniature cannoli from Bensonhurst. I had qualified at a meeting on the East Side. All those Park Avenue snobs Jimmy and I used to pretend to despise nodded at my stories and laughed at my jokes because they understood. They'd been there too. One woman, maybe fifty, wearing a diamond and emerald pin and bracelet from Tiffany or somewhere like it like they were nothing, came over and gave me a hug afterward. You made me cry, she said. Nope, never met her before. Might not see her again unless I go to that meeting. I know her name, though. Hi, I'm Amanda, I'm an alcoholic.

"Nothing," I said.

"Let's go out," she said. She jumped out of bed and started fluffing up her hair. It was bright neon green this week. Chartreuse. All the way down.

"I don't want to go Mac chasing again," I said. "You do that on your own time."

I knew what she thought. I was no fun anymore.

In the street, she hailed a cab. I climbed in after her.

"Go down to Chinatown," she commanded, "and cruise around. There's a place that has the best dim sum, but I don't remember the name, and I don't know where it is."

The driver shrugged and complied. He was a Sikh with a turban. Rajiv Singh, according to his photo ID. Through the bulletproof partition, we could hear him talking on his hands-free cell phone in his own language. Here I was, struggling to stay in the here and now. Working on my spiritual recovery. Thanks to cell phones, everybody else was anywhere but here at any given moment.

Canal Street, the border between SoHo and Chinatown, was teeming. Tourists jostled tiny Chinese matriarchs shopping for fish and bok choy. You could buy a lacquered duck or, farther west, a soldering iron or a set of wrenches. Storefronts opened onto the street, their wares spilling out into the crowd: brocade flip-flops and paper lanterns, red snapper and silvery bass, heavy-duty orange electrical cord and industrial-strength paint stripper.

"Why don't we get out and walk?" I suggested. "If you really want dim sum, there are plenty of places."

"I want the place I know about," she insisted. "Chinatown isn't that big. Heavenly Delight? Imperial Palace? Some name like that."

Chinatown got bigger every year. It had almost completely displaced Little Italy. But the streets were narrow. The taxi had to breast the crowd as if they were a flock of sheep on a country lane in a country that had sheep. England, maybe.

"I could let you off on Mott Street, lady," the cabbie said. "Or Chatham Square."

"No!" Laura said. "Go around the block again."

Traffic stood still on Canal Street, probably backed up all the way to the Manhattan Bridge at one end and the Holland Tunnel at the other. The taxi inched along. The meter ticked. I hoped Laura had brought cash. Before, I had hailed many a cab for a woman who thought I was taking her for a ride until she found out that I was. But Laura could always beat me at the empty pockets game. I did have a twenty for emergencies. I kept it in my shoe. My sponsor's suggestion. Hard to slap it down on the bar that way.

We faced into the sun, already low in the sky. It shed a golden light on the buildings and made glass windows flash like signal flares. The crowd of pedestrians thinned out a bit as the Chinatown part of Canal receded behind us. Laura, head out the open window like a dog enjoying the wind, drew in a sharp breath.

"Stop!" she said. As the driver complied, the light changed to green. Impatient horns sounded behind us.

The driver stuck his head out the front window at the same angle as Laura's behind him.

"Shut up, you bloody idiots," he bellowed. "Where the fuck do you think you can go? Assholes! Stupid bastards! Cocksuckers!"

"Easy does it," I muttered. An AA slogan. The trouble with road rage is that people return it. In the backseat with the windows down, we were sitting ducks.

"Oh!" Laura exclaimed. She craned out the window so far that I grabbed her waist, afraid she'd topple over. She ignored me. "Mac! Mac! Follow that motorcycle!"

"Make up your mind, lady," the cabbie said.

"Just follow it," she said.

I couldn't see any motorcycle. The driver did. I doubted it was Mac.

"How do you want me to do that, lady? This traffic isn't moving."

She took him literally.

"Go around the block," she said. "Cut ahead of him."

"You're the boss," the Sikh said. He added something I suspected it was just as well we didn't understand. He signaled a right-hand turn. The car ahead of us pulled into the intersection, giving us access to the side street and creating gridlock for everybody else. The narrow side street was dim with shadow. Parked cars lined the curb, but we had the street to ourselves. We bumped along over ruts and a few of the original cobblestones.

"Faster! Faster!" Laura urged.

Singh stepped on the gas. As he accelerated, I got flung against Laura so she almost sat in my lap, her back against my chest. I held on. The taxi shot ahead three blocks as if going through a flume.

"That's far enough," Laura snapped. "Make a left."

The taxi squealed around the corner.

"Now a right onto Canal again. Do you see the bike—the motorcycle? Can't you go any faster? We've got to catch up. I'm sure it's Mac."

Like me, Singh read her final words as, "I'm not sure it's Mac." As he made the right-hand turn, he looked back at her, exasperated.

"Lady, this is not my cab. Will you pay the ticket I will get for speeding? Neither will my boss. I tell you now—"

As the taxi poked its nose into the wider street, an SUV impatient to get home to Jersey smacked into the left side of the hood with a sickening thud. The impact flung Laura and me apart. Her head cracked into the upper frame of the window, mine into the partition between us and the front seat. The cabbie hit the windshield, but his turban must have cushioned the blow. He had enough breath left to emit a stream of curses. First in Punjabi or whatever, then in English.

"He's getting away," Laura wailed. "Just go on, go after him!"

"Lady, you are crazy!" the driver screamed. "Look at my cab! How will I explain this fender to the boss? Forget about it, I follow no one. I want you out of my taxi."

Meanwhile, the driver of the SUV emerged, slammed his door, and rounded the front of the vehicle to survey the front of the hood. He bent and ran his hand along the grill. He straightened up and wheeled around to face us, fists bunched.

"Goddamn motherfucking sonofabitch turbanhead, look what you've done to my car!"

Singh flung his own door open and surged out, nose to nose with his opponent.

"Who are you calling turbanhead, cocksucker?" He waggled the offending headgear in the SUV driver's face. "I am not an Arab— stupid dickhead Americans, don't know the difference between a cow and a sheep because they both have tails."

Laura ignored this. She slumped back against the back of the rear seat, rubbing her head.

"Hey, Bruce. Guess what? There are two of you."

I turned my head toward her. It didn't want to go. That and the shooting pain in my neck told me I had whiplash.

"Let me see, Laura. Look at me. Open your eyes and look straight into mine."

I had a vague idea that if someone had a concussion, their eyeballs would be different sizes. No, it must be the pupils. I stared at Laura's. I couldn't tell.

"My head hurts," she said. "I want Mac."

"Laura, I think you have a concussion," I said. "We'd better get you to the ER."

I slid to the right and opened the door on that side. I helped her out and steadied her as she wobbled between two parked cars to the sidewalk. As we limped toward Sixth Avenue, where traffic would be moving uptown toward St. Vincent's, the two oblivious drivers were in each other's faces, bellowing in different languages but communicating very well.

Laura leaned heavily on my arm and whimpered.

"Bruce, you'll take care of me, won't you? You always took good care of me."

Not the way I remembered it. Mutually out of control, we had spiraled down in free fall toward the inevitable crash. I had found a net. Laura had not.

"Sure I will," I said.

Her green nails raked my forearm as she clutched at me.

"I hate hospitals," she said. "They always want to lock me up."

"I know."

"You're the only one who understands," she said. "Don't leave me, Bruce, don't ever, ever leave me."

I already had. It hadn't done me any good. It seemed I was still her yo-yo, bouncing on her string as it came unwound.

At Houston Street, we flagged down a cab for the short ride to St. Vincent's. I squinched over to the left so she could lie down. She eased her body onto the creaking backseat and moaned as she lowered her head onto my lap. We arrived at the ER without incident.

A triage nurse came bustling up. I explained we had been in an accident and thought she might have a concussion. Looking around the waiting room with its tired plastic chairs and baleful fluorescent lights, I couldn't see any gunshot wounds or incipient heart attacks ahead of us. But there might be any number of them beyond the No Unauthorized Entry doors. A fender bender wasn't much of an emergency. I didn't bother to try to make it sound worse than it was. I didn't mention my possible whiplash, and the nurse didn't ask. She took Laura, still limp as a puppet, away from me. Someone shoved a clipboard at my chest. I knew plenty about Laura—her family, her history, her symptoms, what she liked to do in bed—but not if she still had health insurance. A clerk with a computer helped me out. They knew her here.

Time stretched as I hung out waiting for whatever came next. Last time I'd been in the ER, I was the emergency. Now I discovered the true meaning of boredom. A Puerto Rican mom fed an endless supply of junk food—Fritos, chocolate, potato chips— to her flock of screaming children. A black dude in a hoodie jounced to the music in his earphones, shaking not only his own molded chair but the string of three attached to it. I went out to smoke and chose a different seat when I returned. A yuppie couple dressed in tracksuits held a low-voiced argument. They were still at it when I came back in. Hanging out in front of the building beyond the length of a cigarette didn't appeal. I didn't mind other people's smoke, but secondhand cell phone conversations might kill me yet.

More likely, Laura would be the death of me. She got crazier and crazier. If I wanted to get laid, I could find a safer way. Too bad I wasn't gay. Cruising the park with a condom and a dream might be less dangerous. Of course, the sex was not the point, or not the whole point. I could barely remember how I'd come to marry her, but I remembered why. Maybe if she hadn't been bipolar, I would have found her less compelling. It was all Laura, the whole frenetic package. The mood swings. The meds or lack of them. The drugs or more drugs or different drugs. The crackle of energy, all wired together yet fragile too. The zany creative spark, whether she was making a pair of earrings or crafting her body into a performance piece.

I looked at the wall clock for the umpteenth time. The hands gave the illusion of standing still. Maybe hospital clocks suffered from burnout and had to go someplace time flowed normally for R & R. I got up to ask yet another futile question about Laura. As I started toward the desk, a black woman with cornrows and a nostril ring, also a white lab coat and a stethoscope around her neck, came toward me.

"If you are the gentleman with Ms. Dare," she said, "you may come in and see her now." She had an Islands accent. "She has a slight concussion, but you may take her home. The nurse will tell you what to do to make sure she remains stable." Laura Dare. Her name suited her. She hadn't changed it when we got married. Not even a topic for discussion. Her middle name was Deanna. But we used to say the D stood for whatever fit at the moment. Laura Double Dare. Laura Depression Dare.

I wondered why the doctor looked over my shoulder rather than meeting my eyes. Her words had reassured me. Now I wondered if she had held something back. A problem she hadn't told me? News she had to break gently?

"I'll do whatever she needs." A deep voice spoke behind me, hated and familiar. "I'd like to see her now. Then tell me where to find the nurse."

Dammit. Mac. She must have called him on her cell phone. Even though cell phones were *verboten* inside the hospital. Laura Devil Dare.

I walked away without a word.

FOURTEEN

"How's Luz doing?" I asked Barbara.

I was home in my own apartment for a change. I had called to talk to Jimmy. But some guy in Australia had IM'ed him with some information about the transportation of the British criminal classes to Botany Bay. He had been chasing this particular fact for days, and off he went into cyberspace to retrieve it. Barbara, as usual, was already on the extension.

"Still sad," she said. "Still minimizing how awful Frankie was. Trying to go on one day at a time. You like her, don't you?"

"How do you mean?" I stalled. "Sure. She's okay. Nice. Poor kid. Rough time."

"Only okay?" Barbara said. "She could use a corrective experience with a decent man."

"Sometimes I wish you weren't so damn unstoppable," I said. "Though I'm glad to hear you think I'm decent."

"You are, now you've stopped drinking," Barbara said. "All you've got to do now is stay stopped."

"And change my whole life." Another of those little slogans with a sting in its tail.

"Well, please don't stop being sardonic. You wouldn't be Bruce without it."

"I don't have to surrender my whole personality? What a relief."

"Speaking of Luz," Barbara said, "we had better not stop circling the wagons. Those two detectives still drop by every few days. I don't know how they think evidence that didn't exist in the first place will suddenly appear. And if they think she'll change her story, they're wrong, because it's not a story, it's what really happened—at least all she knows."

"What do you want us to do?" I asked. I felt more comfortable when Barbara played detective than when she played matchmaker.

"How about going back to the bakery? We never did talk to Massimo. We could call first—you know, see if he answers the phone. And I bet if I could somehow manage to talk to Frankie's mother, I'd hear things we don't know yet."

"Aw, you just want more of those little cannolis."

"Cannoli. You and Jimmy ate just as many as I did."

"I don't suppose you could get Jimmy to go with you? I didn't do anything but stand around and carry the cake boxes last time."

"It's a miracle he came to the funeral. Getting him on the subway to Brooklyn twice in one calendar year would be a record. Forget it. You're the man."

"Oh, so now I'm the man," I said. "Okay, okay, I'll come with you."

"You can choose the pastries this time," Barbara offered.

When we arrived at the bakery, Massimo was carrying a tray heavy with mini cheesecakes from the back room. A blast of hot air propelled him into the cooler café. He set the tray on the counter and took out a large white handkerchief to mop his brow and forearms. His silver hair was lightly powdered with flour. He wiped his hands on the handkerchief and ran them down the sides of his enveloping white apron for good measure.

"Can I help you?"

We both stepped up to the counter. With an older generation Italian male, I didn't think being a girl carried any advantage. 'Scuse me, a woman.

He tried to form a professionally genial smile. It sat like a mask of comedy on his sad face.

"The cheesecakes are very good today, and we have the chocolate cannoli, both the big and little—but I know you," he said. His face registered recognition, but the sadness didn't lighten. "You are friends of my boy."

It wasn't a question, so we didn't have to lie.

"We are so very sorry," Barbara said, "especially for you and Mrs. Iacone. She must be grieving terribly."

Massimo shook his head, not in denial but in dismay.

"She cries all day long. I cannot comfort her, her sisters and her friends cannot comfort her. Even the children can't make her smile. They say, 'Nonna, don't be sad. Papa is in heaven.' When they leave, she says to me, 'I don't believe in heaven.' Never have I heard such a thing. My Silvia has always been devout. This weeping woman is her ghost."

"Nothing can be worse than losing a child," Barbara said.

Barbara's parents would have been devastated if they had lost a child. On our block, the mothers used to tell the children to go play in traffic. Mine once offered me a hundred bucks to leave town.

"All his friends are mourning, sir," I said. "He was on the brink of such a future, too."

Massimo took that the way he wanted to.

"So much promise lost," he said. " 'It's a turning point, Papa,' he tells me. I think, Now maybe he will come into the business and become a fine baker."

I doubted it.

"He had broken away from the evil companions."

Parental delusion: good boy, bad company.

"Some of them had the *coglioni* to come to the funeral." Indignation colored his voice. "They dishonored my son by being there. They insulted me and his mother. I spit on them!" He added, "I would have thrown them out, but it would have embarrassed Silvia."

So Massimo knew a drug dealer when he saw one. That was interesting. He must think we were a nice, normal couple Frankie had traded up to from the evil companions.

"Please give our condolences to Mrs. Iacone," Barbara said. "Or if it's possible in person?"

We didn't know if Silvia worked at the bakery in normal times. Maybe she was home in bed, with Frankie's aunts flapping around her and making lasagna in her kitchen. Like Luz's aunts.

"She is at the grave," Massimo said. "She goes every day. It makes her agitated, but I can't stop her, no one can stop her. She gets down on her knees and curses God. The priest is understanding. He tells me, 'Give her time. God is patient. He will wait until she is ready to forgive Him.'"

"Do you think she would mind if we showed up?" Barbara asked. "We could pay our respects to Frankie too."

"I think she would be pleased. She talks to Frankie when she kneels there. She calls him her baby boy. She brings fresh flowers every day. She has already planted a rosebush that will grow and flower every year. She tries to forget the bad times, when he became a man and chose the wrong road for a while. It will do her good to be reminded that he had changed—though I warn you she will cry too, thinking how he is gone before taking more than the first few steps. The cemetery is big and confusing. I will tell you exactly how to get there."

"Thank you, sir," I said. "We really are very sorry."

"It will mean a lot to us to talk with Mrs. Iacone," Barbara said truthfully. "And as long as we're here, can we have half a dozen little cheesecakes and six of the chocolate cannoli?"

The day had clouded over when we got outside. A chill in the air reminded me that November was on the way.

"I thought you were going to let me choose the pastries," I remarked.

"You would have chickened out," she said. "After that heavy conversation, you wouldn't have wanted to break the mood by buying cake. And he really is a great baker."

"I notice I'm carrying the boxes again."

"Oh, for heaven's sake," she said, "don't be such a big baby. Here, give them to me. I'll put them in my bag." Barbara's bag was a tote the size of a mail pouch. "Let's buy some flowers to bring. Here's a florist shop two doors from the bakery."

We found the cemetery without any trouble. Its massive iron gates stood open. The gray day suited our surroundings. Some of the monuments were elaborate. Weeping angels. Massive crosses embellished with doves and Celtic knots and crucifixes. Family mausoleums big enough to house the homeless. We both read some of the inscriptions aloud. Some of the verses were unintentionally funny. Some were touching. On the older stones, weathered by pollution, the epitaphs were unreadable.

"There won't be a stone yet, will there?" Barbara asked. "In Jewish burials, it's a year till the unveiling."

"No," I said. "I don't think there's any rule about when you get a monument. They'd have to be up to ordering it. He's gone back to work, but she's still overcome. Then it would take time to get the inscription carved."

"Look at that," she said, drawing closer to me as we passed another recent burial. "They've just dumped the flowers on the grave." The flowers, still in their vases, had withered.

"Depressing."

"I hope they've taken the dead flowers off Frankie's grave."

"Mom's already planted a rosebush," I said.

Just inside the gate, we'd picked up a map with lettered sections and numbered plots. The guy at the desk had scribbled down a series of left and right turns.

"We make a right here."

"Look," Barbara said, "down this aisle, two sections or so farther on. Is that her?"

I squinted into the distance.

"It's a woman kneeling," I confirmed. "Let's get a little closer and see if she's cursing God."

It was Silvia, all right, shrunken and bowed with grief. She wrung her hands and moaned wordlessly, rocking back and forth. Just before she spotted us, she raised her arms and shook her fists at the leaden sky.

"Why?" she howled. "Santa Maria, why?"

It made the hairs stand up on the back of my neck.

Barbara tugged at my arm. She jerked her head at the nearest mausoleum. Plenty of room for a large family. She walked her fingers in a circle. If we circled the monument, we could approach her pretending we hadn't heard. But it was already too late.

Silvia turned her head as if her neck swung on hinges in need of oil. She looked even worse full face, her gray hair stringy and untended, dark smudges under her eyes. She spoke as if continuing a conversation.

"I have no more pride," she said. "My son was my purpose, and he's gone."

The rosebush, its name tag still clinging to a bare branch,

crouched at the head of the plot. But the disturbed earth, roughly the shape of a coffin, looked raw. Six feet under, I thought, that's where Frankie is now. I pictured him with his mouth full of dirt, even though I knew he'd be encased in wood and varnish and baby blue satin for a while yet. They didn't seem much of a protection against worms and time.

"He was the sweetest baby," Silvia said. "Very solid, good to hold. If I squeezed him, he felt dense, like a sack of semolina. He never cried."

Barbara stepped forward and laid her flowers on the grave. When she started to back off, Silvia grasped her hand and drew Barbara toward her. But her eyes went past Barbara to me. Maybe she thought a man would have the answers.

"You were his friend." They kept assuming that. All I had to do was not deny it. "Can you think of any reason? I keep asking God and the Blessed Virgin. They were parents, they should understand. Why now?" Her mouth twisted in a bitter travesty of humor. "Oh, I know that he took drugs. They think because I'm an old woman that I am stupid. Who do they think he came to when he was in trouble? Twice, three times I gave him money when he said that bad men had threatened him. Leg-breakers, he called them. How could a mother let them break her own child's legs?"

In recovery, we called that enabling. If an addict could always count on somebody to pick him up, he never had to admit himself he was facedown in shit and needed to do something different. But mothers were hard to convince.

"That is the thing I keep coming back to," Silvia said. "I do not understand. For this terrible thing to happen, he must have been in big trouble. But he knew he could come to me. Yet he said nothing. He called me the morning he left that place—the rehabilitation center. He sounded renewed, alive. I thanked Santa Maria for looking after him and bringing him safely through. I thought his troubles were over."

And so they were.

"We wonder what happened too," I told her. "As you said, it doesn't make sense. Who else might he have confided in?"

Barbara withdrew her hand, which Silvia had held all this time, and patted Silvia's shoulder.

"Maybe he thought it would be dangerous for you," she said, "if he told you about whatever was going on."

The tears in Silvia's eyes spilled over and tracked furrows down her cheeks.

"You are right," she said. Her voice cracked on the words. "He must have wanted to protect me."

"Who else was he close to?"

"His cousins. There are many in the family. They all played together as children—everybody lived in the neighborhood. Now the younger generation is scattered. They make pizza in New Jersey, they work for big law firms in the city. There were friends, too, since childhood. Now they all have wives and children of their own. I knew them all. They came to Frankie and Netta's wedding." Her voice went dull with despair. "I see them all again at Frankie's funeral." She added, "I look at them and hate them for being alive. I am a terrible old woman."

"Oh, no!" Barbara cried. "Any mother would feel that way."

Silvia looked at her with a spark of interest.

"You think so?" Her eyes slipped from Barbara to me. "Do you have children?" She meant the pair of us. We both sputtered, flustered. I recovered first.

"Not yet," I said. "But we can pray." I told the truth. I said the Serenity Prayer every time I went to a meeting.

"Which of them was Frankie closest to?" Barbara asked. "If we can find one he confided in, we might be able to understand how it happened."

"That would ease my heart," Silvia said. "It is torn out and eaten by dogs. I can never be whole again. But knowing might bring me a little peace. What a terrible world, where mothers have to know so much."

"We'd be glad to help," Barbara said. Silvia didn't know how true that was. "Can you suggest someone we might talk to?"

Silvia thought it over.

"He would not have told a man," she said finally. "If it was a matter of a fight, yes. Defending himself, he would call on his *amici*. But we do not know what it was, this thing that got him—finished him." She couldn't say "got him killed." I could understand that. "If there was nothing he could do—if there was something he was ashamed of—he would tell a woman."

"Netta?" Barbara asked.

"Not Netta." She sounded sure. "Netta was the mother of his children. He would protect her. Especially now, with a new little one on the way."

To me, the logical next on the list would be his girlfriend. I wondered if Silvia knew about Luz the way she knew about the drugs. But if she did, she didn't say so. And if Luz knew anything, she would have told us.

"There is his cousin Carola. As children, they did everything together. They always whispered secrets. Oh, Netta was there too, but Frankie and Carola were older. She tagged after them. Sometimes they let her play, sometimes they chased her away. Only later, when Netta was a beautiful young woman, did Frankie court her."

"And Carola?" I asked.

"We used to joke that they would marry someday," Silvia said with a reminiscent smile. "This would be when they were very small, you understand, no more than six or seven. Frankie adored her. If older boys threatened or bullied her, Frankie would clench his little fists and square up to them, even if they were twice his size. Once he gave a big boy of twelve, a neighbor, not a cousin, a nosebleed by butting him with his head."

Barbara dug her nails into my arm. I wished she wouldn't do that. I got the point: In Frankie's world, even his mother thought it was okay if he got violent, as long as he could justify it. The road from there to "I only hit my woman when she makes me mad" was paved with bloody noses.

"What happened to Carola?" I asked.

"She was Netta's maid of honor," Silvia said, "and almost as beautiful as the bride. But soon after that, she moved away. She got a little apartment in the city, in Greenwich Village, and began to study painting. Frankie took me and Massimo to see her paintings once, in a gallery. It was crowded with people not from Brooklyn, all dressed in black and sipping white wine so bad that we would have thrown it down the sink."

"Did you like the paintings?" Barbara asked.

"They were colorful," Silvia said. "I like a painting that tells a story of nice people—a family, the Virgin with her child."

"And Frankie kept up with her?" I asked.

"I am not sure," Silvia said. "Lately he said no more about her. But if he had a secret, he might have gone to her. Everyone else—they are all here in Brooklyn, they gossip like noisy sparrows, even the men. If you tell one, all the others soon know. But Carola—she has gone her own way."

"Carola's last name?" Barbara asked. "I wonder if we might have seen her paintings."

Any moment, I thought, Silvia would come to herself and the

information would dry up. But she remained docile, like a person in a trance.

"If you live in Manhattan, maybe you have," she said. "She calls herself Bugatti. At least she married an Italian." Her lips pinched together. "She got divorced not even a year later, but she kept his name."

"Would we have seen her at the funeral?" I asked.

"She didn't come." Silvia shook her head with a dragging motion, as if it was too heavy to hold all the way up. "I don't know why. She sent beautiful flowers."

I felt a drop of water on my face, then another. It had begun to rain. Silvia still knelt on the ground. She wasn't young and supple. Her knees must be locked into place by now.

"Can we help you up?" I asked, reaching for her elbow. "You don't want to stay here getting wet."

She shook her head.

"Where would I go? My son no longer feels the rain. I will keep him company awhile longer. You are a nice young couple, kind to talk to an old woman with a broken heart. But now you should go away."

We left her kneeling in the rain.

FIFTEEN

I came into the coffee shop just in time to hear Luz say to Barbara, "I don't understand why you go everywhere with Bruce, like what my aunts would call a *novio*. What about Jimmy? Doesn't he mind? Why doesn't he come along?"

"Jimmy's like some fancy wines—he doesn't travel well. Cross a guy who thinks research is better than chocolate ice cream with a computer nerd, and you get the perfect armchair detective."

"He came to—to Brooklyn," Luz objected.

"A miracle," Barbara said. "We all needed support—I went to support you, Jimmy came along to support me." I could see the sly smile through the back of her head as she added, "I would say Bruce went to support Jimmy, but I have a hunch he really came for you."

"That is ridiculous," Luz said with what I thought appropriate dignity. "And you still haven't explained why it is okay for you and Bruce to run around two by two, like—"

"Like animals in the ark," I supplied. They both looked around, startled. I pulled out a chair, swung it around so I could straddle it backward, and threw a leg across it. "That's how detectives work, Luz. I'm Holmes, she's Watson."

"Like hell you are!" Barbara said. "I'm Holmes, you're Watson."

"Watson is the dim one," I explained to Luz. "You can draw your own conclusions."

Barbara hastened to change the subject.

"I've got Carola Bugatti's address. She lives in Park Slope—nice neighborhood."

"Didn't Silvia say she lived in the Village?" I asked.

"She did. I guess Carola moved back to Brooklyn."

"She's an artist. Maybe she shows in Manhattan," I said. "One of those SoHo galleries down by Laura's."

Barbara's mouth pruned up at the mention of Laura.

"Who wants to come with me to the wilds of Brooklyn?" she asked.

"I'll go," I said, "as long as I'm back by four. I have to make the meeting. My sponsor's qualifying."

I registered Barbara's little smile. She had learned long ago to lay off Jimmy about how he managed his recovery. When I got sober, her controlling tendencies got a second wind. She tried to keep herself in check, but hey, it's a disease.

"Luz? Coming with us?"

"I don't think so," Luz said. "I know it's silly, but every time I think of Brooklyn . . ." She held her clenched fist over her solar plexus.

"It knots you up," I said. "I understand."

"So do I," Barbara said. "It's not silly—you associate Frankie with Brooklyn, so the whole borough makes you anxious. You don't have to come. Do something for yourself—a nap or a bubble bath. Or go to a meeting."

"I have to go to work," Luz said. "They have given me as much time off as I want. But I think I should go back. It helps to be busy—I don't have to think about things. Also, I still have to make a living."

"I don't even know what you do." Stupid of me never to have asked.

"I work in a lingerie shop," Luz said, "on Madison Avenue. I sell, and I fit rich ladies for special undergarments."

"I can imagine," I said. "Accentuate the positive. Sounds like it wouldn't be a good idea to visit you at work. I don't have much call for bras and corsets."

Luz laughed.

"I wouldn't be embarrassed," she said.

"Bruce would," Barbara said. She pushed back her chair and stood up. "If we have to get back by four, let's get going."

"How come you have all this time to go jaunting around, Barbara?" I asked. "You've been awfully available for someone with a full-time job."

"Comp time," she said. "I'm taking all those hours I put in when we had the audit back in January. We don't—" She stopped short and made like a beet.

I could supply the missing words. For once, she'd realized before she said them that they would be tactless: We don't get a murder every day.

Park Slope, along the western edge of Prospect Park, had gentrified more than thirty years ago. Its brownstones with their neat paved areas in front, pocket gardens, and retro Victorian gaslights looked comfortable and settled in. As real-estate prices soared, the neighborhood had swelled, expanding from the three blocks nearest the park to less expensive housing farther west. I would have expected Carola to live closer to the fringe. How much of a living could an artist make? But we found the house only half a block from the park, where golden, red, and bronze October leaves were at their peak. Maybe she had bought in early. Or she might have a rental, half a floor or even less. Almost no one, even owners, occupied an entire brownstone. It would cost a fortune.

"This is nice," Barbara commented. "Too bad it's too early in the day for the gaslights. I love to see the flames. Either she's a lot more of a hotshot artist than we thought, or she has another source of income."

"What's our strategy?" I asked. "We don't have a badge to flash."

"She didn't come to the funeral," Barbara said. "She just sent flowers. People don't always stay close to their childhood friends. How much could she have cared about Frankie? My guess is we won't upset her."

"So we don't make up a story," I said. "We go in and lay our cards on the table."

"And what happens happens." Barbara ran up the reddish steps to the top of the stoop. "Ooh, I like the knocker." The oak door sported a scowling brass lion with the knockable ring between its teeth.

"Use the bell," I advised. "Does she have a floor-through?"

"One name per floor," Barbara reported, reading the row of labeled bells. "Number Two, Bugatti. She has the parlor floor—she must have another source of income. Should I ring?"

"That's what we came for."

"I hope she doesn't have a day job," Barbara said. "Maybe we should have called first."

"You're the one who said if she doesn't know we're coming, she can't tell us not to come," I reminded her.

Barbara rang the bell.

The intercom, a slatted aluminum box above the bells, emitted the rushing sound of an open line.

"Who is it?" a crackling female voice inquired.

Barbara leaned close to the intercom.

"Friends of your cousin Frankie," she said.

After a prolonged pause, the woman's voice said, "Come on in. The outer door's not locked. You'll see another bell by the inner door. I'll buzz you in."

I don't know exactly what I expected, but not the woman who opened the door and stood looking at us warily. Her hand rested on the knob as if to slam it shut if she decided she didn't want to talk to us. She didn't look anything like Frankie. I'd have said she didn't look Italian. But Italians from the north, from places like Milan, could have that ash-blond hair and greenish eyes. She was big, taller than me. She wore paint-spattered jeans with asymmetrical rips that they'd probably come by honestly, not tattered by design. A man's shirt with so much paint on it she could have shown it in a gallery hung from her sturdy frame. Her feet were bare. No makeup. No jewelry except a heavy gold ring on a fine chain around her neck.

"Frankie's dead," she said. "Who are you and what do you want?"

"Just a few minutes of your time." I cocked my head to one side and tried to ooze honey. I hoped she'd find me winning. To myself, I sounded like a snake-oil salesman.

Barbara played the card I should have led with.

"Silvia sent us, Frankie's mom. Can we come in? We won't disturb you for long."

"Silvia Iacone is no friend of mine," she said. Her face stayed shuttered. But she took her hand off the doorknob and turned back toward the interior of the apartment.

With a shove between the shoulder blades that would have knocked me off a subway platform if there'd been one handy, Barbara pushed me forward. She followed so closely on my heels I had to kick her back a pace.

We emerged from a short unlit hallway into a room filled with south light. Spider plants hung from a bar across the top of the window. Philodendrons on strings meandered through the shadowy corners. The shaggy yellow and bronze heads of chrysanthemums squatted on the sill in blue-glazed ceramic pots. One wall was brick, broken up by an immaculate nonworking fireplace, very Brooklyn. An elaborate brass and enamel clock ticked on the marble mantelpiece.

"Nice clock," I said.

"It's old," she said, "but hard to wind. I can't even do it myself." Her lips snapped shut. She hadn't meant to get lured into social chitchat. Crossing the room in three strides, she folded her arms and stood staring at us.

"Take off your shoes," she commanded. "Now, before you step on the carpet."

Easier said than done. Barbara and I both wore sneakers. We wobbled like a couple of drunken storks as we stood there trying to undo our laces. I finally gave up and stepped on my heels so I could wrench my feet out of the shoes by force. Barbara still balanced on one foot, one hand on my shoulder and the other dangling her high-tech running shoe, when Carola's greenish gaze bored into her like a laser beam.

"Are you the girlfriend?" she demanded.

Barbara dropped the shoe. It bounced onto the thick-piled rose carpet. Her fingers clutched my shoulder.

"No!"

She hopped on the other stockinged foot as she tried to retrieve the sneaker. If we'd been alone, I'd have pointed out that pride goeth before jeans too tight to bend. I leaned over, picked up the shoe, and handed it to her.

"Silvia sent us," I told Carola. I met her eyes and tried to look sincere.

"We told you!" Barbara's voice throbbed with indignation.

"You're lying," Carola said. Tough as a week-old bagel. "Why would she do that?"

"She wants to know why her son died," I said. "Don't you?"

I was fishing, but I'd picked a likely pond. I got the impression that Carola was more than a cousin who used to hang with Frankie when they were kids.

"Closure," Barbara piped up. She had to play shrink. But the taut skin around Carola's eyes slackened a bit.

"Stupid word," she said.

"Necessary process," Barbara shot back. "When you love someone."

"What makes you think I love Frankie? Loved." Her voice cracked on the last word. Yeah, Barbara got that one right.

"You're hurting." Counselor voice. Compassion.

Carola's lips pinched.

"Who are you really? Frankie never mentioned you."

"You saw him recently," I said. I made it a statement, not a question. So she couldn't just say no.

"A week before he died," she admitted. "It was a Tuesday." So she kept track. We were onto something. Frankie was important to her. "Are you a druggie?" She aimed that one at me. "From that rehab place?" Yes and no. But she didn't want my substance abuse history.

"And you." She wheeled on Barbara. "If you're not the girlfriend, what was Frankie to you? He didn't have women friends." She added bitterly, "I should know."

"The truth will set you free," I said. I don't know where that came from. "We do know Frankie's girlfriend." We had made Plan A, be candid, when we thought she wouldn't have strong feelings about Frankie's girlfriend. But it beat Plan B. We didn't have a Plan B. "The cops think she did it. We don't. We're looking for something that might change their minds."

"Please talk to us," Barbara pleaded. "You must want to know yourself. What would it accomplish if they get the wrong person?"

About half a tear escaped Carola's iron control and leaked out the corner of her eye.

"Maybe it serves her right."

"Sounds like the one you're really mad at is yourself."

"Oh, the hell with it," Carola said. "Sit."

I looked around. Instead of a couch and chairs, she had ringed the room with giant pillows in shades from pearly pink to a fierce magenta. Great. I hated trying to bend like a pretzel. Carola crossed her legs at the ankle and sank gracefully onto a cushion. Barbara tried to do the same. She ended up collapsing in a heap. Her knees stuck out to one side, and her stiff arms braced the floor like a barge pole stuck in the mud. She would capsize any minute if she didn't watch out.

I lowered myself gingerly, starting on all fours. When my contact with the cushion stabilized, I tried to reverse to a sitting position, one cautious limb at a time. In a mirror that spanned the opposite wall, doubling the light and the sense of spaciousness, it looked like I was playing charades. What am I? Shelob the giant spider in *Lord of the Rings*. I had almost succeeded in turning right side up when my backside touched down, not on the squashy cushion, but on an unexpected protuberance. I fished out the object: a plastic stegosaurus, if that's the one with all the bony points down its back.

As I held the toy dinosaur up, we all heard a wail from another room. Carola stood up as gracefully as she'd folded herself before and hurried down the hall. Barbara and I had a conversation with our eyebrows. We could hear Carola's voice lilt in the cootchy-coo cadences almost everybody uses with young children. The wail turned to contented babbling.

We waited at least ten minutes before Carola came back. Her face looked more relaxed. Not so guarded. She even smiled. Jouncing against her hip she held a little boy. Blue T-shirt, disposable diaper, dark brown hair. His face was hidden as he pulled at her ears and chewed on strands of her hair. Playful.

"Still here, are you? This is Edmund."

At his name, or maybe just the sound of her voice, the baby looked around. He was sturdily built and almost toddler size. His eyes scanned me and Barbara with intelligence and a lively interest in these new people. The beginnings of a widow's peak formed an arrow front and center of his feathery dark brown hair. His eyebrows formed little arches. I knew that face. I had last seen it decked out in baby blue too. Frankie had two-timed Luz as well as Netta. Did Silvia know she had an extra grandchild? Probably not. She thought Carola still lived in the Village.

Carola picked up on my thoughts.

"I couldn't afford a place in Manhattan with enough space for Edmund. I wanted him to have plenty of room to play. The Village is no place to raise a child, anyhow. Otherwise, I'd never have moved back to Brooklyn. I don't hide my address—I suppose you found me in the phone book." Online, not that it mattered. "I didn't send any change-of-address cards to Bensonhurst."

"So you and Frankie—" For once, Barbara was at a loss for words.

I could see Carola decide that putting a good front on her behavior wasn't worth the effort. Been there, done that.

"Yeah, we were an item, far back as I can remember. Frankie and Carola. Went together like a horse and carriage."

She punctuated her words with mock nibbles at Edmund's fat little fingers. Occasionally she pressed her lips to his belly, which peeped out between the T-shirt and the diaper, and blew. Not a full-sized razzberry, but a small whiffling sound. Edmund liked it. It made him giggle.

"So what happened?" Barbara asked. "How come he married Netta and not you?"

"It was my own fault," Carola said, "not that I wasn't probably better off out of it. Marry in the neighborhood, you marry the whole neighborhood. They call a town meeting if you polish your nails a new color."

I looked at her hands. Edmund was playing a primitive version of This Little Piggy with her fingers. They were stained with paint, and the nails were clipped short. Artist hands.

"And God forbid a woman has any ambition. I wanted to paint, and that meant Manhattan."

"Frankie tried to stop you?" I asked.

Her harsh laugh startled Edmund. He reared back in her arms, then put a fat palm over her lips. She smacked a kiss into his hand. He smiled and nestled closer.

"He didn't try to make me stop painting—he knew that much, even if he didn't understand why it was so important to me. Basically, he didn't want me to leave Brooklyn. Ironic, isn't it—nowadays I could paint in Williamsburg—if I still thought it mattered what part of the city I live in. We were very young. We fought, and I stormed away across the Brooklyn Bridge and signed up for the Art Students League."

"Better than the Marines," I commented.

This time the laugh touched her eyes.

"I could have gone to Pratt," she said. "But I was all fired up, and so mad at him for not supporting me. It had to be Manhattan."

"But you came back," Barbara said.

"Yeah, those strings were stronger than I thought. I went back to Frankie first. We always got under each other's skin. I thought we'd outgrow it. I thought once I was living the life I wanted, doing what I loved, and even doing pretty well at it—I show, I sell, a lot of people in the art world know my name—he'd just be part of what I'd left behind. Wrong. The only catch was, by the time I realized I wanted him back, he'd married Netta."

"You started seeing each other anyway," Barbara prompted.

"We were hot, we always were." A reminiscent grin lit her somber face for a moment. "From the first time, when we were fourteen. I didn't care about Netta—well, I did, enough to make sure she didn't know. We were supposed to be best friends. But not enough to stop me. She was a good little virgin all the way to the wedding night. Nobody knew. Rocky and Vince, my brothers, would have killed me."

"When you were fourteen?" I asked. "Or after he was married?"

"Both," she said. "It was none of their business. One reason I put the East River between me and them was they thought they were the morality police. I'd finished with all that."

"You're obviously liberated from that environment," Barbara said. "So why did you have the baby?" If inquiring minds want to know, Barbara will open her mouth and ask. "You could have had an abortion."

"Now here's the stupid part," Carola said, "and the funny thing is, I think you'll understand. I did it so Frankie wouldn't leave me."

I looked around the comfortable apartment. Sun streamed in the window, dust motes dancing in its rays.

"Looks like it worked," I commented.

Carola followed my glance.

"Not really," she said. "I moved back here for Edmund. Frankie started coming around again later, and we'd be a family a couple times a week. That was enough for me, to tell the truth. I'm a painter, I need time to work. No, when I told him I was pregnant, he wanted me to 'take care of it.' That's what he said—he lived off selling cocaine and heroin, but he wouldn't let the A-word cross his lips. I had the baby to keep Frankie—and that's why he left me and took up with that Puerto Rican woman."

SIXTEEN

"I liked her," Barbara said.

She and Jimmy and I sat in their cramped but hospitable kitchen. The remains of Chinese takeout littered the table. In front of Barbara, a hand-thrown silvery ceramic rice bowl sat on a North African woven place mat, with neatly crossed chopsticks beside it. The empty bowl glistened as if she'd licked it. Barbara insisted on dining in what she called a civilized manner. But she liked her food. Equally empty cardboard cartons with forks stuck in them attested that Jimmy and I did too.

"So did I," I said. I cracked open my fortune cookie. "The best is yet to come," I read aloud. "Damn, have they been talking to my sponsor?"

"But I'm not so sure her story hung together," Barbara said.

"Me neither," I admitted. "She painted such a pretty picture."

"What were her paintings like?" Jimmy asked.

"That's not what I meant," I said.

"Woman who keeps silent shows greatest wisdom," Barbara read.

She popped both halves of her fortune cookie into her mouth. "Have you guys been talking to Confucius about me?"

"She had only one big painting in the living room," I said. "It was cheerful but not at all pretty. Almost like a photograph."

"Superrealist," Barbara amplified. "Very fine detail. A bay window in a sunny room with light streaming through the window and a bright red fire engine on the seat. The little boy must love it. Open yours, Jimmy."

Jimmy broke his cookie in half and fished out the little paper.

"Happy is the man who wants what he already has," he read.

"Here's the weird thing," I said. "She made it sound like such a romance. Big Love."

"Even though she admitted to screwing her best friend's boyfriend from junior high through marriage and a couple of kids."

"Right."

"And Frankie wasn't even a faithful cheater," Barbara said, "because he took up with Luz while Carola was pregnant and made Luz think she was the only one too. Carola acted like she wasn't at all pissed off about that, but I don't believe it."

"What about violence?" Jimmy asked. "You would already have mentioned anything obvious like a black eye or broken jaw, but any sign of bruises? Was she scared? Any hint of resentment?"

"Not a peep," Barbara said. "She didn't have that defeated look they get either."

"That's what I meant by too pretty," I said. "Chances are, a guy like that couldn't keep his temper with one woman if he lost it with all the others."

"The little boy looked healthy and happy," Barbara said, "but appearances don't always tell the whole story."

"She also skated lightly over the drug part," I said.

"She knew he was dealing?" Jimmy asked.

"Came right out and said it," Barbara said. "She even mentioned the irony of peddling dope but disapproving of abortion."

"Except she said he wanted her to have one," I pointed out. "That's where I got confused."

"She contradicted herself," Barbara agreed. "Maybe she was simmering underneath the whole time. Maybe he hit her or threatened to hit the kid."

"Could have been emotional abuse," Jimmy said.

"You didn't meet her," I said. "She'd be hard to bully."

"Not every victim of domestic violence looks like one," Barbara said.

"Maybe she'd just found out about Luz," Jimmy suggested.

"Or about Netta being pregnant again," Barbara said. "Though she did strike me as the kind of free spirit who wouldn't care if he wasn't monogamous, and not just because she said so. I got a gut feeling that she was an empowered kind of woman—at ease in her own skin."

"I thought so too," I admitted. "But it could have been an act. She implied that she knew about Luz all along. As if it didn't bother her, since it started while they weren't seeing each other. But maybe she didn't know he still had that going till just before the murder. She could have gone up there to confront Luz, found Frankie there, and lost her temper."

"Or she could have known he'd be there," Jimmy said, "and gone up there to kill him, knowing Luz would be suspected."

"I'd like to talk to her again," Barbara said.

"I'd like to see her paintings," Jimmy said. "Do you know if she shows at one particular gallery?"

"I'm not sure," I said. Barbara shook her head.

"Give me a minute." Jimmy pushed back his chair and galloped out of the kitchen. A few seconds later, we heard his computer talking to him. He talked back. In a couple of minutes, he called, "Found it!"

Barbara and I got up and went to look over his shoulder. Carola had a show in a gallery less than a block from Laura's loft.

"Want to go look at pictures?" I asked. "Any day but Saturday."

I had told myself firmly that I would *not* spend another Saturday in SoHo.

"Anyone else you want me to look up while I'm at it?" Jimmy asked.

I shook my head.

"How about Netta's brothers?" Barbara asked. "Avenging the family honor?"

"Vinnie said to stay away from them," Jimmy said.

"Vinnie said to get the hell out of Brooklyn, all of us," Barbara retorted. "Did we listen to him?"

"I think he was issuing a friendly warning. We don't know what those guys are into."

"Why, because they're Italian? Come on, don't be a bigot. At least find out their names and what they do. Maybe Vinnie was just trying to scare us off."

"If Netta and Frankie had a wedding site," I said, "her maiden name will be all over it."

"Find the name, Jimmy," Barbara said.

"Yeah, yeah. I'm on it." Jimmy's fingers flew on the keyboard.

"I'll call Carola and ask her what she thinks of Netta's brothers." Barbara started to paw through her bag. "They were neighborhood kids like the rest of them. I know my cell is in here somewhere."

"I'm going out for a smoke," I said.

When I came back, Jimmy was printing out a Web page.

"Sal and Vito Gaglia. They run a body shop on Coney Island Avenue." He read from the screen. " 'Hell on Wheels. Auto body repair and custom detailing. Classic and exotic—or we can just hammer you. Body parts available.' What's the message here?"

"It could be a chop shop," I said.

"It could be a perfectly legitimate business," Barbara said. "I'm going to ask Carola about them." She waggled the cell phone at us and marched out of the room.

"Hey! Where are you going?"

"Bedroom. I can do this better without an audience."

"Jeez, what is she planning to say?"

Jimmy shrugged and brought up a virtual Civil War reenactment site on the computer.

"With Barbara, you never know."

By the time she came back, 8,163 soldiers, Union and Confederate, had died at Antietam. Jimmy clicked Save and laid down the mouse reluctantly.

"Poor guys," I said. "You haven't killed enough of them?"

"Nope. Both sides together lost 23,000 in a single day at the real battle."

"Never mind that," Barbara said. "Carola said she's known Sal and Vito Gaglia her whole life, and they're harmless."

"That's what Luz said about Frankie," I said.

Barbara's cell phone, still in her hand, played the first fifteen notes of the "Ode to Joy" from Beethoven's Ninth. She flipped it open, listened, made a few soothing noises, then thumbed the mute button.

"Luz. She's had a fright. A man followed her in the park. Okay if I ask her to come over?"

"Sure, sure," Jimmy said. He'd already gone back to Antietam.

It wasn't my apartment. And I liked the idea of seeing Luz again.

"I might have imagined it," Luz told us ten minutes later. She refused Chinese leftovers but accepted tea. Her small hands circled the ceramic mug, making the handle look oversized. "It was stupid of me to go through the park this late, but it wasn't dark, and the crosstown bus didn't come and didn't come."

We all nodded. Every New Yorker knows how that is.

"I didn't realize until I got to the Great Lawn how deserted it was. Nobody playing ball, no mothers with kids in strollers. I walked as fast as I could. The sky was beautiful—all gold looking downtown and pink to the west. I was admiring it, not thinking where I was going but not slowing down, you know?"

Jimmy and I nodded again.

"Road trance," Barbara said, "you got kind of dissociated."

"Yes, exactly," Luz agreed. "Suddenly I found myself back under the trees, almost up to the bridle path, without exactly knowing how I'd come that far. And I heard footsteps—it was probably silly to think anything of it, but it was so gloomy under the trees, and they kept pace with mine exactly. When I walked faster, they sped up. I was afraid to run."

"Did you look back?" Jimmy asked.

"At first I was afraid to do that too," Luz admitted. "As if showing fear or making eye contact would make things worse. I thought about all the stories I've heard of people being attacked in the park, especially women. I was so mad at myself—how could I have been so stupid?"

"Women should be able to walk in the park at sunset," Barbara asserted. "It's not our fault if we can't."

Jimmy gave her a not-now look.

"You were freaked out," he told Luz. "I can understand that. But you did look?"

"Yes, very quickly—and that frightened me more, because when I did, the footsteps stopped, and I could see no one."

"What did the steps sound like?" I asked. "High heels, heavy boots? Lots of people wear running shoes to the park. It would be hard to hear someone sneaking up on you."

"At first it was a brushing sound, like someone sweeping the leaves," Luz said. "There are many on the paths right now. It was too regular to be a squirrel."

"Not so hot with left and right, squirrels," I said, trying to win a smile from her. She still looked very tense. "But you got here okay. I'm glad."

"I was lucky," she said. "My back felt all nerves, as if someone had painted a target between my shoulder blades. I wanted to scream and run. I think I would have done so in a minute. I had trouble breathing, and my heart was going so fast." She pounded her fist against her chest in illustration.

"Panic attack," Barbara murmured. "Sorry, go on. What happened?"

"Just as I reached the bridle path," Luz said, "two cops came along on their horses."

"Did you tell them someone was following you?"

"No, I didn't. All of a sudden, things felt normal—the horses trotting, one cop talking on a cell phone. My panic disappeared. The other cop said hello as I crossed the bridle path."

"They were up high," I said. "If there'd been anyone behind you, they'd have seen them."

"Yes, that is what I thought," Luz agreed. "But whoever was following me must have heard the hoofbeats, as I did, and hidden or run away. I heard no more after I crossed the path. Then I did run, all the way to Central Park West."

"Only an idiot would attack someone with mounted police right there," Barbara said. "And since the stable on Eighty-ninth closed, they're the only folks on horses in the park."

"I'd suggest no more sunset strolls in the park," Jimmy said. "It's not fair, but there are too many predators out there."

Luz rubbed her fingertips across her forehead as if to smooth out the wrinkles of anxiety.

"That I have already told myself," she said. "But there is more."

"What, Luz?" I prompted.

"What if it wasn't just a mugger picking any foolish woman walking alone? Whoever killed Frankie has been in my apartment."

"You mean the same person might want to hurt you? Oh no!" I protested. Unfortunately, I didn't mean I thought it was impossible.

"That's terrible!" Barbara sounded as appalled as I did. "But why? Frankie was—you aren't—"

Frankie was a son of a bitch and Luz was a very nice woman. Jimmy found a nice way to put it.

"We can't assume that the murderer's motive for killing Frankie would apply to you."

"This too I tell myself," Luz said, still troubled. "But we still do not know why Frankie died. Someone jealous might hate me too. Someone with a secret might think I knew it."

"All the more reason," Barbara said, "for us to go on trying to find out what really happened."

"And until then, Luz," I said, "please be extra careful. I don't want anything to happen to you." I meant to say "we." Really.

SEVENTEEN

Barbara couldn't stay out of work indefinitely, so Jimmy agreed to come and look at paintings with me in SoHo. He waited till she wasn't around to suggest we combine it with a trip to Coney Island Avenue. We both knew Barbara thought she was Wonder Woman, and we didn't want to risk her confronting the Gaglia brothers, in case they turned out to be dangerous.

"Do you think Luz knew about Carola and the baby?" I asked. We emerged from the subway at Spring Street into a blindingly bright day.

"She said she didn't." Jimmy looked dazed and a little cross, like a bear coming out of hibernation. "But if she did, it's another motive for her."

"You can't believe Luz killed him. She couldn't. She's too— too—" I fumbled for a word and came up with a lame one. "Too nice, dammit."

"Hi, I'm Bruce, I'm susceptible," Jimmy said.

I elbowed him in the gut.

"Smile when you say that," I warned him. "Creep."

"Asshole."

We grinned at each other. For a moment, we were eight years old.

On a Tuesday afternoon, the galleries were empty, but the restaurants were packed. Locals, not tourists, wearing black like a uniform.

"Doesn't anybody in this city have a day job?" Jimmy demanded.

"Why, you want to be special? Times have changed. Look at all the laptops and cell phones."

"I don't see how they can get any work done, cramped together elbow to elbow like that."

"So maybe the laptops are just props and all they really do is schmooze," I said. "What's wrong with that?"

Jimmy's brow furrowed.

"They might spill coffee on their laptops."

I hooted. Trust Jimmy to champion the hardware.

"Look, that must be it. That's her painting in the window."

Displayed behind sparkling plate glass against a white velvet backdrop was a companion piece to the one we'd seen at Carola's. Same bay window, same red fire engine. But in this one, everything else was gray. Rain streamed down the windowpanes, each drop meticulously detailed. Gloom shrouded the street outside. Carola had managed to paint the very air dreary.

"Wow, this is technically brilliant," Jimmy said. "No wondering whether the artist knows how to draw. Depressing, though."

"She kept the cheerful one at home," I said, "where the kid could see it. Let's go in."

The cavernous warehouse space had the usual high white walls and glossy wood floor. Overhead, a tangle of pipes receded into shadow. Track lighting made the paintings glow. A small desk to the left of the door held oversized postcards of some of the paintings in the show and a laminated catalog identifying the works displayed. The chair behind the desk had rolled back three feet, as if its tenant had gotten up in a hurry. A pink cardigan slung over the back and a half-moon of red lipstick on a cardboard coffee cup on the desk indicated a female receptionist. Taped music played, repetitive and probably electronic. I found it disturbing. The paintings matched.

Jimmy peered at the largest canvas.

"Hard to believe she can do cheerful," he said, "looking at this. I'll have to take your word for it."

In the same meticulous style, Carola had rendered a crucifixion scene. Some of the details could have come from a Renaissance painting. The crowd of men and women with their bright clothes and anguished faces. The theatrical composition. The irrelevant life-goes-on elements: two little boys scuffling, a bedraggled mutt stealing a hot dog. Yes, a hot dog. Not too many of those in the sixteenth century. And in the distance, bathed in light and untouched by the drama in the foreground, not a medieval Italian walled city, but Manhattan. What really socked the viewer in the eye, though, was not the New York skyline. It was the figure on the cross: a woman.

Jimmy's lips pursed in a low whistle. He shook his head.

"I'm surprised the Church isn't picketing outside."

"Hey, it's a SoHo gallery, not Saint Patrick's Cathedral. I bet the Church doesn't even know this painting exists."

"Let's see the rest of them," Jimmy said.

We circled the gallery. I wanted to stop and stare at each one. I also wanted to close my eyes and not look at all. But Jimmy's comments drew me on.

"She's gender-reversed the saints," he said. "Arrows, that should be Saint Sebastian."

A female nude, bristling with quills like a porcupine. The scene was one of those English tea parties you see in the movies. Edwardian or Victorian, whatever. The women were archers in frilly long dresses and big floppy hats.

"Here's one with a man," I said. "Oh, shit, I wish I hadn't seen it." The poor guy was getting castrated. "I hope I don't dream about it."

"Saint Agatha," Jimmy said. "She had her breasts cut off. Jesus, Mary, and Joseph, I think it's Frankie."

I looked again, glad to focus on the face. Allowing for the agonized expression on a face we'd last seen embalmed into repose, it was him all right.

"Didn't you and Barbara say she didn't seem angry?" Jimmy asked. "Uh, I think we've found her anger."

I backtracked to the crucifixion scene to peer more closely at the faces in the crowd.

"You know what? I recognize a lot of these faces from the funeral. Look, that's Silvia and Massimo. The Roman soldier with the spear, that's Cousin Vinnie. The women holding the mother up, Stella from the bakery and a couple of her gum-chewing friends. And who's Netta supposed to be?"

"Red robe? Mary Magdalen. I think she's pregnant, too."

"Just the way we saw her," I agreed. "Do you suppose these people have seen these paintings?"

"They would be ready to crucify her," Jimmy said.

"She's already done it. Portrait of the artist. The gal on the cross is Carola."

"Maybe she figured they'd never know, since they never leave Brooklyn."

"Frankie would have seen them," I said. "How do you hide a body of work this big in a long-term relationship?"

"He probably didn't care," Jimmy said.

"She said he didn't take her painting seriously."

I squinted toward the opposite wall, far enough away I could have skated there if I'd had the skates.

"What are these about? Not Bible stories." I moved in closer. "Fairy tales. Come see what she did with these."

The biggest was a Rapunzel. She'd given it quite a twist. Rapunzel was still a girl, up in her tower with the fifty-foot hair hanging down. As I remembered the story, her father locked her up there. The prince used to climb up her braids to visit her. Nobody ever said it hurt. In Carola's version, the guy must have weighed 250 pounds with his armor on. Tears of anguish sprang from the corners of her eyes as he tugged on the hair. In a minute, he'd either topple her or pull her scalp right off her head. It was Carola's face again, and the prince was Frankie.

"Look behind her," Jimmy said. "In the shadow inside the tower. A second guy is tearing off her dress."

"Gee, do you think she's making a statement?" I bent down to read the little title card. "She calls it 'Rape, Puns, Hell.'"

"They're not all fairy tales," Jimmy said, moving on. "Here's Lady Godiva—or rather, Lord Godiva."

"Naked on a horse? Is it Frankie again?"

"Nope, wrong eyebrows. Lots of body hair."

The people in the crowd were eating chocolate. Godiva. I got it.

"Humiliation as a spectator sport," Jimmy said.

"We're very proud to show her work exclusively." We hadn't heard the receptionist come back. Now she stood behind us, gazing at Carola's paintings with proprietary satisfaction. Maybe she was the gallery owner. Her expertly made-up face looked a little too old for the glossy blue-black of her hair. She wore flowing black drapery and a couple of pounds of the kind of art jewelry that sells for thousands at high-end craft fairs. It was different from Laura's, the way a Picasso is different from a Matisse. I bet they knew each other. "She sells well, so if you are interested in a particular work, you may want to look at the catalog. If you have any questions, please feel free to ask me."

"Do you have something that will match my couch?" That got me a haughty stare from the gallery lady. Some people can't take a joke.

Since the whole place was far above my price range, and Jimmy wasn't about to pay five figures to take home a bunch of Brooklyn Italians getting tortured, the sales pitch kind of drove us out of there. The midafternoon sun still dazzled. The restaurants had mostly emptied, and more people milled around on the street.

"On to Brooklyn?" Jimmy asked.

Anywhere but past Laura's loft.

We turned back toward the subway. A block or two ahead, a crowd blocked the way.

"Some kind of street performer, maybe," Jimmy said.

My bad luck. The street performers were Laura and Mac. They were putting on quite a show.

"So why do you bother to stay with me?" she screeched as I reached the back fringe of the crowd and peered over the dandruff-speckled shoulder of a Hasidic Jew with a black hat and sideburns nearly as long as Rapunzel's braids. "If I'm so fucking lousy in bed, maybe it's for the money!"

"I don't need your money, you overmedicated little twat!" Mac roared back.

Off her lithium would have been undermedicated. Too much antidepressant this time, then.

"Who are you calling a twat, you unmitigated cocksucker?"

"Who do you think?" Mac jeered. "The pathetic little bitch who begged me to give it to her not an hour ago."

"You're such a moron you don't know faking when you hear it. That must be because that's all you've ever heard from women. If we didn't lie to you, your dick would fall off."

Someone jostled my shoulder. A couple of Japanese tourists with cameras hustled their family away. I hoped the kids were too young to have learned much English yet.

Mac ran out of words and self-control at this point. With a wordless growl, he raised a meaty arm. I remembered that big fist. The crowd gave a collective gasp, as if at some daredevil high-wire act. I started forward, shaking off Jimmy's restraining hand on my shoulder. A couple of big guys who looked like construction workers got in ahead of me. They loomed up on either side of him.

"Take it easy, buddy. Leave the lady alone."

Mac grunted and shook his head and shoulders like a dazed bull. Laura swung her hips past him, almost touching, like a tore-ador making a pass. Part of me admired her panache. Part of me thought she was crazy. I mean, to provoke a maddened animal like that. I always thought she was crazy.

"Yeah, leave me the hell alone! I've had it, I don't care what you say. I'm leaving."

She thrust her way through the crowd. I needn't have worried she'd notice me. Her attention was still focused on Mac. She looked back over her shoulder, her face ablaze with triumph at having the last word. She stepped into the street, stumbling on the curb, just as the light on the corner changed to green. A delivery truck rumbled past. Kosher chickens. It picked up speed as the light on the next corner changed and the cars at the other end of the street began to roll forward. Behind the truck, a little Honda Civic that had been blinded by the truck's bulk gunned its engine and pulled out on the wrong side. I squawked out a warning. The crowd groaned, like when the outfielder catches the pop-up on the last out with bases loaded. Stepping out into the street, Laura walked right into the Honda's hood.

Brakes squealed like hyenas as the impact flung her up into the air. Her body twisted with a corkscrew motion. What goes up must come down. I didn't know I'd moved until I was sliding into home plate, desperate to interpose my body between hers and the unyielding pavement. She thudded down onto me. It knocked the breath out of me, but I was okay. And she landed soft. Sort of. More like a sandbag than a sofa cushion. But thank God, her head didn't crack on the pavement.

I lay there with my eyes closed. The alarmed and angry cries of bystanders sounded far away. I could hear Jimmy, very calm, talking to the 911 operator. Laura mewed a little, her body lax against mine. Not unconscious, anyhow. If she'd broken anything major, I thought, she would have been screaming. My arms were wrapped around soft skin stretched over sharp bones. It felt like she had no intervening meat on her at all. Her warm breath panted against my left eye and blew up into my nostrils.

"We've got to stop meeting like this," I said.

"Smartass," she whispered.

"It's one of my best qualities." My hand trembled as I stroked her hair. I had scraped my arms raw from knuckles to elbow on the uneven pavement. With surprise, I noticed blood welling up in the grooves. I hadn't felt a thing. A sore hip on my sliding side probably meant I'd be black-and-blue there by evening. "Jimmy's calling an ambulance. All you have to do is hang on."

Taking me literally, she clutched at my forearm. I winced but didn't stop her.

"They'll get tired of me at St. Vincent's," she said in a thread of a voice.

"What did you think you were doing?" I heard my scolding tone but couldn't help it.

Her lips moved against my cheek.

"You think I don't try to leave, but I do."

"There's got to be a better way than walking into traffic." Anger boiled up in me. "You could have been killed!"

Her mouth quirked in a faint smile.

"That would solve the problem, wouldn't it?"

"Don't talk like that. Where is the son of a bitch, anyhow?" I looked around. Concerned bystanders pressed as close as they could, but Mac wasn't one of them. I could hear a siren wailing. The ambulance, a few blocks uptown and coming closer. A cop car had already arrived. Its roof lights whirling, it pressed close against the downtown end of the truck.

"He probably went home," Laura said. "He isn't much of one for hospitals."

"And I am? Thanks a heap."

"Don't fight with me," she said. "Not now. You could always make me feel better."

My jaw clenched on all the things it wouldn't help to say.

"I wish I could."

"It's no use," she said. "I'm a lost cause. Save yourself, Bruce. You should walk away."

Then she kissed me on the cheek, her soft lips parted. The tip of her tongue darted out for a little lick at the corner of my mouth. So I knew she didn't mean it.

EIGHTEEN

After the fiasco down in SoHo, Jimmy and I had to start the visit to the Gaglias all over again. I spent the interim mostly on the couch, draped in ice packs and turning interesting shades of black and blue. And popping Tylenol, which didn't have much kick without the codeine. My sponsor advised me not to risk it. "You can take a little pain," he said. Tough love. "It's not worth experimenting and ending up in relapse."

We decided to bring the Toyota for artistic verisimilitude. It had a plausible collection of dings and dents from what Jimmy called fender benders and Barbara called slight disagreements with inanimate objects.

"I've never hit a person or a car," she said with indignant pride.

"Parked cars don't count?" Jimmy asked.

"We live in Manhattan!" Where parallel parking is more than an item on your road test and even a Beetle or Mini gets used to being shoehorned into spots too tight for it.

"They can give you an estimate, but don't let them do any work on it" was her parting shot as we saddled up and headed out. "Body work is highway robbery no matter where you get it done."

"Yes, dear," Jimmy said.

"We'll just have them paint a few flames on the hood and maybe put on a spoiler," I said. She threw a bagel at me, but we were already out the door.

Coney Island Avenue was a treeless strip of auto repair shops, gas stations, pizza places, discount stores, and commercial ventures of various kinds. It was nowhere near the beach.

I had pictured a dusty lot with a chain-link fence topped with coils of barbed wire and a couple of Dobermans. But Hell on Wheels was all interior, a cavernous space like a giant's garage. The wide doorway yawned, spilling darkness out rather than letting daylight in. A massive steel door perched overhead, ready to chomp down.

"Nice portcullis," Jimmy said, ever the medieval knight.

He pulled the car up on the ramped sidewalk to the left of the open doorway. We got out and stood peering into the dim interior, getting our bearings. The shop consisted of three bays, each roomy enough for a couple of eighteen-wheelers. In one, a guy in a face guard—"Visor down," said Jimmy, still in the Middle Ages—wielded a blowtorch spitting sparks. An SUV swam in midair on a hydraulic lift. From beyond it came a helluva racket that sounded like a hammer on metal with a lot of muscle behind it.

"Yeah, what?" The speaker was rangy and balding, his face pitted with acne scars. Once I saw him, I remembered him from the funeral.

"Mr. Gaglia?" Jimmy asked.

"I'm Sal. What can I do you for?"

While Jimmy went into his pitch about getting an estimate, I looked around. I couldn't name most of what I saw. As a Manhattan native, I had never belonged to the rest of America's car culture. To tell the truth, Jimmy and I had both learned to drive joyriding with older boys, a six-pack on the dash. God knows who I owed amends to for those excursions.

"Bruce." Jimmy beckoned to me. "He wants to show us something."

We followed Sal as he strode past the elevated SUV and whisked a grimy tarp off a sleek vehicle that had been hidden in the shadows.

"Tell me that ain't a beauty," he said.

Even I could see the car was a classic, low to the ground and gleaming with fresh paint and chrome. Half the length of it consisted of outthrust hood, no doubt housing a powerful engine.

"Sixty-nine Dodge Charger Daytona Hemi," Sal said.

I gave a low whistle. He expected it. Call me a people-pleaser.

"Best I ever had is a Corvette," Jimmy said. Like hell he did.

"Corvette!" Sal spat on the ground. "The Daytona's a muscle car."

"You said it. You work on engines too?"

"Only the ones like this baby." Sal gave the Dodge's hood an affectionate slap, then pulled a wild rag out of his pocket and wiped away his fingerprints with finicky care. "It's a hobby."

"More like a passion," Jimmy said, "and why the hell not?"

"Looking for a deal?"

"Not today. My sister's husband had a Daytona." Right. Jimmy's sister and brother-in-law lived in Patchogue and were putting away every cent they could for the baby's college education.

"No kiddin'. The Sixty-nine?"

"Not as well restored as this one," Jimmy lied. "Beautiful detailing you've done."

"What happened to it?" Sal asked.

"The bastard cheated on my sister and then took off," Jimmy said. "Left her with three kids and a mortgage. Traded her in for a newer model."

"You can't do better than a Sixty-nine Daytona," Sal said. "Especially if you take your time and fix her up right."

"Oh, he's still got the car," Jimmy said. "My sister took up with a bimbo twenty years younger. Two years later and she's still knee-deep in lawyers, trying to get what's hers."

"Sucks."

"Sisters are a big responsibility." Jimmy heaved one of his gusty ACOA sighs. "Man's gotta take care of family."

"Tell me about it," Sal said.

"Never too old to need pulling out of trouble," a new voice chimed in.

"My brother Vito," Sal said.

"Sir," Jimmy said, extending his hand.

Vito shook. He carried the face guard tucked under his arm and clutched the blowtorch and a pair of padded asbestos gloves. He looked a lot like Sal. A couple inches shorter, a couple shades grayer.

"Sisters," Vito said.

"They gotta marry some scumbag," Sal said. "Hope yours has got a good lawyer. Squeeze his nuts and wring 'em dry."

"Or you could just hammer him."

The brothers guffawed. *Har har har.* It didn't last long.

"Sisters," Sal said, glum again.

Vito growled low in his throat.

"Rip the fucker's throat out."

"So you wanna get the little Jap tin can back in shape?" Sal asked. "You'll need new sections, but we can order them for you. Or are you interested in some real muscle?"

Vito tapped on the Daytona's hood. Sal handed him the wild rag. No smudges allowed.

Jimmy sidestepped with a shtik about asking the wife that made the Gaglia brothers eye him with disgust and pity. We got back in the car, and Jimmy started it up. Before he could shift into reverse, Sal tapped on the window.

"Lemme give you a card," he said. "If your sister pries the Daytona outta shithead, I could give her top dollar."

"Thanks, man," Jimmy said. "More likely it'll end up he sells it and makes her a settlement. He won't be looking for any recommendations from me."

"Tell her not to take a penny less than half a mil," he called after us as we rolled down the street.

NINETEEN

I walked through the park, kicking at the mounds of fallen leaves. Barbara and Luz, one on either side of me, chattered across me as if I were one of those little tables at Starbucks. The air was soft and smelled of musty oak. I used to know a guy who brewed a homemade beer with oak leaves. He probably still did it. I hadn't seen him in a while. Bar friends don't meet sober friends unless they hit bottom and cross over. Jimmy was still my only real friend. Now and forever, amen.

Barbara had a hundred friends. No topic of conversation was *verboten*. As we dawdled along, she and Luz covered aging female relatives, boot styles, perimenopause, and the best way to cook a turkey.

I waited for an opening. Even Barbara had to breathe sometime.

"Yo. Ladies. Luz, I want to know—are the cops still hassling you?"

"They seem to have given up for now," she said. "I was afraid, but at least when they came around, I knew they were doing something. Now I don't know if they even go through the motions." She gestured like a temple dancer, rotating her wrists and fluttering her fingers. "I still want to know who killed Frankie. I need to know."

I nodded.

"You want to shut the drawer and move on," I said.

"Yes, that is it exactly. This way I stay—"

"Stuck," Barbara supplied. "It feels like we're all stuck. We ought to be going somewhere or doing something or talking to someone. The trouble with New York City is the container is too big. You can't take the whole bowl of soup and swirl it around to see what's on the bottom."

"Not like a small town, huh?"

"It would be a lot easier," Barbara said, "in a place where everybody in it has lived there since birth and knows all there is to know about everybody else, except for a bunch of secrets that come out when whoever it is investigates the murder, if there is a murder."

Having used up all her air on one of her inimitable sentences again, Barbara drew a deep breath.

"There are still places like this?" Luz asked.

"Probably not," Barbara admitted. "Americans move a lot, and families don't live or even think the same from generation to generation. Too many options, too much television, and with the Internet, forget it—the kids growing up now don't even need to walk out their doors into the street to find communities of their own."

"This small town sounds like Frankie's neighborhood in Brooklyn," Luz said.

"Good point, Luz," I said.

"Except we don't belong to their little enclave," Barbara said. "We're on the outside looking in, which makes it hard to find anything out." The corners of her mouth turned down, and she kicked at a Diet Coke can that had rolled into the middle of the path.

"Frustrating," I sympathized. "Let's kill all the litterers—that'll help a lot."

Barbara smiled. Luz laughed aloud. Not at my feeble joke, I thought, but to please me. That made me happy. What was so bad about what the Al-Anons called "people-pleasing"? I'd have to ask Barbara sometime. Or not.

When we reached the Great Lawn, I stopped to admire the pale blue bowl of the sky, fringed with the skyline to the south and the trees turning color and beginning to bare their branches to the east and west.

"I don't think we have done so badly," Luz said. "We have talked to a lot of people. Not just Frankie's friends and relatives in Brooklyn, but his friends from rehab too." She twinkled at me. I liked being twinkled at. "We have even discovered what we needed to know about his—" Her forehead creased in a frown. She didn't like talking about Frankie's drug connections.

"His dark side," I offered.

At the same time, Barbara said, "His other world. You're right, Luz, we should think positively. Let's brainstorm. Who have we *not* talked to, and how might we get to them?"

Luz's face relaxed.

"It feels better to have something to do," she said. "Brainstorm—I like this."

"We haven't talked to his friend Vinnie   the nice one from the funeral," Barbara said.

"I didn't think he was so nice," I objected. "I didn't like his eyebrows." I waggled mine like Groucho Marx.

"At least he showed us around," Barbara said. "And he didn't blow the whistle on us. That would have been excruciating. I hate feeling embarrassed."

"So you tell us. Frequently."

"I hate feeling embarrassed too," Luz said. "No, Barbara is right, Vinnie was kind. I had met him many times with Frankie, and he always acted like we were a real couple. I am grateful for that. He knew I loved Frankie, and I think he liked me well enough."

"How could you tell?" I teased. "He always wore that hairy black frown."

"Oh, stop it," she said, more comfortable with me than she'd ever been. Good.

"Let's get practical," Barbara said. "Could you call him? Do you have his number?"

"I am not sure," Luz said. "It might be in my Rolodex. What would I say to him if I called?"

"We'll cross Brooklyn Bridge when we come to it," Barbara said. "One day at a time. How about Netta?"

I could see the anxiety roll back across Luz's face. I glared at Barbara.

"You don't have to talk to her, Luz. Nobody with any sensitivity would ask you to."

"I wouldn't ask Luz to talk to her," Barbara protested. "I just meant one of us needed to. Who's a better suspect than a cheater's wife? Sorry, Luz, but from her point of view, he did cheat on her."

"It's okay, Barbara, I can face it. With me he was unfaithful twice over, to two women who had borne his children. I accept my—my inventory. I should have known better. I *did* know better, but I loved him so much. He didn't mean to hurt me, but he carried so much rage inside."

"It is a good idea to talk to her," I said, "but you don't have to do it." With a scowl, I aborted Barbara's lecture on the cycle of abuse. "We'll figure out how one of us can reach her."

We scuffled through the leaves in silence for a minute or two. I could hear faint yelps, kids playing touch football at the south end of the Great Lawn. A very friendly golden Lab dropped a drool-coated chartreuse tennis ball at my feet and looked up at me hopefully, plumed tail wagging.

"Taxi!" The Lab's person came panting up, a gray-haired woman wearing sweats that matched the tennis ball. "He doesn't want to play. How many times have I told you not to talk to strangers?"

The dog frisked over to her. When she grabbed for its collar, it circled back to me.

"Cute name," I said. I let the Lab sniff my hand. That didn't mean I would pick up the tennis ball.

The dog owner scooped up the ball without hesitation. The dog's tongue probably spent more time on her hands and face than inside its mouth. When the Lab went after the ball, she lunged for its collar and got hold of it. The dog didn't carry a resentment. It looked adoring and delighted as it pranced around her legs.

"Thanks," she said. "Come on, Taxi, let's go play with the fellas." She led him off toward the big sloping field just north of the West Eighty-sixth Street entrance, which serves as a dog run.

"I can do it," Luz said suddenly. "I have thought of a way."

"To do what?" Barbara asked, turning. She had walked ahead a little way. Barbara is not a fan of dog saliva.

"To see Netta. It will have to be me, though. You know that I work in the lingerie store."

I had forgotten about the temple of rich ladies' underwear.

"Yes, of course."

"Don't you see?" Luz's eyes sparkled. "I can get her to the shop. We often have specials. We send fliers."

"You've showed me," Barbara said. "Glossy, Bruce, and very pink."

"We used to get them printed up. Now that we have computers, we make them ourselves. I can send Netta an announcement for a sale she can't resist."

"It's a great idea." I smiled at Luz. "But Netta saw us at the funeral. What if she figures it out and makes a scene?"

"That's why it has to be me," Luz said. "You two and Jimmy met her at the funeral, but I did not. Remember? I stayed far away from her."

"Then I guess it'll be okay," I said. "If you're sure you don't mind. I could understand it if you didn't want to see her."

"I want to do it," she said. "If she killed Frankie, I want to know. The same if anything she says helps us find out who did."

"If there's a sale on, won't you be too busy?" Barbara asked. "How can you have a real conversation with her if the store is packed with women pouncing on the bargains?"

Luz looked pleased with herself.

"Oh, this will be a very special sale. I will make up the flyer myself. Only Netta will get one."

"Can you get away with that? You don't want to lose your job."

"No problem," she said, "as long as I set it for a date and time when I am in the store alone."

I thought of another objection.

"At the funeral, Netta looked like a beached whale. Will she be interested in sexy underwear?"

Luz and Barbara looked at each other and laughed.

"She is still a woman," Luz said.

"Don't tell anyone I said it," Barbara said, "but when gorgeous lingerie goes on sale, feminist principles fly out the window."

"It is true, we have beautiful things," Luz added. "Silk and satin, handmade lace, and some of the new microfibers feel so soft and wonderful. You can even put them in the washing machine."

"But she's just lost her husband," I said.

Luz and Barbara exchanged another glance and shook their heads.

"It has nothing to do with men," Luz said with authority. "It is how we feel ourselves—beautiful in our skin." She ran her hands down her brief but sweetly rounded torso in an unconscious gesture. My body stirred in response, like a sleeping lion shifting position. I hoped to hell they didn't notice.

"She is very pregnant," Barbara admitted. She sketched elephantine curves in the air with her hands.

"Oh, we have maternity things," Luz assured us, "flowing robe and nightgown sets. And underwear for afterward, when they want reassurance they can get their old body back. Also nursing bras."

"Nursing bras are sexy?" I asked.

"Ours are," Luz said.

"It's not about sexy," Barbara said, "we're trying to tell you. Sexy is something you put on for someone else—men."

"That lesser breed that you put out with the trash," I murmured.

"Now you get it. This is aesthetic—no, spiritual."

"Spiritual?" I squawked. "I know the whole universe is One, but lingerie? That's going too far."

"No, she is right." Luz sounded certain.

"It's the inner feminine," Barbara explained. "Think Jung if it makes you feel better. Sensual, opulent, at peace with our own spirit. It's the same with belly dancers, but I digress."

"So you do. All the time."

"So it is settled," Luz said. "I will make the flyer tomorrow. I often stay to close up, so I can make sure I'm alone at the end of the day."

"If we could be sure you'll be safe," I said.

"What, in my own shop where I work for three years?" Luz scoffed. "Surrounded by filmy garments? The most dangerous object in the whole boutique is a corset."

"Luz, did you ever tell the cops you thought someone was stalking you?" Barbara asked.

"Oh, Barbara, not stalking," Luz protested. "It was only a feeling. What could I have told them?"

"What kind of feeling?" I asked.

"A nervous feeling," she said. "A kind of chill between the shoulder blades, as if someone is watching me."

"Do you feel it now?"

"Oh no, I feel safe with you. I have not gone into the park alone since that time I told you about. And I try not to come home too late at night. But I can't become a prisoner in my apartment. I go to meetings. I visit my aunts."

"Can't one of your cousins take you home?" I remembered she had a lot of cousins.

"They usually do."

"Speaking of home," Barbara said, "Luz is coming home with me for brunch. Bruce? Wanna come? We'll lure Jimmy away from the computer with bagels and lox."

"Are you sure it is okay to interrupt Jimmy's work?" Luz asked.

"You have to interrupt Jimmy," Barbara explained, "or he wouldn't have a life."

"I promised to go downtown and see Laura," I said. "Don't give me that look, Barbara. She got hit by a car the other day. The hospital said she's lucky. She got off with bruises and a broken thumb." I didn't say she'd landed on top of me. "She's still having trouble getting around and lifting, though. The least I can do is give her a hand. My ex," I told Luz. "Just a friend now."

Barbara opened her mouth and closed it with a snap. Not a good example for her sponsee if she bad-mouthed Laura. Or maybe she realized that if she told Luz I was still hung up on my sicko ex-wife, I would wring her neck.

"I'll walk the two of you over there and then take the train," I said.

Luz had enough tact to change the subject. I entertained her with stories from my recovery jobs doing office temp work as we wound our way past yelling kids, beleaguered parents, and gossiping nannies. More dogs like Taxi, high on being off leash. Squirrels storing acorns for the winter.

"I always wonder how they manage to remember where they've hidden them," I remarked.

Luz laughed.

"Maybe they forget."

We crossed the bridle path and reached the main park road. It was Saturday, so the road was closed to cars. There were plenty of bicycles, and runners were out in droves, with the New York Marathon only a couple of weeks away. But we hit a lull. For the moment, the road was clear.

As we started across, Barbara fell back.

"Go ahead," she called after us. "Pebble in my shoe."

"Want to wait?" I asked Luz. "Need a rest?"

"Whatever you like. I am fine."

Luz, on my right, turned her head to smile at me. So I was looking north when a car came tear-assing down the road, headed straight at us. I stopped, but Luz, still smiling, stepped right into its path. At the last moment, I got hold of her elbow and jerked her backward. We both cannoned into a knot of helmeted cyclists on racing bikes, streaking by behind us at just the wrong moment. All of us went down with a crash, punctuated by the whir of spokes and a stream of curses from the cyclists, who had been hugging the bike lane and hadn't even noticed the speeding car.

In no time at all, a crowd gathered, like people at the beach when someone spots a shark. Some helped disentangle us from the bicycles and their riders. Others whipped out their cell phones. The rest provided commentary. They seemed to be enjoying themselves.

"Are you all right?" I asked Luz.

"Just a little shaky." She held up her hand, palm down, to show me the slight tremor. "But you—your leg!"

I looked down. The right leg of my pants was ripped from knee to cuff, exposing a long gash, dirty and bleeding.

"You must wash it," Luz said, "or it will become infected."

I hadn't even felt it until she mentioned it, but it hurt like hell now.

Barbara caught up to us just then.

"What happened?"

"A car tried to run Luz down," I said.

"Bruce's leg is injured," Luz said at the same time.

"Luz, are you okay?" Barbara had her priorities straight, thank God. "Was it a park van? There are no cars in the park on the weekend. And how did the bikes get into it?"

"Wrong place at the wrong time," I said. "We jumped backward—"

"Bruce saved me," Luz put in.

"—and a protruding bike pedal took a bite out of my leg. It wasn't a park van. It was a car that shouldn't have been there and it was going about ninety miles an hour. Luz could have been killed."

"Did you see what kind of car? I don't suppose anybody got the license plate."

"All I saw was running lights glowing like the eyes of a mad bull and then a black streak going by. And the crowd didn't gather until the bikes crashed."

"Let's see your leg." Barbara squatted down to examine my wound. I held out a hand to steady her and realized it was shaking.

"Maybe we should all sit down."

The crowd was dispersing. Excitement over. Luz and Barbara helped me limp over to a bench. Barbara brought out a wad of tissues and a bottle of designer water and dabbed at the dirt around the wound.

"Ow! It stings! Take it easy, will you?"

"It really needs disinfectant and maybe stitches."

"Forget it," I said. "We'll bandage it when we get to your place. I'll be fine. I'm more concerned about Luz. This could be the same stalker who scared her before."

"In the park?"

"It happened in the park the last time."

"In a car? We didn't plan to walk across the park," Barbara said. "How could someone have followed us?"

"What goes up must come down," I said.

"What do you mean?"

"The road circles the whole park," I said, thinking it through as I spoke. "Cars go uptown on the East Side behind the Met, across at the north end, and downtown parallel to Central Park West, right past where this guy almost got us. What if the stalker was following Luz? He could have picked her up at her apartment."

"And followed her into the subway? By car?"

"I took the bus," Luz said. "It was such a beautiful day."

"But we spent more than an hour at the meeting," Barbara said.

"So he waited. Followed her to my apartment, waited again, and followed us into the park. Then all he had to do was zip around the top at 110th Street and intercept us."

"He could have taken a break while we were in the meeting," Luz said. "If he knew it was a meeting, he'd know how long it would last."

"Who would know it was a meeting?" Barbara asked, then answered her own question. "Only somebody in the program."

TWENTY

Luz looked up, biting her lip, as the bell that signaled a customer's entrance pinged. She stroked the smooth satin of the slip she had been folding. It was warm in the shop. Maybe that was why she was sweating. The boutique's owner, an impossibly thin Park Avenue matron who didn't need the money, often said, "Ladies don't perspire." If a woman stained her bras and camis beyond a dry cleaner's abilities, she wasn't good enough to buy them here.

The women surged into the shop. Four of them—four and a half: Netta's gargantuan belly preceded her like a dignitary's motorcycle escort. A woman with platinum-tipped and rigidly sprayed hair, earrings far too large for the East Side, and a bright pink sweater spackled with bling-bling had already found the high-priced and artfully displayed items in the first showcase. The flaw in Luz's plan had been that she could not actually put anything on sale. She hoped the ladies from Brooklyn would assume the price tags represented a reduction in even more expensive garments.

"Oh, look at these," she cooed. "Netta, you gotta see. If they don't have it in maternity, you could get it for afterward." *Chomp, chomp.* "You can wear it for you know who."

Luz shuddered, hoping her reaction didn't show on her welcoming-saleswoman face. She recognized the voice and the sound of the ruminating jaw. She had last heard it as she cowered in a bathroom stall.

"Don't be silly, Shirley," Netta said. "I'm not thinking about afterward. I don't know what you're talking about."

"Listen to huh!" Shirley said. "'I don't know what you're talking about,'" she mimicked in a mincing voice. "Doncha?"

The third woman still held the door open, letting in a blast of frigid air as she ushered an older woman in.

"Come on, Mamma Silvia," Netta said. "It's warm in here."

Madre de Dios, Frankie's mother! Luz's bowels turned to water. *They've never met me, they've never met me.* She said it like a rosary.

The woman at the door turned a glossy head of sculpted auburn hair. These women must spend a fortune at the beauty parlor. Maybe they could afford Chez Ashleigh's wares, on sale or not.

"Come on, Aunt Silvia. There's a cute little chair here. You can sit down, get comfy while we look. Wanna Tic Tac?"

Luz recognized that voice too.

"Let Netta sit. Do your ankles hurt, darling?"

"They're a little swollen. But you sit too, Mamma Silvia." She raised her voice. "There must be another chair."

"Of course, madam. I'll get it for you right away." She schooled her face and tone not to betray her anger. Frankie had given her plenty of practice.

"I don't know why I let you children talk me into this." Silvia sank onto a little gilt stool with a tapestry cushion. "My heart is broken, and you want me to look at nightgowns."

My heart is broken too, Luz thought. She looked at Netta. Had she still loved Frankie? She continued to bear his babies, but that didn't mean she couldn't be relieved that he was gone.

Luz placed another gilt chair, this one with a low scrolled back-rest, next to Silvia's.

"Let me help you, madam."

Netta sat, one hand pushing at the small of her back and the other curved protectively over her enormous belly. She neither thanked Luz nor met her eyes. Good, Luz thought. It would be horrible to like her.

"I wanna see this in a twelve," the gum chewer demanded. Shir-ley. "And the robe that comes with it. I can see Tony getting hot and bothered if I wore this." She gave the irritating little giggle Luz remembered.

The one who had called Frankie's mother Aunt Silvia snickered.

"I should be so lucky. My Rocco gets hot and bothered when the Giants win, and that's about it. But it is cute. Ya got the same one in ivory in an eight?"

"An eight!" Shirley scoffed. "You gotta be kidding, Patti. You haven't been an eight since seventh grade."

"Gimme the eight," Patti ordered. "We'll see about that, Miss Shirley. You got a fitting room?"

"Behind the mirrored wardrobe to the right, madam." Luz kept her eyes down and her hands busy, pulling the silky garments from their drawers and refolding them with practiced speed. "Let me also show you one that is a little different—you may like it better."

Soon Shirley and Patti were tucked away in the fitting room. Squeals emerged from behind the wardrobe. In minutes they had thrown half a dozen rejected garments onto the plush carpet. Nightgowns and peignoirs spilled out under the latticed half-door. Luz bent to retrieve them.

"What did I tell you? An eight, honestly!"

"I am so an eight. This gown is cut small."

"Listen to huh. Or is there something you're not telling me? Maybe you should make an appointment with Dr. Feingold."

"Shush! Netta will hear you. She has a fit if you mention him, after that mess last year."

Luz frowned. What were they talking about? Luz's gynecologist was Dr. Feingold. Frankie had asked her for his number last year. He'd made it sound as if Netta needed a hysterectomy. Female trouble, nothing to suggest they still had a sex life. She hadn't questioned him because she wanted so much to believe him. He'd been lying, or Netta wouldn't be pregnant now. But what had happened last year? A mess. Did they mean an abortion?

"Miss! Miss! Can we get some service here!"

Luz hurried back into the showroom.

"May I offer you some espresso, ladies?"

"No caffeine for me," Netta said, "until this one decides to come out." She patted her swollen belly. "Oh, look, Mamma Silvia, he's awake."

Sure enough, a little cone-shaped ripple traveled across Netta's belly like a shark's fin moving through the water. Luz started the noisy espresso machine, glad of the excuse to hide her face. She brought the tiny cup with its sliver of lemon and minuscule sugar cubes to Silvia. Frankie's mother had two fingers pressed to her forehead, just above the bridge of her nose.

"Your coffee, madam." She turned to Netta. "She is ill? Or she has lost someone, perhaps?"

Netta thrust her elbows out and dug her hands into the small of her back.

"Actually, I'm the one that's lost my husband."

"Oh, I am so sorry. I did not know."

"Well, how could you?" She didn't add "stupid girl," but her tone supplied it.

Silvia opened her eyes and took the coffee.

"You cannot imagine a mother's grief. God should not allow a child to die before his parents."

"Well, I have a wife's grief." Netta sounded sulky. "I can't help it if everybody says I have to pull myself together and move on. A man is not supposed to leave his wife and children to manage on their own, either."

The corners of Silvia's mouth pinched together.

"As if he died on purpose, out of spite! You have no respect. And you are not left to manage on your own. You have plenty of help from family and friends—all kinds of help."

She means financial help, Luz thought. She bent down and picked an imaginary grain of sugar off the rose colored carpet to hide her face.

"When I had babies at home," Silvia said, "I still had to work long hours in the bakery. For thirty years I got up with Massimo at four in the morning."

"I can't help it," Netta pouted, "if my brothers love me and my kids enough that they're trying to make it a little easier for me to give them my full attention. Times have changed since your day."

So Netta's brothers supplied the financial support. If they dealt in half-million-dollar cars as a hobby, they could afford it. They had been angry about Frankie's infidelity to their sister. Did they disapprove of Frankie's drug dealing? Or were they part of it? Vinnie had said they were dangerous. They'd seemed aboveboard to Bruce and Jimmy.

Luz smiled a little as she thought of Bruce. She hadn't known a man in early sobriety could be so nice. The frozen heart she had carried around since Frankie died thawed a little whenever he was around.

All at once, Silvia gave a keening cry. Luz whipped around just in time to catch the empty espresso cup. The saucer fell to the floor and bounced once on the carpet as Silvia clasped her hands on her breast.

"Oh, my heart! My heart!"

Shirley and Patti popped out of the fitting room.

"What happened? Is she having a heart attack?"

"Aunt Silvia? What's the matter? Are you all right?"

"She's fine," Netta drawled.

"Heartless, heartless," Silvia breathed through stiff lips. She pounded her clasped hands against her left breast, as if to emphasize her broken heart and Netta's lack of one.

"Oh, all right, I'm sorry," Netta snapped. "Though don't ask me what for. Look, we're both upset. Maybe this trip wasn't such a good idea. Get yourselves changed," she ordered Shirley and Patti. "We gotta get her home."

The two women disappeared with little squeaks.

"Would you like me to call you a cab?" Luz asked, struggling to sound polite rather than eager.

"No, we came by car. Are you okay now, Mamma Silvia?" She tugged at her hand, now gripped firmly in Silvia's. The brief storm between them seemed to be over.

"I want to go home," the older woman said.

Netta pulled away and stood up, rotating on the fulcrum of her huge belly. As Shirley and Patti emerged, bundled up and ready to leave, she waddled over to the door. She opened the door, letting in a blast of cold air, and stuck her head out.

"Vinnie!" she bellowed.

"Oh, no!" Luz's hand went to her mouth in an unconscious gesture of dismay.

Frankie's cousin Vinnie, dressed in a brown leather bomber jacket and rugged jeans, peered over Netta's shoulder into the hot and intensely feminine room. His heavy brow made his genuine frown more menacing.

"So ya ready to go already?" he began. "I'd a bet you'd be ages. Didja buy—" He stopped short as his gaze fell on Luz.

She stood helpless in the middle of the rosy space like a maiden staked out for a boutique-stalking dragon. Her eyes pleaded: *Don't tell them who I am.* The frown bulged downward as if his eyebrows might reach the tip of his nose. His jaw set like a slab of concrete. His gaze bored into her, then passed with slow deliberation from Silvia, drooping martyred on her gilt stool, to Shirley and Patti, twittering obliviously. He looked down at Netta, who stood as close to chest to chest with him as her belly would allow. Her face tilted upward under his chin like a buttercup.

"Oh, Vinnie, take us home."

"You got it." His face softened. Then the squared chin came up. His glance ranged over Netta's head and back to Luz. "Lemme go bring the car right up to the door, a guy just pulled out. Miss, wanna come help? You can hold the spot."

"Certainly." She shouldn't leave these ladies alone in the store. If the boss knew, it could mean her job. "Of course, sir."

She followed him out, his disapproving back looming like a wall ahead of her. In the street, he turned and faced her.

"I don't know what you think you're doing," he said.

"I didn't—it was a a coincidence," she faltered. "I didn't know." She gestured to the women inside the shop. Shirley and Patti still chattered as they picked up the delicate garments, shook them out, held them up, and exclaimed over them. "It's not my fault, they just came in."

"You're not a good liar, Luz." Vinnie shook his head sorrowfully. "I like you, Luz, but I'm telling you for your own good. It's over. You've gotta get out of our lives."

Her chin set with defiance.

"All right, then. I loved him. I want to know what happened to him."

"Let the past rest."

"I can't." Her chest felt tight, her breath constricted. Her eyes brimmed with unshed tears.

"Then I can't help you," he said.

TWENTY-ONE

Jimmy breasted his way through the usual crowd around the church door toward where I stood talking with my sponsor.

"What's happenin'?" I gave him the ritual greeting. Jimmy usually gave me a lot of space when he saw me in serious conversation with Glenn. He approved of my sponsor, who had an even shorter way with my bullshit than Jimmy did.

The ritual answer was, "What's happenin'?" Jimmy didn't give it.

"I need to tell you something bad. Sorry, Glenn."

"No problem," Glenn said. "Take it easy, man, and think about what I said." He do-si-doed around a couple of smokers standing close by and fell into effortless conversation with two women just beyond them. I didn't know if he knew them or not. In AA, it didn't matter.

"What? Is Barbara okay?"

"Oh, no, no, nothing like that." Jimmy patted my shoulder. "Didn't mean to scare you. I just ran into Mars, remember Mars?"

"The god of war," I said. "So he hasn't picked up."

"I saw him in the beginners' meeting next door. He told me Kevin is dead."

"Your new sponsee? He picked up?" I had become interested in whether anybody I knew had relapsed. Just like every other sober alcoholic.

"I don't know." Jimmy shook his head with an impatient snap, as if a pesky fly kept trying to land on it.

"Come on, let's go down the block for coffee. Tell me what's bothering you. Anyhow, I know. This poor guy croaked and you feel responsible."

"You're right. I do feel responsible."

"So come on." I started down the path. This particular church had a postage stamp of a front lawn, surrounded by wrought-iron fence.

Jimmy didn't follow.

"The meeting isn't finished. The break is over. They're going back in."

"There'll be another meeting tomorrow," I said. "Tonight, even, if you want to find one instead of going home after we get some coffee. You want to talk. I want to hear it. I'll even comment in nothing but program slogans if you like."

"Don't be a dork."

"Hey, I'm powerless," I retorted.

"Okay, okay, I'm coming."

The greasy spoon around the corner had good coffee. The thick white cup and saucer with the thin green line didn't hold much, but they didn't call it "tall" or charge three dollars and change for it. And an old-fashioned waitress in a green cotton dress came right to our table and filled it up again for free. The name embroidered on her pocket was Galadriel. You can't have everything.

I tapped a cigarette out of the pack. You couldn't light up even in a coffee shop anymore. But they wouldn't stop me from playing with it. Jimmy tore off strips of paper napkin, twisted them into thicker strips, and twiddled with them. He'd done that forever. Since we were too young to drink coffee.

"Okay, bro, what's on your mind?" I asked. "You always say nobody's sponsor is their Higher Power. So how come Kevin's death is your fault?"

"He was doing so well. Maybe I overpraised him, so he thought if he admitted he was struggling, he'd be letting me down."

I nodded.

"So how did he die? Did he OD or didn't he?"

"Mars said no. He talked to Kevin's parents. The cops called it a mugging. They found him down on West Street around four in the morning."

"Where the far-out gay bars all used to be. A gay bashing, maybe? Love gone wrong?"

"I don't know." Jimmy took a sip of cooling coffee. "They've cleaned that neighborhood up a lot, rebuilt the whole waterfront. And he was supposed to put relationships on the shelf for the first year."

"Most of what happened in some of those bars wasn't what you and I would call a relationship," I said.

Jimmy laughed, but he still looked unhappy.

"So what's bothering you, bro? They didn't find drugs in his system. So he was clean."

"I think he went down there to cop," Jimmy said. "And I know he had zero money. He was crashing with his parents out in Queens and waiting tables a few hours a week."

Galadriel the waitress came over with the brown coffeepot in one hand and the orange one in the other. She gave us an inquiring look.

"No, thanks," I said. "Not even unleaded. I'm awash."

Jimmy shook his head.

"No, thank you." We watched her retreat behind the counter and start putting doughnuts from a box into one of those clear plastic domed display containers.

"Dude, I hate to tell you," I said, "but there's a time-honored way for gay guys to get drugs without money."

"I know that. But Kevin was deathly scared of HIV. He'd survived both IV drugs and the old gay sex scene without getting the virus, and he wouldn't do anything that might put that at risk. He said if he did have money, he'd rather spend it on crack than on the HIV cocktail."

"Sounds to me like the guy was all but waving a sign in front of your face that he was planning a mission."

"It does now!" Jimmy said. I hadn't seen him lose his equanimity like this in ages. "I thought he was being dramatic, making a point. How could I have been so stupid?"

"Oh, Lord, have mercy!" I exclaimed. "James F. X. Cullen is human like the rest of us."

"You don't have to rub it in. I feel bad enough already."

"I still don't get what you think the scenario could have been. If he wasn't copping drugs or renting his ass out, what was he doing there?"

"I think he went there to cop, he just didn't get the chance before someone killed him. Maybe a mugger took the money off him."

"What money? He had no money."

"I think he got some," Jimmy said. "I think it had to do with Frankie's murder."

"Why would you think that?" I asked.

"He hinted," Jimmy said. "I don't know how he got the idea we were looking into it."

"That would be me. When I asked him and Mars all those questions at the meeting, I must have been less subtle than I thought. It's not your fault."

"It's my fault if he got involved and it got him killed." Jimmy groaned aloud. The couple at the next table swiveled to stare, then turned back to their coffee and their conversation. New Yorkers.

"He wanted to find something out," I said. "And lay his little triumph at your feet, like a cat bringing you a mouse. You can't help being such a fucking good example of recovery that your pigeons idolize you."

"I told him to let it go!" Jimmy was too agitated to sit still. He stood up and shrugged his jacket on. He wound a scarf around his neck. Unwound it. Wound it on again. Pulled his gloves out of his pockets and stuffed them back in again a couple of times. "I told him to keep the focus on his sobriety."

"But you couldn't make him. Powerless, remember? So what do you think he did instead?"

"I can think of two possibilities," Jimmy said. "Let's say he knew or found out something about the murder, a connection between Frankie and whoever. One, he tried to blackmail the person because he needed money to score. Or, two, he just wanted to talk to them."

"Who do you think it was?"

"It would have to be somebody from rehab. Kevin didn't know all those Brooklyn people."

"He could have been wrong," I said.

"If he was wrong, why did he get killed?" Jimmy asked. "Suppose Kevin thought he knew who killed Frankie. Someone they knew from rehab. What would he do?"

"Code of the streets," I said. "You don't squeal."

"Don't forget the TC model," Jimmy said. "Rehabs use it too, they're just not as brutal about it."

I knew exactly what he meant.

"You confront the person directly."

TWENTY-TWO

"This time I swear it's over," Laura said as she whipped us up a postcoital omelette.

I was there against my better judgment, beating eggs and trying to believe her. Her bruises had faded to a streaky green and yellow that would have blended well with the autumn leaves in Central Park if Laura ever went uptown. They hadn't splinted her broken thumb or put it in a cast, but she was supposed to stay off it. My own hand clumsy in a padded oven mitt, I steadied the pan as she flipped and poked.

"Especially after he walked away without waiting to find out if that car had killed you." I knew Laura's capacity for forgetting past experience.

"It was just a Honda Civic."

"You could still be dead."

"Aren't you glad I'm not? This thing is done—hand me that plate. I mean hold it for me."

She flipped the omelette onto the plate, tossed the spatula in the sink, and managed to glue herself to me all the way down the front with one leg laced around my waist. All without moving an inch away from the stove.

"Can I put the plate down, please? And are we coming or going here?"

"Oh, all right. I guess we should eat while the eggs are hot." She thrust her hips at me, managing to arouse me and push me away at the same time. Story of my life with Laura.

I still hadn't told her one word about the murder. Beyond asking if Jimmy was still "seeing that tight-ass Jewish do-gooder," she had shown no curiosity about our renewed friendship. She didn't even remember Jimmy had been there when the car hit her. That, at least, could be chalked up to concussion rather than narcissism. But whatever wasn't about Laura died of inattention, like the houseplants well-meaning short-term girlfriends kept giving me before I got sober.

Once she'd accepted the ground rule of not getting high in front of me or asking me to drink with her, my recovery became another topic we never mentioned. Laura had a knack for bringing out the old Bruce, the guy who always took the course of least resistance. Sometimes it seemed like SoHo was a different planet. Visiting Carola's gallery twined a couple of threads together. But thanks to the Civic, that trip downtown had ended up being all about Laura too. When I rode the lumbering elevator up to the loft, I never knew if I'd be visiting the mental hospital. I wanted Laura away from Mac. The guy was scum. But did I want her to lay it all on me? The needs, the demands, the suicidal depression, the scary manic swings?

I took my cell phone out as soon as I stepped into the street, like a space shuttle contacting Houston. I had one new message. I thumbed the buttons to retrieve it as I walked toward the other Houston, the broad street that separated SoHo from NoHo. Had

I ever given Luz my cell phone number? No. Maybe I should. I'd never even seen her alone. But I had begun thinking about her a lot. I worried about her. Her boyfriend had been murdered in her apartment, and now she had a stalker. Maybe.

The message was from Jimmy, to say he'd see me at the meeting. Barbara wouldn't make it to Al-Anon next door—she had to work. That evening, I sat lost in my own thoughts through most of the qualification. Jimmy, bulky in a down vest, gave the speaker his full attention. The guy had just made ninety days and sounded a lot shakier than me. Jimmy was great at squeezing curds of wisdom out of the most unpromising share. It must be those extra fifteen sober years that I would never catch up with.

AA and Al-Anon let out at the same time. We ran into Luz right outside the door. Jimmy invited both of us back to the apartment. Barbara should be home from work by now, he said. While he talked to her on his cell, I took out my own cell phone.

"I'd like to give you my number," I said to Luz as we trailed behind. "If you're ever in trouble, you could call me."

"I wouldn't want to bother you," Luz said.

"No bother. Honest. I'm always up half the night anyway. Recovery has screwed with my sleep pattern."

Luz trotted along beside me in little purple ankle-high boots. Cute.

"For me, I had trouble right after—right after."

"And now?"

"It is funny, but I begin to sleep like a baby."

"You're not scared?"

"When I go out, yes, a little. But I think maybe I imagine, what to call them—shadows in corners. In my apartment I feel safe."

"Like before—before?" I didn't want to say "Frankie's murder" any more than she did.

Luz examined her toes.

"Better than before. With Frankie, often I felt afraid. I guess that makes me stupid for loving him."

"No, you're not stupid! Being a person who's capable of loving— how could that be bad?" I glanced sideways at her. "You may want to pick a little better next time."

"You are lucky to have an alcohol addiction." She added, "You do not mind?"

"What? Talking about my alcoholism? Not at all." We were having a real conversation. I wanted to keep it going. "How do you mean, lucky?"

"You have a disease," she said. "You know what it is, and you can fix it."

"You don't believe in love addiction?" I nodded toward Jimmy, still on the phone. "Barbara would say it's all the Disease."

Luz waggled her hand.

"Sometimes yes, sometimes no. Sometimes I think I understand this thing that makes me act so much against my best interest. Then I have hope, because if I can abstain, someday I will get a chance to make a better choice. But then I think no, Luz, you are making excuses, it is all your own stupidity."

"Oh, don't abstain from love. From addictive behavior, yeah, sure, but don't—" I wanted to say, "Don't close your heart." I hovered on the brink, feeling like a total jerk.

"Let us not talk about this anymore," she said. "What about the—what Barbara calls the sleuthing? Do I have that right?"

"It's more a joke than a real verb," I said. "Barbara loves to play detective. You don't have to get involved anymore if you don't want to."

"It is painful to think about that woman. Frankie's wife. There, I say it. You are *simpático*. I know I must make amends to her. That frightens me. And to find a way to do it without more harm being done."

"I know what my sponsor would say," I said. "You're a long way from Step Nine, so it's not today's problem. Anyhow, I think you're allowed to do it by changing your behavior."

Luz's anxious face cleared.

"That I can do. I take a vow—no more married men, not ever!"

I opened my mouth and then closed it. I didn't want to screw things up by saying the wrong thing. Was "Shut up and be grateful" a slogan? It ought to be.

After a silence, she said, "I would help. I want to. But you have met the brothers and the other woman with the child. You talked to his parents. So many important people he never talked about."

"Try not to worry about it."

"What about the cousin Vinnie and those awful women?" she asked. "At the store the other day, he was mad at me, but he didn't give me away."

"You must want to leave the whole crew of them behind."

She didn't answer, but she tucked her hand into the crook of my arm.

When we got to Jimmy's, Barbara insisted on recapping all of it, including the phony lingerie sale.

"Now we know for sure," Barbara said, "that they weren't one big happy family. They all had problems. Frankie was the scapegoat, that's all."

"I must be a bad person," Luz said. "I was glad to see them fighting."

"You're only human," Jimmy said.

"I'd have felt the same," Barbara said.

"Me too," I said.

"I think the most important part," Barbara said, "is the conflict and tension between Netta and her mother-in-law that Luz saw. I'm not sure what it means in terms of what happened to Frankie, but I bet it means something."

"So what next?" I asked. "Back to darkest Brooklyn?"

"Stella's our best bet," Barbara said. "She knows all of them, and she likes me, she'll talk to me. If necessary, we can tell her who we really are. She didn't come shopping with Netta the other day, did she, Luz?"

"No, just the restroom girls. They're called Patti and Shirley."

"So maybe Stella's not so close to Netta anymore. She might even sympathize with Luz's story if we tell it right. And we know where to find her—at the bakery."

"It's a plan," I said.

"It's a plot," Jimmy said. "I knew Barbara would find a way to get some more of those cannolis."

TWENTY-THREE

Luz trotted down the street, trying to hurry without appearing to. It would take only a couple of minutes to reach her apartment. Ordinarily, this block felt safe enough, even though the whole neighborhood knew it as a crack block. Luz had negotiated it without difficulty just that morning. When the sun shone and addicts hung out in the street as if it were a block party, waiting for their drugs to arrive, Luz did not feel fear. She had gone to school with some of them. They looked frail and desperate, arousing only her impatience and compassion. At night, the orange sodium lights usually provided a measure of security. But three of them were out, and the street was striped with shadows.

Luz wondered if the dealers had deliberately broken the streetlights. Maybe not. Down on Madison Avenue where she worked, and even around Barbara's on the Upper West Side, the city was quick to replace a burned-out bulb. They weren't so eager to venture into Spanish Harlem. She hiked up her purse a little tighter under her armpit. Not that mugging was the only danger. Everybody knew someone who'd been killed in the street. Kids shot for a jacket or knifed for a fancy pair of sneakers. Luz struggled every workday to maintain the balance between looking too expensive in the neighborhood and too shabby down in midtown.

She caught a flash of movement in her peripheral vision and whirled to face it. It was hard to know which would work better, acting fearless and defiant or oblivious. This time, it was only a cat. She watched as it squeezed under the chain-link fence that blocked the street's one empty lot. The fence didn't do much good. The cat hadn't bothered to use the front door, a hole where the wire had pulled away from the metal post. Luz knew an old lady who got in daily to leave open cans of food in there for *los gatos*. She was a friend of the *tias*, now gone a little crazy. Or maybe she was only kind. Kindness could seem crazy enough in this *loco* city.

Kindness made her think of Bruce. She thought he was attracted, but she wasn't sure. It made her feel shy. Frankie had filled her world so that weeks after his death, she still felt a pang of terror at the thought of touching another man. Frankie had been so jealous. He would interrogate her for half an hour if she was ten minutes later than she'd promised coming back from visiting the *tias* or an outing with some of the cousins. *Who was there? Who paid attention to you? Did you encourage him? Did he lay his hands on you?* All in the name of love. The punch line was always *Don't you know I love you?* If she answered wrong, it ended in a punch. Frankie did love her in his way. And they had had some good times. When she walked down this block at night with Frankie, she was never scared.

A deeper patch of shadow loomed ahead, where one streetlight was out and another smashed. Half hidden by the bulk of a high stoop, someone lurked in the area used outside most brownstones for garbage cans or a few pitiful plants in pots. None of the brownstones on that stretch of the street had lighted windows. How could everybody not be home? Maybe they were all in their kitchens, which faced onto the hidden yards and gardens between this street and the next. Was he watching her, waiting for her to pass? Would he snatch at her purse? Or at the gold chain around her neck? She always tucked it underneath her blouse when she got on the bus to come home, but she patted her neck to make sure. That was not the worst, though. What would she do if he had rape in mind? Her crotch liquefied with terror at the thought. Any woman who wasn't afraid of rape was a fool. In denial, anyway.

She couldn't tell if he was looking at her. No definition of the face, no gleam of eyes. As she got closer, she saw why. He was bundled up, more than the brisk fall night deserved. A dark watch cap pulled down over his ears met a dark scarf wrapped so it covered not only his neck, but his mouth and nose as well. His coat, a heavy wool jacket with the collar turned up, and his trousers were also dark. He had jammed his hands into his pockets, so she couldn't tell if he was black, white, or brown. What should she do? March steadily past him and not look back? Break into a run and scream? Use her cell phone? It was in her purse, tumbled among her keys and lipsticks and all the junk that lived in there. While she fumbled for it, he might grab her.

Panic seized her. For a moment, she imagined herself running wild, howling with fear as she raced down the street. Would that merely provoke him? Would he turn out to be the kind of hunter who got excited at the scent of prey? Luz thought this not in words, but in a vision of herself fleeing from wolves. She set her jaw and went on marching forward, her eyes on the traffic light at the far end of the block. She sent a brief prayer up: *Please, God, just help me reach the light.* She thought she saw the man begin to move toward her. Where was everybody? Had some evil force put the whole neighborhood under a spell? Her step faltered, and she almost broke and ran.

At that moment, she heard the jiggling rhythms of a rap song coming from behind her. She risked a swift look back. A group of kids rounded the corner, boys and girls not more than thirteen or fourteen. One carried the boom box on his shoulder. The others were horsing around, mock fighting, flirting—she could see the body language from here—showing off with little break-dancing moves.

"Change the station, man." A lightly accented voice came floating down the block. "Let's have a little salsa. Let's do some real dancing to real music." A mixed group, then, blacks and Hispanics together. That made it not a gang, just a group of kids who probably went to school together. Maybe change was possible in this world. Maybe God would get her to the corner.

TWENTY-FOUR

"Did you know," Jimmy asked, "that Diocletian was the only Roman emperor who died in his bed?"

"How did the others die?" I asked. I didn't really care about a bunch of guys who'd been gone two thousand years. But Jimmy has a way of sucking you in.

"Most of them were murdered by the army or their own bodyguards."

"So how did he manage not to be?"

"Smart enough to retire at the right moment."

"Well, don't look at me," I said. "I can't retire. I haven't started yet."

"Started what?" Barbara came into the living room balancing two mugs of coffee and a plate of oatmeal cookies. She felt guilty about not letting me smoke in the apartment, so she fed me. "Did you want milk in your insomnia?"

"The career I haven't picked out yet. No, ma'am, gimme a straight shot. You know me."

She handed me a mug. I snabbled a couple of cookies and dunked them in the coffee.

"I do know you, and I've been thinking about that. It's about time you traded up from your recovery job."

"Aren't we here to talk about the murders?" Jimmy acted as if he'd never mentioned ancient Rome. He got away with it because Barbara is the designated digressor in our triumvirate. "And what's happening with Luz?"

I got serious immediately.

"Someone's stalking her, and I don't like it," I said. I hadn't meant that to come out sounding so proprietary. I frowned at Barbara, daring her to comment.

"Who could it be?" Jimmy asked. "Who might still be mad enough at Luz to want to hurt her even now?"

"Netta," Barbara said. "But Netta doesn't know who Frankie's girlfriend is. Was. Is."

"The same goes for Netta's brothers," Jimmy said. "Unless somebody told them."

"Cousin Vinnie could have told," Barbara said. "But why would he make trouble? He wants her to get out of their lives. He didn't give her away when they all showed up at her shop."

"That was in his own best interest," Jimmy said. "I wouldn't have wanted to make a scene among the lingerie myself."

"I can never get you within a block of a lingerie shop," Barbara said, "so it's moot. What do you think about Luz maybe calling Vinnie? We need more of a handle on Netta's brothers."

"I don't like it." I snapped.

"It was just an idea," she said.

"All your ideas put Luz out front in uncomfortable situations."

"Come up with another idea, then."

"I have one," Jimmy said, "but neither of you will like it. Are we a hundred percent sure that Luz didn't kill Frankie herself?"

"Jimmy!" Barbara said. "I thought you liked her."

My throat constricted and I could feel my face turn red. I couldn't say a word.

"I do like her," Jimmy said. "But she had plenty of motive. She couldn't get herself to leave him. If she had, he'd have reeled her back in with no trouble. His getting sober didn't stop the battering. You know how that goes."

Barbara's grim nod went for me too. Some of the women's stories in AA made me want to crawl for being a guy.

"She could be making up the stuff about being stalked," Jimmy said.

"We saw a car nearly run her down," Barbara protested.

"You saw a car speed past while she was crossing the road."

I felt depressed. I hid my face behind the coffee mug.

Jimmy went on.

"She said she didn't know about Carola and the kid. What if she lied? That would give her even more of a motive."

"She lied to me about knowing he had kids with Netta," Barbara admitted.

I banged the mug down on the coffee table. Quick on the draw, Barbara slid a napkin underneath it before it touched down. Saving the furniture from rings and solving a murder at the same time. Jimmy's not the only multitasker.

"Maybe it was Carola," I said. I didn't care about Carola. "He was a hitter. If she thought he might hurt the little boy—"

"Edmund."

"Right. If he knocked that kid around, she'd have killed him, no problem."

"Yes but," Barbara said. "She was always there when he saw Edmund. It's not like she went out and left him to babysit."

"As far as we know."

"It was their time together as a family," Barbara said. "If he'd threatened or hurt Edmund, she'd have clobbered him then and there. It's like what we said about Netta. Would Carola hire a sitter so she could follow him all the way from Park Slope to East Harlem? Why bother?"

"To set Luz up." I leaned forward, excited. "No, listen, it makes sense. Luz didn't know about Carola, but Carola admitted she knew about Luz. We have only her word for it that she didn't mind Frankie playing away from home."

"Playing away from away from home," Barbara corrected. "Like off-off-Broadway."

"Whatever." I thought hard. Anyone was likelier than Luz. "And let's not forget Netta's brothers."

"Who we still have to figure out how to follow up on," Barbara said.

"I can't stop thinking about Kevin," Jimmy said. "We could try to find out what he knew."

"How do we do that?" I asked.

"You could go downtown to the gay meeting again, Bruce," Barbara said.

"Why can't Jimmy go?"

"No whining." Barbara said. "I would go myself, but it's a closed meeting."

"That didn't stop you when I first got sober," Jimmy said.

"I've grown a lot since then. I *have*—I've got a lot more respect for the traditions now. I wouldn't go in there and pretend I'm an alcoholic. Besides, I might run into someone I know from work or from the other program who'd know I'm not, and I'd feel—"

"Embarrassed!" we chorused. We knew her very well.

"Why would we go to the gay meeting anyhow?" Jimmy asked. "Kevin wouldn't be there. Kevin is dead."

"You could talk with Mars again," Barbara said. "Maybe we're missing something about that crew from rehab."

"We don't need a meeting to contact Mars," Jimmy said. "I have his number."

"And that woman Marla," Barbara said. "She said she identified with Frankie. Maybe she was close to Kevin too. Rehab is intense, right? People get close."

"So how do we find Marla?"

"I'll call Mars," Jimmy said, "and ask him for her number."

But he didn't have to do that. The next day, I ran into Marla at a lunchtime meeting near my current temp job in the East Fifties. More churches than you'd think are tucked away among the glass and steel office buildings. Office work makes a good recovery job for folks whose sobriety is still shaky and who want to get to a lot of meetings. In fact, it surprised me that I'd never run into her before. I found out why when she raised her hand and shared.

"I'm five days back," she said. She'd relapsed.

Everybody clapped. In AA you get a lot of points for even one day without a drink.

Marla held up her hand in a Stop gesture.

"Thanks for the support. It's hard for me to believe I deserve it. A few weeks ago I went through rehab. Bared my soul for twenty-eight days, borrowed money from my folks, which I hate." That drew sage nods and murmurs from around the room. "And I went back out." Her voice got husky. "I will not cry!"

A couple of the women's purses clicked open as they searched for tissues.

"Do I still have time?"

The guy who'd volunteered to be "spiritual timekeeper" for that meeting nodded and held up one finger. She had a minute left to speak.

"A friend of mine got killed," she said. "A friend from rehab, clean and sober the same amount of time as me. I'm not saying it as an excuse. We can always find an excuse to drink. I mean, *I* found one—or didn't need one, same thing, I know. If he hadn't died, maybe I would have stayed clean. Or maybe he'd have his ninety days and I'd still be telling you I'm five days back."

She left before the meeting ended. At lunchtime meetings, people do. I hurried after her. I caught up with her as she stopped in the street to light a cigarette. Her match kept going out.

"It's Marla, right?" I flicked my lighter on and held it out to her. "Hi, I'm Bruce," I said, giving the password.

"I know you. Wait a minute, I'll get it. I'm still so mokus. Bad case of CRS—Can't Remember Shit. I can't believe how clear my head felt when I left rehab. I guess you heard me in there, huh?"

I nodded.

"Frankie's funeral," I said.

"Oh, yeah, right, of course. You and the other guy knew Mars. You know, I need to make amends to everybody from that funeral. I was so freaked out I made all of us pretty conspicuous."

"No, I don't remember you doing anything bad."

"Nice to run into somebody I don't owe amends to, then," she said. "I made a bit of a scene over the coffin. Must have been after you left."

I drew a long pull on my cigarette and blew it slowly out.

"Well, as long as they make people look at their friends all dolled up with blue satin and embalming fluid, people are gonna react. It doesn't sound so terrible to me."

"Thanks for saying so. I have a tendency to guilt-trip myself— me and every other addict, huh? I wish I hadn't picked up. And then—you remember Kevin? Little Irish guy who came to the funeral with us? He's dead too."

"I heard. It sucks. I guess some of us make it and some of us don't."

Could Jimmy be right about Kevin? Had he accused someone of killing Frankie?

"Were you in touch with Kevin?" I asked.

"Yeah, I feel guilty about that too. I guess I'm the queen of guilt. He left a message on my machine, said he wanted to run something by me. I never returned his call." Her face twisted in self-mockery. "Of course not. I was high as a kite. The last thing I wanted to do was talk to program people."

I understood that all right. Story of my life until a few months ago.

"If only. My sponsor says 'if only' is as useless as 'should.' Too bad we don't come with an off button."

"Amen to that," Marla said. "My way of turning off 'if only' was to score a bunch of pills and wash them down with vodka. I was already ripped up about Frankie getting killed. When someone's got the same number of days you do, they're special. Frankie and I connected. I didn't know about his bad side. I never saw that side of him."

"I can relate to that." I thought of a detox buddy, dead now too.

"Hey, can I get your number?" Marla asked. "I need to make a lot of calls if I'm going to make it this time. My mom was a drunk. I'm older now than she was when she died. I don't want to end up like her."

There was no way to refuse. She pinched the half-smoked cigarette between her lips as she fished around in her bag and whipped out a pad and pen. She scribbled her number, tore off the sheet for me, then handed me the pad and pen to write mine. I had gotten used to calling Jimmy and my sponsor when the inside of my head started getting too dark. I had trouble imagining unloading my shit on strangers. Maybe I'd better not ever relapse, if that's what I'd have to do to get back.

"I don't know if I have another recovery in me," Marla said, "you know?" She let the cigarette fall from her lips and ground it into the pavement with the toe of her shoe. "I've gotta give these things up."

Me too. Only somehow it's never today. Booze was hard enough.

"I'm trying to smoke only half," she said. "But who am I kidding? You know how AA fucks up all your addictions. This relapse was no damn fun."

A silence fell as we both thought about that. I stubbed out my own cigarette.

"I used to see him at meetings," Marla said. "New York can be such a small town, you know?"

"Big city's got the skyscrapers," I said, "small town's got the church basements. It is kinda mind-blowing."

"I saw Frankie at a meeting the night he died," Marla said.

"Are you sure?" When you go to a lot of meetings, they can kind of blur together. And the clear head comes slowly.

"I remember that night," she said. "I'll never forget it, because Frankie was so nice to me. It was pouring cats and dogs, and he helped me get a taxi after the meeting."

I remembered that downpour.

"Yeah, it can be hard to get a cab in Brooklyn late at night."

"Brooklyn? No, this wasn't in Brooklyn. Oh, you mean because of the funeral. Yeah, that's where he lived. His whole family lived there, like, they owned the neighborhood. Not owned owned, but you know. This was uptown. You know how you're willing to go to meetings all over town when you first get clean."

I nodded. I knew how Jimmy and my sponsor told me I should be willing to go to meetings all over town. Okay, they didn't say "should." They suggested I pray for willingness.

"This was uptown," Marla repeated. "There were plenty of cabs out, but the drivers don't want to stop at night in Spanish Harlem."

TWENTY-FIVE

"Finally!" Barbara said. "Do you realize how important this is? We actually know something the police couldn't possibly have found out—what meeting Frankie went to the night he died."

We had just come out of another of those His and Hers AA and Al-Anon meetings and were walking toward the crosstown bus. Jimmy had stayed home to chair a real-time meeting in cyberspace.

I stopped to light a cigarette.

"Yeah, now we just need to figure out what to do with it."

Barbara wrinkled her nose and brushed away smoke with her hands.

"Hey, stop taking my inventory," I said. "Nonverbal counts. I'll quit when I'm ready."

"Isn't the last person who saw the victim," Barbara said, taking a final swipe at my exhalations, "usually a suspect? That's either Marla or whoever Frankie left with. Did you ask her if he was alone?"

"Damn. I didn't think of it." My shoulders slumped. The cigarette drooped in my fingers and dropped ash on the pavement. Barbara whisked her toes away. Ostentatiously. "Wait a minute. Wouldn't she have mentioned anybody else from rehab?"

"You'd think so. And she didn't know any of his or Netta's family. Or Luz."

"As far as we know."

"Did you get her number?"

"I did."

"So call her and ask."

"Why don't you call her? You're the one that likes to play detective."

"Why did you take her number if you aren't going to call her? Wait a minute, let me guess. You didn't ask for her number, she gave it to you."

"We-e-e-ell—" Sometimes Barbara is too quick. "Since you're so smart, you call her. Here, I'll give you the number." I had stuck Marla's scrap of paper in my pocket, and I hadn't changed my pants since then. I thrust it at her.

"Wait, let me put it in my phone, so I can give the paper back to you." She scrabbled in her bag. "You *could* make a program call, you know. Damn, the pesky thing is playing hide-and-seek with me." She stuck two pens behind her ear and a small notepad in her mouth. That left only a couple dozen items to rummage through. "How am I supposed to explain about having her number? I'm not an alcoholic."

"She probably thinks you are," I said. "Yeah, yeah, you won't lie about that. Be creative. You'll think of something."

"Found it! Huh, I thought I had it on. I usually put it on vibrate when I'm in a meeting."

She pressed a button. The phone lit up, flashed, and sang like a slot machine in a miniature Vegas. As soon as that subsided, it began to emit an insistent high-pitched peep.

"Somebody left a voice mail. I have to get myself another phone—this one has an annoying habit of nagging when it has a message waiting."

She punched in the code and pressed the phone to her ear.

"From Luz. Hold on, let me listen to the whole thing. I might have to call her back."

"Take your time." I lounged against a flashy Lamborghini parked tight against the curb. The owner must be crazy to leave it on the street. Or made of money. Or a drunk.

Barbara listened. One hand pressed the phone against her ear. The other made impatient circles in the air, fingers waggling. Long message.

"What? If you can tell me."

Since Barbara was Luz's sponsor, the message might be none of my business. On the other hand, Barbara's incurable love of talking didn't always trump anonymity. She shook her head at me.

She finally clapped the phone shut and dropped it back in her bag.

"Program call?"

"Not really. Guess what—Carola called her."

"But they didn't know each other. Carola didn't know who Luz was."

"I told her," Barbara confessed.

"When?" As I said it, I knew. "At her place. While I was in the can."

"I couldn't stand her talking about 'the Puerto Rican woman.' I thought if they could only talk to one another, they'd find they had a lot in common. I was working on Luz, trying to get her to reach out. I figured here were two people who actually mourned Frankie—they could help each other. Carola had the same idea."

"What did she want? To share her feelings?" I didn't have ninety days free of sarcasm. That might be the last frontier for me. "She didn't strike me as the warm fuzzy type."

"Of course she didn't put it that way. She said they both loved Frankie, so maybe they could help each other through. It's not like either of them made him cheat on the other—they didn't know."

"Yeah, he did that all by himself."

"Carola invited her out to Brooklyn. She said why doesn't Luz come and have a drink or some coffee, at least meet the baby. He looks a lot like Frankie, and he's much nicer."

"Luz said Carola said that?"

"I say that," Barbara said. "She wanted to know if I thought she should go. I'll have to call her back, tell her it's her decision."

As we talked, we had started walking again. The wind was picking up, the temperature dropping. I zipped up my denim jacket as we reached the bus stop.

Barbara stepped out into the street and craned her neck to the east.

"I can't see the bus. We'll wait twenty minutes and then four of them will come along. Are you coming with me?"

"Call her now, then. No, I'll keep you company till the bus comes and then go home." I had stuff to do around the house. When I was drinking, I'd never done a lick of cleaning or organizing. Maybe I'd traded alcoholism for OCD.

Barbara fished out the phone again. She punched a few buttons and listened, not as long as before.

"Luz, it's Barbara. I got your message. Sounds like Carola was trying to make amends. Up to you what you do about it. If you're not sure, you don't have to decide today." To me, she added, "I got her voice mail—she must have turned her phone off."

"When did she leave the message?"

"I didn't look. A while ago—I've had the phone off for a couple of hours. Want me to check?"

"No, just curious."

Fifteen minutes later, having seen Barbara onto her bus, I headed for home. I planned to stop in at the corner bodega. I needed cigarettes, orange juice, and maybe some V8 too. I was working my way up to fruits and vegetables.

As I crossed the final street, my cell phone rang.

"Yeah."

A faint, strained whisper reached my ears. I couldn't make it out.

"Say again. I can't hear you."

"Yoda," I thought the person said. Yoda? Someone who'd seen *Star Wars* too many times?

"You've got the wrong number." My thumb hovered over the hang-up button.

The strained voice got urgent.

"No! No! *Ayuda!*"

"Who is this?"

"*Ayúdame!*" Then, "Bruce—help—help me."

"Luz?" A pang of alarm shot through my gut. "Where are you?"

"Brooklyn," she whispered.

"Are you hurt? You sound scared. Where in Brooklyn? Tell me where." Brooklyn is huge. A city in itself. It's got something like the twelfth-biggest population in America.

The phone went dead. Damn! "Can you hear me?" has become a mantra for our times. She must have gone out of range.

She'd called me for help. That touched me. Barbara for moral dilemmas, Bruce for action. Barbara doesn't approve of damsels in distress, but she always says it's okay to ask for help. Thank God Luz had taken that in. Now all I had to do was find her.

As far as I knew, the only folks she knew in Brooklyn were Frankie's relatives and friends. She could have gone to visit the grave. Twisted her ankle or even broken it falling in a hole or tripping over a monument. But she had sounded scared. Had she gone to see Massimo or, more likely, Stella in the bakery? We'd told her where it was. I had trouble imagining anyone being scared in that bakery. The sugary, yeasty smells enveloped you like a kid's blankie. She couldn't have braved the Gaglia brothers by herself, could she? She must have gone to Carola's. Carola had invited her. She'd sounded friendly. When Luz couldn't reach Barbara, she'd remembered on her own that it was better to make your own decisions. So she'd gone.

I wheeled and started trotting back toward Lex. The subway would be a helluva lot faster than a cab. I just hoped I'd be in time. In time for what, I didn't want to think about. Damn! I knew Carola's I-don't-mind-the-other-girlfriend act was bullshit. She must have hated Luz. Here she is saddled with this baby. And there's the guy she's loved since they were kids giving her only a third of his attention. Maybe less. Maybe she goes uptown to confront Luz.

Luz isn't home, but Frankie's there. He has his own key to Luz's place. Of course he lets her in. He wants to know what the hell she's doing here. They fight. She loses it and stabs him with a kitchen knife. Then she scrams. Takes the subway back to Brooklyn. Maybe she washed the knife and put it back. Maybe she threw it on the tracks on the way home. Only rats go down onto those tracks voluntarily. Sure, guys who work on the tunnels. Change the lights. Fix the tracks. But nobody cleans New York subway tunnels. If they saw a bloody knife, they'd let it lie.

The police won't think to question her, I thought. They don't even know she exists. Besides, the murder's in East Harlem. She's so far out of her briar patch she's home free the second she steps on the train back to Brooklyn. It has nothing to do with her. Probably she thought somehow she'd feel relieved to get Frankie out of her hair. But instead she feels worse. I could imagine what Barbara would call "a whole range of feelings." She loved the guy. She misses him. Maybe she didn't expect losing him to be agonizing, since he's left her before. But before, she didn't murder him. So she's mourning. And on top of that, she discovers she's still angry. More than angry.

She's probably furious at Netta as well as Luz. But she knows Netta, she knows her family. She knows Netta has brothers. Besides, it's all too close to home. She can't be a hundred percent sure nobody will tell the cops about her. They might even seek her out just as an old friend of Frankie's, a cousin who might be able to tell them more about him. That's what we did. If Silvia told us, she could have told the cops. She's mad at Netta, but she won't commit a Brooklyn murder. It's a whole lot safer to go after Luz.

I'd made it halfway down the subway stairs when the phone rang again. I snatched it out of my pocket and flipped it open.

"Luz! Where are you?"

"What are you talking about?" The irritable voice was Laura's. Good thing I'd never said a word to her about Luz. "I can't hear you. Are you in the subway?"

"Yes, I'm about to take the train. What's up?" I didn't need Laura at all right now.

"I need you. Bruce, I can't go on. Mac keeps leaving, I keep getting hurt, it's all too hard. I can't do it anymore." I'd been wrong. Not irritable. Hopeless. Laura depressed and desperate, same as usual. I felt impatient first, then guilty, then irritated myself.

"Laura, I don't need this now. It's just the depression. It always passes. You know that."

"I can't," she wailed. "I can't do it alone. How can you be so mean to me? You're the only person who can always talk me down. Come down here, Bruce. I really, really need you."

"I can't, Laura." I tried to keep the exasperation from my voice.

"But I might cut myself. Or worse. I have plenty of pills. I've been stockpiling."

"Call 911," I said. "Or grab a cab and go to St. Vincent's. They'll take care of you." In spite of myself, I added, "Or call Mac."

"He doesn't understand," she said. "You're the only one who does. I'm scared what I might do if you don't come down and be with me."

We'd been through this a thousand times. Laura needed limit setting, not enabling. I began to get what that meant. She might go down the drain, but I didn't have to go down with her. I had a choice. We weren't even married anymore. It wasn't about that, anyway. I could feel the tidal pull of her overwhelming need. I couldn't let her suck me in.

"No!" They said no was a complete sentence. Right now, it felt like a better sentence than the hard labor I'd already served: rescuing Laura over and over again. "Laura, I can't come. I'm busy. I have my own life to live, and you've got to pull yourself together and live yours. You're beautiful, you're talented, you deserve a lot better than me. It's over. No more emotional blackmail."

"It's over," she repeated. The two words thudded, final as coffin nails. Oh, shit, what if this time she really meant it? But she never did. She'd do anything to keep me on the merry-go-round. "There's someone else. Oh, Brucie, how can you do this to me? I love you so much. I've always loved you, you know that."

At that, I got mad. It was easier than feeling guilty.

"So much you hooked up with that Neanderthal turd Mac. You never loved me, Laura. Okay, maybe in your way. But you needed someone to lean on, and sometimes I've thought that any scratching post would do. I'm sorry. I hope someday you figure out how to be happy, joyous, and free." The AA words tumbled out as if from a stranger's lips. The truth was, Laura didn't want the person

— 240 —

I had a chance of becoming now. Only the person I had been. "I'm the one that can't do it anymore. I'm sorry."

I shouted the last words into the phone, barely able to hear myself as the train rumbled into the station. I didn't have the heart to hang up on her. But I knew the signal would cut out the moment the train doors closed. I'd expected the connection to break a lot sooner. Maybe cell phones, like guys addicted to beautiful bad girls, had trouble letting go.

At least I tried. If I didn't always embrace the new behavior, I knew the right direction to go. That's what I liked about Luz. She tried too. That didn't mean she didn't ever fall back into the arms of past illusions. In fact, she was a lot like me. And I could help, if only this train would get its electrical ass in gear and get me there. Jimmy would say I'm powerless over the subway. *God give me patience—now!* That was a joke, not a real prayer. I said it under my breath anyway. And then a prayer for Luz and one for Laura. Just in case Someone was listening.

TWENTY-SIX

When Barbara let herself into the apartment, Jimmy was hunched over the computer. The only indication that he'd moved in the two hours she'd been gone was a row of empty soda cans lined up on the floor in a soldierly fashion and stripped stems bristling with twigs sticking up out of a bowl that had been filled with grapes when she left. The lilting felicities of uilleann pipes and pennywhistle, Celtic harp and bodhran filled the room.

"Chieftains? How was your meeting?"

"Fine, my peach." Jimmy used the remote to lower the sound without taking one hand off the keyboard or the other off the mouse. For Jimmy, this hardly counted as multitasking. "How was yours?"

Barbara scooped up an armful of soda cans and came around behind him to kiss the top of his head. She unbent her elbow, letting the cans fall with a pleasant clinking, harmonious enough with the Irish music, into a metal wastebasket a foot from Jimmy's chair.

"Wastebasket—Jimmy. Jimmy—wastebasket." She waved her hand, performing introductions. "Oh, what's the use? It was a good meeting."

"What use indeed, my pet?" Jimmy said, his eyes twinkling. "Acceptance is the answer. Did anything interesting happen?"

"Not at the meeting. But I talked to Bruce afterward, and I want you to make a phone call. Did you ever reach Mars, to get Marla's number?"

"I left a message, but he hasn't gotten back to me."

"Never mind," Barbara said. "I have it—she gave it to Bruce, and he gave it to me. It's what she told him that's interesting. She knows where Frankie was the night he died—at a meeting up in East Harlem, so not far from Luz's apartment. We can look it up in the meeting book if we need to."

"She was there?"

"Yes, and she talked to him. He got her a cab. Remember how it was pouring?"

"Did she tell the cops?"

"She didn't tell anybody. She's been in relapse. And there's more—she was in touch with Kevin. She said she didn't answer his voice mail when he called to ask her advice, probably about the confrontation or whatever he was planning, because she was drinking and completely wasted. But don't you think she's bound to know more?"

"Yes, I do," Jimmy said. "We need to ask her who else she saw at that meeting the night Frankie died. What he said to her. Who he left with. Whether she had any other conversations with Kevin that might have given something away."

"I can't make a program call," Barbara said, "but you can. You can say you got her name from the book at some meeting or other."

"I won't even need to," Jimmy said. "Give me the number."

"Use the landline, so I can listen."

"Don't forget you can't make a sound," Jimmy said. "Only in extraordinary circumstances would I make a program call when I knew someone was eavesdropping."

"I know, baby," Barbara said. "We'll figure out a way to make amends later. And don't worry, I'll be quiet." She kissed him and vanished into the bedroom.

"Marla? Hi, it's Jimmy from program. You got time to talk? I hear you've got a few days back. Congratulations!"

The conversation turned to Frankie's and Kevin's deaths quickly and without prompting. Marla started to sob, apologized, blew her nose audibly, and sobbed some more. Jimmy made no attempt to soothe or stop her. Barbara, listening with compassion, thought, it isn't all about playing Sherlock. If we can find the truth of what happened, maybe Luz won't be the only one who can start to heal.

"Kevin went to that uptown meeting with me," Marla said. She drew in a tremulous breath. "We both felt pretty shaky coming out of rehab. You know how it is."

"I sure do," Jimmy said. "The stresses, all the pressure of regular life that you get away from in rehab, and the temptations on every street, the bars and liquor stores."

"That's it," Marla said. "Only someone in recovery can understand—that's why it's so great to go to meetings. Kevin and I were supporting each other. We wanted to do a ninety in ninety if we could." Ninety meetings in ninety days: total immersion in the program.

"And you ran into Frankie."

"Yes, I felt so close to both of them. I know it's no excuse, but I fell apart when they died, one right after the other like that, and that's when I picked up."

"Hey, it happens," Jimmy said. "They don't call it a chronic relapsing disease for nothing."

Barbara, quiet as a mouse on the extension, was moved by Jimmy's kindness as much as by Marla's pain. Her eyes filled with tears. She knew she had no right to share this private moment, the intimacy of two alcoholics talking.

"I keep thinking about that night," Marla said. "Obsessing, wondering if anything I could have done would have made a difference. He got me a cab. If I'd insisted on him sharing it—if he hadn't gone to his girlfriend's apartment—Do you think she did it?"

"I don't know. Did Kevin take the cab with you?"

"No, he ran into some people. They were going out for coffee. He liked that strong Puerto Rican coffee, wanted to go to some neighborhood place with these other guys. But it was raining and I was tired, and I wanted to get home."

Barbara's mind raced as Jimmy searched for the right question. Who had Kevin wanted to confront? It had to be one of the people from rehab. Could going for coffee have been an excuse? No. He'd been killed downtown, at the edge of the West Village. That must have been where he'd met his killer. But the killer had come to Luz's apartment. So he knew his way around East Harlem. Had Luz herself known any of them? No, of course not. She would have said so at the funeral if she'd recognized anyone.

"Was Frankie all alone at the meeting?" he asked. "Or did he come—and leave—with someone else?"

"Oh, yeah, one of those guys from the funeral came with him. He waited inside while Frankie got me the cab, so I guess they left together. Kevin was pissed off about it. It was a closed meeting, so this guy Frankie knew shouldn't have been there—unless he was an alcoholic too. I don't know if he was."

"One of the men we saw at the funeral in Brooklyn left the meeting in East Harlem with Frankie the night he died?"

"Yeah. Wow, I never thought about it that way. It sounds freaky.

When you crawl into a bottle the way I did, you don't do much thinking, do you?"

"No, you don't," Jimmy said. "You crawl into the bottle because you don't want to think or feel."

"You got that right," Marla said. "I pray to God I never have to do that again. I know, never say never—one day at a time."

"Marla, listen, this could be important. Can you identify the guy from Brooklyn? Do you know who he was?"

"No," she said. "Do you think I should tell the police anyway? Nobody introduced me to all those people. They didn't really want to meet Frankie's friends the drug addicts, and I was too busy freaking out at the time anyway."

"If you know something," Jimmy said, "it would be better if you told."

"Like being honest?" she said. "Yeah, I don't want to rack up any more guilt for my Fourth Step inventory, if I ever get that far. Hey, I just smiled—talking about it with you has really helped. I feel better. 'We're as sick as our secrets,' right?"

"Yeah, honesty is good," he said, "and I'm thinking safety too. You didn't know the guy's name, but could you describe him?"

"I think I could," she said. "Oh, shit, you know what? Kevin had met a bunch of them on family day at rehab. Frankie introduced him as one of his friends from men's group. That wife of his didn't want to know from women friends. Civilians don't understand."

"Kevin had met Frankie's family at the rehab?"

"Yeah, so of course he had to pay his respects at the funeral. He knew all their names."

TWENTY-SEVEN

The package lying in the street caught my eye right away. Park Slope was the kind of neighborhood where they kept the streets clean. The thick parcel of heavy paper tied up with twine could have been anything. It had probably been carried in the plastic supermarket bag that would have long since flown away on the wind if the package hadn't trapped a corner of it. It lay like an illegally parked car in the gutter near a hydrant. It might have been tossed from the trunk of the black Mercedes pulled up a tad too close to the yellow line that marked the curb a couple doors down from Carola's.

It didn't look like garbage. Someone's laundry? Someone's dinner? Curious, I went over and picked it up. I caught the plastic bag, too, before the wind whisked it away. It was white with black lettering, the letters crumpled in on themselves. I pulled the bag out flat between my hands. Not supermarket. *Supermercado*. I didn't think there were any *supermercados* in Park Slope. Maybe a bodega or two on Seventh Avenue or farther away from the park. The package felt soggy but not completely soft, like half-defrosted food. I held it up and sniffed. Was I imagining a faint spicy aroma? I thought of Proust. Well, I thought of all I know about Proust, which is that the guy in his book remembered seven volumes worth of shit from his past because he sniffed some cookies. Not only was the scent familiar, but I had seen a package exactly like this recently.

Pasteles! I flashed on Barbara turning from the kitchen counter, saying, "Oh, Luz, you shouldn't have." And Luz saying, "You told me once your mother said a good guest never comes empty-handed. My *tias* say the same." And Barbara wailing, "Ohhh, I just ordered Chinese. Shall I call them and cancel? I love *pasteles*!" And Luz convincing her to freeze them, saying her own freezer was full of them, Tia Rosa always made too many, and she loved Chinese food.

If Luz's *pasteles* hadn't made it to Carola's, then neither had Luz. What had happened? Had the stalker followed her to Brooklyn? Had he attacked her? Had she run? But if she ran away, why wouldn't she have run straight to Carola's? If she'd gotten there safely, either the guy would have given up and gone away, or they would have called 911. No cop cars. No sign of disturbance on the street except the discarded *pasteles*. And no one had retrieved the package. It was well wrapped, and it had thawed only a little.

What next? Ring Carola's bell? I still clutched the package of *pasteles* in both hands. I put it down on the closest surface, the trunk of the black Mercedes parked too close to the hydrant. It bounced. The package bounced. For a moment it didn't compute. Then I heard the thumping on the inside of the trunk door. Every time it thumped, the package jumped. After half a dozen more thumps, the package slid off the polished metal surface and fell to the street again. By that time, I had my mouth down close to the keyhole. Stupid of me, because trunk keyholes don't have holes in them like the locks on old-fashioned wooden doors. But it was all I could think to do.

"Luz!" I shouted. "Luz! Are you in there?"

"Bruce? I can't get out." I could hardly hear her.

"Hang on, Luz. I'll get you out. Isn't there a safety catch inside the trunk?"

I thought she said, "I can't." Then I realized it was, "No hands."

Shit! Was she tied up in there? Who had done this to her? Carola? Then I'd better not ring her bell and ask to borrow a crowbar.

In our misspent youth, Jimmy and I had acquired a number of skills they didn't teach in school. Jimmy's talent for electronics reached its full maturity when the Internet came of age. I'd picked locks since long before then.

"Hold on, Luz. I'll get you out, but it may take a few minutes," I shouted, my lips close to the sheet of metal between us. Maybe it would conduct sound, like those telephones kids used to make out of string and orange juice cans back in the days before instant messaging. "Can you hear me?"

I laid my ear against the cold metal.

"Yes! Hurry!"

Now what did I have on me to tease open the damn lock? It had been awhile since I'd needed this skill. I dug my hands into my pants pockets. I hadn't emptied them in a long time. My fingers read Braille over a ton of junk till I found a nest of paper clips. Someday I'd have enough recovery to stop stealing office supplies. I fished them out. They were fluffy with lint. I blew on them, straightened a couple out, and got to work.

It didn't help that my hands felt like two bunches of sweaty thumbs. Luz had stopped thumping, but I felt hyperaware of how near she lay. *Easy does it.* "Thanks for sharing," I growled back at the still, small voice. I didn't know I'd said it aloud until I heard Luz's anxious query. "It's okay!" I shouted down to her. I knew she could hear me jiggling the lock. What had the fucking woman done to her? Where had she meant to take her? Had she stashed her in the trunk and gone calmly back into the house to read the kid a story? The nerves at the back of my neck jumped at the thought she might come out again.

Easy does it. Maybe she didn't mean to take her anywhere. Once she had Luz tied up, she could do whatever she wanted right here. If she smothered her or bashed her on the head, she wouldn't even lose the parking spot. As far as she knew, no one knew Luz had come. Carola could wait till the alternate-side parking changed and then drive somewhere and dump her. New Jersey. Bear Mountain. Smart of Luz to use her cell phone. How had she managed it? Carola was twice her size, but she must have fought her off as long as she could. I remembered Carola was bigger than me. Better get Luz out and scram before she came out again.

Ahhh. The lock yielded at last. The trunk door swung slowly upward on its own. I reached for Luz before I could see her. Her trembling hand shot out and clutched my forearm so hard it pinched the skin. She wasn't tied up? She almost fell out of the trunk, scrambling up with most of her weight on me. I grabbed her by the shoulders. She gave a cry of pain.

"Sorry!" I gripped her around the waist instead, drawing her up and forward as she got first one leg and then the other over the rim of the trunk and eased herself to the ground. She looked grimy and disheveled but unharmed. "Are you okay?"

"No, I am sorry. I think he broke my arm."

"Don't try to move it. How's the other one?"

"Pins and needles. I was lying on it. I couldn't reach anything."

"Hey, you managed to let me know you were in there. What did you bang with?"

"My knees. My head. They hurt, but my arm is the worst."

"Listen, I have a bandanna. We'll make you a sling and get the hell out of here. We can get a cab back to Manhattan. Or take it straight to the nearest hospital—that would be better." I was babbling. And I didn't realize until I thought *bandanna—pocket* that I still clasped her around the waist. She kept pouring out the story.

"He waited for me outside. I don't know how he knew. I tried to think while I lay there in the dark." She shuddered and nestled closer. Her head fit right in under my chin. "She told him, or maybe he tricked her into calling me. I never saw her."

My arms tightened around her.

"It's okay, it's okay. It's over. I'll get you out of here." Comforting her seemed so important that it took me all that time to do a double take. "He? It wasn't Carola? Who—"

About a ton of muscle landed on my back. A hairy arm locked tight around my neck. Vinnie! I reeled from the blow. Luz spun free and fell back against the trunk. I wrestled with a mass of writhing muscle. I felt like the Greek guy with the couple of king-size snakes. I fought back with teeth and elbows and stomping feet. We fought dirty back in Yorkville. Brooklyn, too. I narrowly defended my crotch from a knee like a mallet striking upward. I wrapped a leg around the back of his knee and punched him in the gut. If I could trip him, that would help. Even better if he cracked his head. He fell back with a grunt. I felt pleased until I saw him use the breather to pull out a knife.

"Vinnie! What are you doing? Stop! Stop!" Carola's horrified screech distracted him. I risked a quick glance. She stood on the stoop, the kid in her arms. His wail added to the commotion. Vinnie gathered himself for the kill. I could feel it. The knife in his clenched fist glinted as it started downward. Before it could strike, a berserker joined the fray. Luz had picked up the *pasteles*. She used them as a weapon, whacking him over the head and shoulders again and again. They weren't frozen solid enough to do any damage. But she got his attention. Then she sank her teeth into his knife arm and hung on like a terrier.

Meanwhile, Carola sat the kid down on the steps. She ran

screaming toward us. I landed blows wherever I could as she seized his other arm. He twisted from side to side, roaring like a wounded bull as he tried to shake off the three of us. He hadn't dropped the knife. I tried to grab his wrist. He whirled away from me, jerking his arm free from Luz's clinging jaw. The momentum threw him against Carola. The tip of the knife sliced down her cheek. He checked it, but too late. She clapped a hand to the cut. Blood ran out between her fingers. At that moment, Luz charged in again, head lowered. Vinnie saw her and leaped out of her way. Carola didn't. Luz's head butt hit her in the solar plexus. She reeled back into the street just as a gangsta car, an airbrushed Eighties Caddy with a hip-hop station blasting, screeched around the corner. It hurtled down the block at twice the speed limit.

Carola tripped and fell against the car's aggressive hood as it flashed past. The impact flung her into the air. Like Laura, except that nobody broke her fall. The car didn't stop. They never do. The Caddy fishtailed around the corner, trailing taunting lyrics. Neighbors began to come out on their stoops. Maybe somebody had caught the plate number. More than one would have called the cops. Carola lay like a broken doll.

Behind me, I heard something metal clatter to the ground. With a howl of anguish, Vinnie stumbled past me. Luz squeezed in against my side. My arm moved without volition to hold her close. Vinnie fell to his knees. He gathered Carola up in his arms. Nobody could have stopped him. I didn't try. I hoped her spine would be okay. Vinnie rocked her in his arms. Emotion wrenched the sobs out of his chest and forced them through his throat.

"No," he sobbed, "I didn't mean it. Not you, not you. Anyone but you."

TWENTY-EIGHT

Carola wasn't dead. I was glad. The first ambulance rushed her away, while a neighbor, finally attracted by the commotion, took charge of the little boy. We would find out soon enough how Vinnie had worked her into his plans. In the meantime, the cops booked him for assaulting Luz and locking her in the trunk. He'd said enough to tag him as Frankie's killer. Now that they knew, the cops seemed confident they could find the evidence. I stuck to Luz like glue while the cops and the second set of EMTs duked it out over whether she went to the precinct or the hospital. The hospital won, even though it turned out her arm wasn't broken, just badly sprained. The cops asked as many questions as they could before the painkillers kicked in. Someone would get in touch tomorrow, once they'd worked things out with the Manhattan homicide guys.

They let me come in the ambulance. She threatened to throw a fit if they didn't.

"Considering," I told her, "you did a damn good job of saving me. You went charging into battle wielding the mighty *pasteles*."

"When I thought he would kill you, I forgot my arm. It hurts now, but it didn't then."

"Adrenaline," I said. "Here. I rescued them. What do you want me to do with them?" I held out the now completely soggy package.

It was good to see her laugh.

"I think you came too late to save them. Throw them out, please. Only you must never, never, ever tell Tia Rosa."

This conversation took place in the ER of the nearest hospital, New York Methodist. Before it could continue, a young woman in a white lab coat with a stethoscope slung around her neck came in.

"Ready to go home?" she asked Luz.

"Oh, yes!" She wrinkled up her nose. "I don't like hospitals. Oh! Sorry, I do not mean to insult you."

The doc laughed.

"No problem. I'm not responsible for the décor—or the smells. Or managed care." She turned to me. "You with her? We're not admitting her, but she still needs an escort to leave."

"Oh, Bruce, no," Luz protested. "You have already done so much. I can call one of my cousins to come and get me."

"And wait till they get here all the way from East Harlem? No way. I'll call a car service and see you home."

I didn't like the idea of leaving her alone in the apartment. It was still the place where Frankie had died. She insisted on making me soup. Or rather, since she had a bum arm, I opened the can and made it under her supervision.

We sat at her kitchen table. I slurped, she sipped. I let the whole day go and considered the joys of comfort food.

"I should call Barbara," she said. "So much has happened that I forgot about her. I left a message asking her if she thought I should accept Carola's invitation."

"I know. I was with her when she listened to it. She left one back. I guess you never heard it. What happened with your cell phone?"

"Oh, I was so lucky I had your number. I had only a moment to call, then he snatched it away and smashed it against the curb."

"I didn't see it. I bet it spun away beneath the car. The cops will find it." I thought about it. "You remembered my number? You must have dialed like lightning."

Her lashes came down over her eyes.

"I had you on my speed dial."

"Oh. I see." Yeah. I did. "Luz."

She looked up. For a moment our eyes met. Then we both turned away.

"I wish   ," she said. "I can't— I'm sorry."

"I know," I said. "Bad timing."

"Yes." She jumped up. "Let's call her now."

I pushed back my chair.

"You got a landline?"

I knew all Jimmy and Barbara's numbers by heart. I dialed their landline.

Jimmy answered.

"Where are you, dude? I've been trying to get you for hours."

"My cell phone went. I'm up at Luz's. We've had quite a time, but we got the murderer. It was Vinnie. You won't believe what happened."

The soup had put fresh heart in me. All of a sudden images and feelings flooded in. I couldn't dam them up. I didn't want to. I started pouring the story out to Jimmy. It took him several tries to stop me. Finally, he drowned me out.

"Whoa, dude!"

I pulled to a verbal halt.

"What?"

At that point, a familiar click heralded Barbara's arrival on the extension.

"Did you tell him?"

"Not yet."

"For God's sake, Jimmy!"

"Vinnie killed Frankie, he attacked Luz, they're both at Luz's, and I've been trying to get a word in edgewise."

"Let me tell him," Barbara said.

"No, I'd better do it," Jimmy said.

"Yoo-hoo," I said. "Can I join this conversation? Do what? Tell me what?"

"It's bad, buddy." Jimmy's somber voice chilled me out in a hurry. But how bad could it be? Luz and I were fine. So were Jimmy and Barbara. We were all right here.

"Laura's dead."

The trouble with shutting the door on one compartment of your life while you go and deal with another is you can't see what's happening behind that first door. And if you don't know, you can't stop it. All of a sudden, Luz's homey kitchen felt like a soundproof room. The refrigerator stopped humming. The water she'd put up to boil for tea or coffee steamed silently. The air took on a shimmer, flashing between dark and bright as if someone had turned on the strobe lights.

"She called me." My voice came out a croak. "And I didn't go. Luz had just called. In trouble. I thought it was just Laura's usual bullshit. Oh, God, what have I done?"

"It's not your fault," Jimmy said. "She'd cried wolf a hundred times."

"You couldn't have stopped her," Barbara said. "Not if she really meant it."

"I should have known," I persisted. "I was just so mad—"

I didn't want to go into the whole sex and jealousy drama. Not with Luz listening. I didn't want her to know I'd kept sleeping with Laura. Even though Luz and I had just agreed our being an item wasn't going to happen. But I was such a bonehead. This wasn't about my love life. Laura was dead. This time she had really gone and done it.

"Killed herself," I said. Maybe if I said it enough times it would sink in.

"Who?" Luz cried.

"My ex-wife," I said. "Laura."

"Bruce." Jimmy's voice called me back. "Are you still there, man? Are you okay?"

"Of course he's not okay," Barbara snapped. Then, "Sorry. Sorry to both of you—I'm upset too."

I felt stupid. I didn't know what to say or what to ask. How? I knew how. I had always thought the bucket and the knife were just props for her histrionics.

"How did you find out?"

"The boyfriend, Mac, came in and found her," Jimmy said. "He called the cops. The cops found my number on her cell phone, I guess because she called you here so many times. They'll want to interview you, but I'm sure it's no big deal. Mac would be way up ahead of you on the list."

"There is no list," I said. "She did it herself."

"He found her in the bathtub bleeding out," Barbara said.

"They said 'apparent suicide' as if they meant it," Jimmy said. "They must have found the knife in the right place."

"Did she leave a note?"

"They didn't say."

"What did she say on the phone?" Barbara asked.

"Same old drama queen threats as always," I said. "I was going into the subway. I told her I couldn't come."

"She meant to succeed," Barbara said, "or she wouldn't have gotten in the tub."

"She did that after she talked to me. It *is* my fault. If I'd gone down there, she'd still be alive."

"If you had, I would be dead." I'd forgotten Luz was there. She had moved up close enough to hear what Barbara and Jimmy said.

"I can hear Luz," Barbara said. "Let me talk to her. It sounds like she had a rough day too."

"I did," Luz said. "Vinnie locked me in the trunk. He would have killed me if Bruce hadn't gotten me out."

"My God! Look, this is silly. Give Luz the receiver," Barbara said. "No, wait, I want to tell you this first, Bruce. It wasn't your fault! What Laura did was shitty. She's dead, I'm sorry, I know you're sad. But suicide sucks. She let you believe it was the same old histrionic act she always pulled. She knew, you knew, she knew you knew how it went. And then, when you finally stopped enabling her, she up and did it for real. She knew how bad it would hurt you, and she chose to do it. She punished you good for saying no to her, and it was a cruel, selfish thing to do."

"Thanks, I feel a lot better," I said, my voice bleak. I couldn't even summon up the sarcasm that used to fuel everything I said.

Barbara has a good heart.

"Oh, Bruce, I'm sorry, I really am," she said. "I didn't mean to make it worse. Suicide makes me mad for the survivors' sake, but if that doesn't help you, I'll shut up."

"Really?" I surprised myself by laughing a little. "Jim, you want to get that in writing before she changes her mind?"

"Why don't you go home and get some sleep?" Jimmy said. "Come over in the morning."

"We'll have bagels and lox," Barbara said.

"And maybe take in a meeting," Jimmy said.

Barbara being Barbara and Jimmy being Jimmy—now that did make me feel better.

TWENTY-NINE

I woke with a furry tongue and dragon breath. But no hang-over. Nice change from my old bad habits. I grabbed a cup of cof-fee at the corner bodega and caught the crosstown bus with my eyes still sticky.

Luz had decided to spend the day hanging out with her aunts and cousins. I suppose she had uncles too, but they didn't seem to count. I wondered if she had alcoholism in the family. She'd never said. Maybe with Frankie gone, she'd withdraw from the whole world of recovery. Barbara would be disappointed. She be-lieves everybody in the world could use Al-Anon. But I could see Luz eventually marrying some nice Puerto Rican boy who went to church. She might come to remember this part of her life as a bad dream.

After breakfast, Jimmy talked us into going to a meeting. The closest His and Hers lay on my side of the park. We decided to walk across.

"What are you thinking about?" Barbara asked.

"Luz's future," I said. "Without me. Without any of us."

"Daydreaming about someone else's life?" Barbara said as we skirted the Great Lawn. "You *do* need Al-Anon."

"Riding Bruce instead of thinking how you'll feel if Luz pulls away from the program?" Jimmy teased. "So do you."

She swatted him on the arm.

"You're getting too smart."

"I've always been smart."

The damp, gray day hovered just above freezing. Now maybe it dropped a degree, because lazy, wet snowflakes began to drift down. Those that fell on the path melted as they landed. But the faded grass began to take on a powdering of white.

Barbara stuck out her tongue like a little kid and caught a snowflake on the tip.

"I guess my inner child will feel abandoned," she admitted. "Not Luz's fault."

I wasn't up to a discussion of Barbara's inner child this morning. I changed the subject.

"So Vinnie killed them both, Frankie and then Kevin."

"I think he did," Jimmy said. "Marla said she'd tell the police everything she knows." He added, "I think she's going to make it this time. She's really working her program."

I'll never be like Jimmy. He finds recovery more interesting than any other topic in the world. Except maybe the fourteenth century. No, not even.

"Kevin was mad at Frankie for bringing an outsider to a closed meeting," Barbara said. "Apart from that, he probably didn't think anything of it. But once Kevin knew that Frankie had been murdered, he must have wondered. Then he spotted Vinnie at the funeral."

"Poor Kevin," Jimmy said. "The disease killed him. He tried to stay clean, but he still wanted desperately to get high."

"He needed money to score," I said. "And once he thought of blackmail as a good way to get it, that was it. Bad move, blackmailing a murderer. 'Stinkin' thinkin'.'" Another AA expression.

"If he'd asked me for the money," Jimmy said, "he might still be alive. Kevin knew who Vinnie was, but Vinnie wouldn't have given him a thought if Kevin hadn't made contact."

"Nonsense," Barbara said. She hugged him to show she meant it nicely. "You'd never have given him drug money."

"You're right," Jimmy said, "but I almost wish he'd lied to me about what he needed money for. If only he'd gone to the police and told them he'd seen Vinnie with Frankie the night he died."

" 'If only' gets you nowhere," Barbara said.

"I know, I know."

"Can we get back on the main track?" I asked. "Vinnie was Frankie's best friend. Why did he kill him?"

"Love," Jimmy said. "One more guy who loved his sister."

"Let's visit Carola in the hospital," Barbara said.

"Who, me?" I said.

"You know I won't get Jimmy out to Brooklyn again so soon."

"The Web is lovely, dark and deep, and I have promises to keep," Jimmy said.

So that afternoon, Barbara and I made our way to Brooklyn one more time.

Carola lay propped up on the bed with several parts of her in traction. The blue-green shadows under her eyes matched the hand-woven throw flung over the hospital sheet.

"Pull up a chair," she greeted us. "And hand me that Styrofoam cup, the one with the flex straw sticking out of it."

Barbara handed. I pulled. Barbara sat. Carola sipped. I lounged against the radiator, enjoying the warmth against my buns.

"Please don't take it personally," Carola said as she set the cup down, "if I say I wish I'd never met you."

"I can understand it," I assured her.

"Me too," Barbara said. "On the other hand, we didn't even come into it until Frankie was dead."

"Frankie was asking for it. I can't argue with that. But Vince! Finding out my brother is a murderer is an experience I wouldn't wish on anybody."

"You mentioned your brother Vince when we visited you," Barbara said. "We might have put two and two together."

"Why?" Carola said. "Not everybody in Brooklyn is related. Not even everybody Italian." She flashed a wan grin. "Even if it seems that way. And at home, we never called him Vinnie."

"Do you mind talking about it?" Barbara said. "It would help if we could understand why." She didn't specify who it would help. Barbara's inner T-shirt says, "Inquiring minds want to know." To my relief, Carola insisted she was glad to have us to talk to. The family, she admitted, was driving her crazy.

"Do you think Vinnie saw himself as an avenger?" Barbara asked. "You know, killing the guy who did his sister wrong."

"We aren't quite so medieval in Bensonhurst," Carola said. "But the code still exists, even though most of us know it's crap. I *told* my brothers to butt out. I thought they had."

"Men!" Barbara said. "You can't tell them anything." I tilted back my chair and let her and Carola have their moment of female bonding.

"It wasn't all about me," Carola said. "Vince was in love with Netta. His whole life."

"We never heard a word about that."

"Nobody talked about it," Carola said, "because everybody knew it. Netta dangled him. She gave him nothing, but she liked having him around."

Like a spider with a fly wrapped up in the pantry.

"Poor Vince didn't get it," Carola said. "She liked things just the way they were."

"He thought she'd turn to him," Barbara said, "once Frankie was gone. It happens in books all the time. Faithful Dobbin gets the girl on page 850 or so."

I didn't think Vinnie had ever read *Vanity Fair*. I supposed most people wouldn't think I had either. In our predrinking days, when Jimmy and I played hooky, he had always made a beeline for the library. Two choices: read or die of boredom.

"It's not enough," I said. "Faithful Dobbin didn't kill to get the girl. Vinnie and Frankie were friends, right? Best friends. Something had to shatter that."

"It did." Carola shifted under the sheet. The hand-woven throw slid halfway off the bed. She strained to reach behind her.

"Can I help?"

"Under the pillow."

Barbara slid her hand past Carola's back.

"This?" She held up a small leather picture frame, the kind that hinges.

Carola took it from her hand. She snapped it open and held it up.

"Look."

The frame held two photos. One was a studio portrait of Carola's little boy. The other was a snapshot. Taken outdoors, it appeared to be a scrimmage. I peered closer. Several kids, all too young for football, tumbled like puppies on and around a figure on the ground: Vinnie. I recognized Edmund and the boy and girl, Frankie's kids, from the funeral. All of them were laughing. Vinnie too.

"Vince was crazy about kids," Carola said. "Especially mine and Netta's kids."

"How about Frankie?"

"Not like Vince." She tapped Edmund's picture. "If I'd had an abortion, Vince would have gone ballistic." She caught her breath. "Sorry. I still can't take it in. You don't expect your brother to become a killer."

"Of course not." Barbara's voice warmed and soothed. "Frankie wanted you to get an abortion."

"He offered to pay." She and Barbara exchanged another of those "Men!" looks. I squirmed.

"You told Vinnie?" I asked.

"Of course not. But I made the mistake of telling my sister-in-law. Patti could never keep her mouth shut."

"You were pregnant by a married man," Barbara said. "You needed to talk to someone."

"Something like that," Carola said. "It kind of knocked the halo off Frankie for Vince. The fact that Frankie played around didn't bother him so much. He didn't like it that the girlfriend was his sister, but none of us were fourteen anymore."

"He made Netta have an abortion, didn't he?" Barbara asked. "Not this time, obviously, but maybe a year or two back?"

Carola nodded.

"How did you know? He was heavy into drugs, and he didn't want to think about another twenty years of shoes and bicycles and orthodontia. Vince was furious about his not wanting Edmund. But to do that to Netta? It tipped him over the edge."

"Did you talk with Vince about it?" Barbara spoke softly. She sat back in her chair beside the bed, not pressing for the answer. Her intent face was still. Her hands, usually in motion when she talked, lay relaxed along the wooden arms of the chair. She must look like this when she did counseling.

"I did. Netta told him—trying to make trouble, if you ask me. And he came to me. He wanted me to talk to Netta. She'd already done it, I don't know how he thought I could help—maybe just show some solidarity. He kept saying, 'He shouldn't have killed the baby.'"

I could imagine Vinnie saying it. *He shou'n'ta killed the baby.*

"I underestimated how far he'd go." Carola snapped the photo frame shut and dropped back against the pillows.

"You're tired," Barbara said. "We've stayed too long. We'd better leave and let you get some rest."

"No, no." Her eyes drooped. "Well, maybe. Funny how tiring lying in bed can be. Or maybe it's getting hit by a car that's so exhausting—worse than welding. I did some monumental sculpture a few years back. But I wanted to tell you what happened that day, before I ran out there."

I did want to hear about that. Barbara caught my eye and shook her head very slightly. She didn't want me to say I'd suspected Carola. I hadn't intended to.

"Please do," Barbara cooed. "And then we really will go."

"I never meant that woman to get hurt," Carola said. "I wouldn't have called her if I'd known what Vince had in mind. It never occurred to me he'd lie to me like that."

"What did he lie about?"

"He told me he had a crush on her. Luz. He'd never let on he knew about her—that far he still felt loyal to Frankie. But once Frankie was dead, he thought I'd grieve less if I knew what a two-timing bastard he was."

"Three-timing," I put in. "Sorry, go on."

"He told me he'd met her a lot of times. At first he felt sorry for her, but then he realized he'd been attracted all along. At least—"

"Lies," Barbara said.

"You know, I think he did feel sorry for her."

I agreed. Luz had told me how Vinnie had tried to get her to back off. Stop looking for Frankie's killer. Leave the family alone.

Get the hell out of Brooklyn. Still, if he had succeeded in killing her, his being apologetic about it would not have helped. Dead was dead.

"He planned to kill her because she wouldn't stop looking," I said.

"It should have been us," Barbara said. "He didn't know Luz would never have gone sleuthing on her own."

"No point feeling guilty," Carola said.

Have you murdered anyone lately? my sponsor had asked me once. *Most guilt feelings are bullshit. Resentment is the killer.*

"Easier said than done," Barbara said.

Carola nodded.

"I feel guilty myself," she said. "Vince used me to set up an alibi. I've already told the cops. It makes what he did premeditated. He meant to kill her."

"The alibi?"

"First he had to get me to make the call. He told me he wanted to ask her out, but he was afraid she'd say no. He thought—he said he thought she was afraid of him. So he told me to invite her over and he'd drop in, maybe offer to drive her home."

"That puts him right on the scene, though," I said. "How did that make an alibi?"

"He never meant her to come inside," she said. "It was Saturday—do you know what day it was?"

"Almost Halloween?"

"Daylight saving time!" Barbara exclaimed. "I mean, no more daylight saving time. The day we put the clocks back."

I hadn't done mine yet. I'd better. I still didn't care what time it was, but the law firms I temped at did.

"Exactly," Carola said. "I always forget. Ever since I got my first alarm clock, I've counted on Vince to remember and do it for me. He didn't make a big deal of it, either. Most times I didn't even notice, just expected the clock to be right. I only have one clock, anyway, and I don't wear a watch."

She was an artist. No day job.

"I remember your clock," I said. "Brass and enamel. Old. Hard to wind."

"You must have some kind of schedule with Edmund," Barbara said.

"Sure," Carola said, "but it didn't matter, because Vince's setup started *before* he changed the clock. I always put Edmund down for his nap at the same time. Vince knew that. While I was in the other room, he put the clock back an hour. I don't have one in the baby's room, I never wanted the ticking to disturb him. And I don't like digitals."

"What if Edmund only napped for an hour?" Barbara asked. "Wouldn't you have noticed if it was the same time when he woke up as when you'd put him down?"

Carola smiled.

"Edmund's a good napper. Vince knew that too. If he slept one hour, I'd just think he'd slept two."

"So he made an invisible hour," I said.

Carola's smile reversed into an unhappy droop.

"He walked in while I was putting Edmund down and said, 'Didn't she come?' He already had—he'd already—"

He already had her stashed in the trunk. We took our leave without making her finish the sentence.

Barbara, who worked in a hospital herself, predicted the elevator would be slow. The crowd that accumulated by the time it came could have fielded a football team, though some of them didn't look fit enough for dodgeball. The doors slid open at a majestic pace. We all squeezed in. Several people pressed the button for the ground floor. The elevator went up.

Visitors, hospital workers, and the occasional patient got on and off. We all shrank back into the corners to make room for a gurney twice as big as the shriveled, pasty-faced old person who lay on it. I had begun to wonder if we had enough air to reach the lobby when Barbara said loudly, "Oh, shit!"

Everyone looked at her, even the moribund patient on the gurney.

"What?"

"Later," she told me. Our companions looked disappointed.

Five minutes later, we revolved through the hospital doors. We shared a section roomy enough for a wheelchair. In its illusory privacy, Barbara began to talk.

"I forgot to ask her about the gynecologist."

"What gynecologist?"

We emerged into air at least thirty-five degrees cooler. It would have been more but for the thick fug of smoke. The huddled cigarette addicts included patients still hooked to their IVs as well as doctors, some of them no doubt oncologists. I would have stopped to light up, but Barbara, one hand clapped over her mouth and nose, hurried me along. I couldn't understand her muffled answer.

"Say again?"

She shook her head without removing the hand. With the other hand, she grabbed a fistful of my coat and tugged me along. Fifty yards from the hospital she stopped, let go, and drew in a double lungful of relatively untainted air.

"When Netta and her friends came to the lingerie shop, Luz overheard them talking about Netta's abortion. That's how I knew. They didn't say the A word, but they mentioned Dr. Feingold. Luz had given his name to Frankie, not knowing that was why he wanted it. I've been encouraging her to switch to my gynecologist, but Luz says she has a horror of a woman touching her 'down there.'"

"Thanks for sharing. I can't tell you how glad I am you didn't say this in the elevator."

"Don't be silly. Anyway, I'm trained. When you work in a hospital, it's a big confidentiality no-no to talk about a patient in the elevator, so you learn discretion."

"If that's your idea of discretion," I started. "Oh, never mind."

I threw an arm out to keep her from starting across the street just as the light turned red.

"Whoa! I've had enough hit-and-run karma to last a lifetime in the past few weeks. Dr. Feingold, huh?"

"That's what she said. Why?"

"I think he was Laura's gynecologist. It doesn't matter now."

We started down the subway stairs. As we fished out our Metrocards, we heard the rumble of an approaching train. Grateful for the distraction, I jammed the card into the slot and tugged it through. The digital readout gave me a hard time. *Please Swipe Again.* Damn. I missed the old days when I used to jump the turnstile. But nobody had to tell me getting arrested would be bad for my sobriety.

Barbara held out a hand as I burst through on the third try, and we ran for it. We just made it into the most crowded car and had to stand. Barbara tried to shout at me over the racket of the train. I pointed to my ear and shook my head. Swaying practically on tiptoes as she hung from a metal strap a little too high for her, she took my earlobe between the thumb and fingers of her free hand and pulled my head down close enough to speak into my ear. Her breath tickled.

"You'll have to talk about Laura eventually."

"Not now!"

It came out more of a bellow than I'd intended as I jerked my head away from her touch. New York subway riders are notorious for ignoring any kind of drama. But two people turned their heads to see if we'd provide any entertainment and three shifted slightly farther from us.

For once, Barbara shut up. I didn't feel like telling her, even in private, that I knew damn well that Feingold was Laura's gynecologist. He'd done abortions since before *Roe v. Wade*, which was okay by me. But he didn't ask a lot of questions. He had believed Laura's mother when she brought her fourteen-year-old daughter in, saying the pregnancy they needed to terminate was the result of a schoolyard rape. Like hell it was. Laura's stepfather had started coming to her room when she was eight. Unlike Netta, Laura had never been able to conceive after the abortion. She hadn't spent most of her time since then trying to stay high or die for no reason.

THIRTY

I didn't let Barbara take me to my first Al-Anon meeting. I told her I was going, so she could kvell, as she would say, like a proud mother whose little boy takes the bus alone. But I had to do this by myself.

Once the thing with Luz unraveled, I could let it go. But if my life was one big show, Laura still held the spotlight. Barbara refrained from scolding me about it. She didn't even remind me more than once or twice a day that codependency is a disease.

"You're entitled to grief," she said.

Jimmy, troubled by something an AA meeting couldn't fix, offered me his company, his virtual ear 24/7, and all the simple wisdom of the program. I *knew* "this too shall pass." I even found it comforting. Staggering evidence of how much I'd changed. But Laura still upstaged every other act and character. Even mine. Even me.

If I'd chosen differently that day, would Laura be alive? Would Luz have died? Would anything be better? Would I feel any less responsible? My head had sensible answers to all those questions. My heart just hurt.

I wondered if Laura would ever have succeeded in leaving Mac. She couldn't leave him. I couldn't leave her. I kept thinking I had, but it took death to cut the cord for good. That made me no different from her at all.

My sponsor advised me to go back to the First Step. Oddly, Step One is the same in Al-Anon as in AA: "We admitted we were powerless over alcohol and our lives had become unmanageable."

I told him I didn't even feel like drinking.

"You will," he said. "If not now, during some other crisis, or maybe sometime when everything is ticking along nicely. For now, think of alcohol as a metaphor. We're powerless over *everything*—except our ability to choose the next right action."

So I chose to attend this meeting. The church basement was no different from the church basements of AA. I even saw a few familiar faces. The same Twelve Steps and Twelve Traditions, only a word or two different here and there, hung from the wall behind the speaker. I liked the opening someone read, especially the part about taking what I liked and leaving the rest. I could do that.

When they opened the floor to shares, I raised my hand. I still had trouble doing that in AA. I didn't plan it this time. For a moment, I became God's marionette. And that was all it took. The speaker called on me.

"Hi, I'm Bruce, I'm an alc—" I bit back the rest. "Sorry. Damn! 'I'm Bruce and I'm sorry.' I guess I do qualify for this program."

That got an encouraging ripple of laughter.

"Yeah, I'm in the other program," I admitted. "That's not why I'm here, though. I'm here because someone I loved is dead."

As if the D-word flipped a switch, the quality of the silence changed. No one fidgeted. Nobody's chair creaked. No one rustled any papers. Even the knitters in the front row stopped clicking their needles and waited motionless for me to go on.

"She's not my only qualifier, though she did do drugs and alcohol," I said. "But she's the one I never could let go of."

"You're in the right place," someone in the back row murmured.

"We got a divorce. It didn't make any difference. I got sober. That didn't work either. I didn't even love her anymore. Not that way, whatever way that is. I still couldn't stop hanging on."

Now I saw the nodding heads that meant the listeners could identify. A couple of people said softly, "Keep coming back."

"The other day she killed herself," I said, through a lump in my throat that felt the size of a fist. "I couldn't save her." I fought back tears. They all sat quietly and waited for me to cry or not. Whichever I wanted. Whatever came. *Acceptance is the answer.* Not only theirs, but mine.